THE ULTIMATE TREASURE

CHRISTOPHER BULIS

BBC BOOKS

Other BBC DOCTOR WHO books include:

THE EIGHT DOCTORS *by Terrance Dicks*	0 563 40563 5
VAMPIRE SCIENCE *by Jonathan Blum and Kate Orman*	0 563 40566 X
THE BODYSNATCHERS *by Mark Morris*	0 563 40568 6
GENOCIDE *by Paul Leonard*	0 563 40572 4
THE DEVIL GOBLINS FROM NEPTUNE *by Keith Topping and Martin Day*	0 563 40564 3
THE MURDER GAME *by Steve Lyons*	0 563 40565 1
BUSINESS UNUSUAL *by Gary Russell*	0 563 40575 9

DOCTOR WHO titles on BBC Video include:

THE WAR MACHINES *starring William Hartnell*	BBCV 6183
THE AWAKENING/FRONTIOS *starring Peter Davison*	BBCV 6120
THE HAPPINESS PATROL *starring Sylvester McCoy*	BBCV 5803

Other DOCTOR WHO titles available from
BBC Worldwide Publishing:

| POSTCARD BOOK | 0 563 40561 9 |
| THE NOVEL OF THE FILM *on audio tape* | 0 563 38148 5/Z1998 |

Published by BBC Books
an imprint of BBC Worldwide Publishing
BBC Worldwide Ltd, Woodlands, 80 Wood Lane
London W12 0TT

First published 1997
Copyright © Christopher Bulis 1997
The moral right of the author has been asserted

Original series broadcast on the BBC
Format © BBC 1963
Doctor Who and TARDIS are trademarks of the BBC

ISBN 0 563 40571 6
Imaging by Black Sheep, copyright © BBC 1997

Printed and bound in Great Britain by Mackays of Chatham
Cover printed by Belmont Press Ltd, Northampton

CHAPTER 1
VISIONS AND PORTENTS

The only illumination in the Seers' chamber came from the ring of nine tall thick candles mounted in brass cups on the floor at its centre. Surrounding this, seated cross-legged on the black marble that lined the chamber, was the assembly of Seers themselves, numbering one for each of the candles. They were robed in black, leaving only their faces and hands uncovered, so they appeared to float disembodied in the darkness. All were adepts of the Seventh Circle. None of lesser mental power would be capable of the feat they were now attempting.

'It is time, brothers and sisters,' said Shalvis softly, her words echoing back in whispers from the invisible walls.

The Seers closed their eyes and bowed their heads and the thin silver tendrils that rose curving backward from each of their high foreheads began to lift and stretch. The trembling hazy air over the candle ring rippled as though disturbed by a sudden wind. The smoke swirled into a funnel and then it seemed a black pit opened within it – not the blackness of clear air, but something far, far deeper. It was as though a hole had been opened in the very fabric of time and space. For a moment the smoke flowed downward into the candles, even as the rivulets of wax on their shafts ran back up to reform about the flames. Then the process reversed and the candle flames brightened as they began to burn down the wicks again with astonishing speed. A cluster of sparks drifted slowly within the dark void like stars, which perhaps they were. The image of a blue-and-white-speckled orb appeared: a world as seen from space. This was replaced by a cluster of buildings, then a group of faces, then frantic activity and accelerated action. Behind the figures suns seared across the

1

sky and moons flashed through their phases in seconds. Each scene flickered past faster and faster, eventually dissolving into a blur of light and colour that finally resolved itself into a shimmering white globular opacity.

'The way is open,' said Shalvis, noting the rapidly sinking candles. 'Begin.'

The first Seer on her left sent his mental projection into the vortex, sampling the myriad twisting currents of time that flowed within it. 'I see journeys beginning with death... five parties of seekers shall set out but only four will arrive.' He withdrew his projection, trembling from those few seconds of intense effort.

The second in the ring cast forth her projection. 'I see them also,' she confirmed. 'But some of their forms are peculiar... uh, machinery intervenes...' Then she also drew back, gasping with relief.

'Two travel with the rest but are also apart,' said the third.

'One is bound up with a quasi-living thing. Its nature I cannot determine,' said the forth.

'The other will arrive transformed but purposeful... a facsimile,' said the fifth.

'What of their fellow seekers' natures?' Shalvis asked quickly. The candles were burning lower by the moment.

'Simple greed for some, a desire for personal gain intermingled with duty for others, two who follow out of loyalty, one with a youthful sense of adventure...' the sixth Seer reported.

'And one whose motivations I cannot quite fathom... ambition, but also a curious detachment...' said the seventh.

'But there is also another who has a mind of power... ah, I recognise the type now,' said the eighth with satisfaction.

Now it was Shalvis's turn. As always she held her projection longest in the time stream.

'I see their names clearly now... and the two others who

are apart. One is a troubled intelligence caught between worlds... a lost spirit. Both have gone beyond death, but will not relinquish their hold on life. Each in their own way are seekers, their destinies intertwined...' The candles were mere stubs guttering in their cups as she strained to read more. 'The first we must aid, the second –' With a moan she shrank back, withdrawing her projection just as she was about to lose control.

The white globe collapsed in upon itself and was gone in a swirl of smoke as the candle flames were snuffed out. For a moment there was total darkness. Then artificial lights flared into life at a wordless command, illuminating the black chamber with a cool steady radiance. The nine candles in the centre of the room stood tall and whole once more, looking as though they had never been lit.

The other Seers crowded anxiously round Shalvis, who had slumped back on one elbow, and helped ease her upright.

'You should not exert yourself so,' said the fifth.

'Remember the danger,' said the second.

Shalvis smiled wearily, and gently pushed aside their supporting hands. 'I am unharmed,' she assured them. 'The last sight was deeper than I would have wished.'

'What did you learn?' asked the eighth practically.

'I glimpsed the true nature of the second who is apart,' said Shalvis with a slight shudder, looking up at their anxious faces. 'Our powers alone will not defeat such evil – and we can do nothing to prevent its coming!'

CHAPTER 2
THE PRICE OF KNOWLEDGE

The public phone in corridor 25 of Astroville's Delta tower was little used, which was why Hok had given its number to his buyer. He had good reasons for not revealing his personal phone code. So he had lurked within earshot of the booth, cursing silently whenever somebody passed by. But at almost exactly the agreed second the phone rang. Hok reached it before the second tone had died away, punching the 'Sound Only Selected' key even as he accepted the call.

'Buyer?' he asked simply to the blank screen.

'Yes. Seller?' came the reply, in a voice Hok tentatively classed as humanoid.

'Speaking. You will meet me in exactly one standard hour at Chocky's Inn, central concourse, level 3, corridor 14. You will each be wearing green trillis blossoms on your persons. Bring the full payment in the manner agreed. Do not be late. That is all.'

Hok broke the connection and shuffled away from the booth as fast as his stubby, aged locomotor limbs would allow. As he went he rubbed a pair of his manipulator tentacles together in a gesture of anticipation he had learnt from some of his human acquaintances. The item had cost him a great deal to acquire, as had the computing time needed for its deciphering, but its sale would ensure he spent his declining years in luxury. This transaction alone would cover his expenses and leave a modest profit, but owing to the nature of the commodity in question there was no need to stop there. His merchandise was genuine and the provenances he had provided to all his potential customers were honest. But he had promised none of them that they would be his *only* customers.

* * *

'How about this one, Doctor?' Peri asked, sweeping out of the changing cubicle and striking a pose.

The Doctor looked up from his chaise longue in the fashion house's main salon and benignly appraised the floor-length ballgown-like creation in diagonal stripes of crimson and cobalt blue.

'Ah, yes. Most fetching. Of course, on Gamma Ceffilos 12, that style and combination of colours means you are a recently widowed mother still in mourning, but would be accepting new suitors after the next lunar conjunction.'

Peri returned to the cubical to try on another costume.

'Perhaps modom would care to try something slightly less formal?' the robot attendant suggested deferentially, lisping slightly. Yes, it actually had said: 'modom', Peri decided. Where had it been programmed to talk like that?

Nevertheless, Perpugilliam Brown (Peri to her friends) admitted to herself that she was having the time of her life.

Only a few days ago, relatively speaking, she had been on twentieth-century Lanzarote, Earth, and desperate to get away from her stepfather's boring archaeological expedition. Well she had certainly managed that – and then some. Who would have expected a disguised space-time machine known as the TARDIS to be waiting for her on the beach? After a dangerous excursion to the planet Sarn, the Doctor, the TARDIS's owner, had agreed to let her travel with him for the remaining three months of her holiday. Of course, that three months could be spent virtually anywhere in time and space. Currently, at the Doctor's suggestion, she was getting acclimatised to mixing with alien races and cultures on Astroville Seven; a thirty-first-century spaceborn trading post many light years in space away from her own Earth. And, as she'd left with only what she'd be been wearing, wasn't it perfectly reasonable that she had to shop for some new clothes first? The Doctor had shown her the huge store of costumes for all occasions that the TARDIS carried, but she'd really wanted to chose her own from new. Once he understood, a mild indulgent look had spread across the Doctor's face, and so here she was.

Peri caught sight of herself in the cubicle's multiple mirrors. She had clear skin, lightly tanned by the Lanzarote sun, with regular features framed by collar-length dark hair. Her figure was compact and well developed in a manner she was quietly pleased with. But at that moment, she decided, her most notable feature was the broad grin of sheer delight at the adventure she had found herself in. And she was determined to enjoy every second of it.

The attendant produced a sort of silver metallic jumpsuit.

'Perhaps this would be more to modom's taste?'

For a moment Peri eyed the design with interest, then the silver glitter reminded her of Kamelion and she frowned. The shape-shifting android had been the Doctor's companion when she joined him. But it had come under the influence of the Master, the Doctor's arch enemy, who had turned it against them. It had tried to take over the TARDIS and then chased her across Sarn's rugged landscape, first looking like her stepfather, then as the Master, and sometimes a hybrid of them and its true form. Eventually, stricken with remorse at what it saw as its disloyalty and knowing it could no longer be trusted, Kamelion had begged the Doctor to put a merciful end to its tortured existence. It was a sad experience she'd prefer not to be reminded of.

'Uh, no thanks,' she told the attendant. 'I think I've got all I want now.'

The Doctor was paying for her purchases with some sort of futuristic credit system, which was fortunate because the plastic cards she had with her would probably be accepted only by a museum here and now. She watched him as he thumbprinted the transaction pad and arranged for the purchases to be sent by cargo tube to their docking bay.

He was a tall man with collar-length, straight, blond hair, and amiable clean-cut features. He appeared to be in his early thirties, but she guessed he was much older. His eyes were dangerously deep and very intelligent. His preferred costume was a white period frock coat, striped trousers, and a V-necked English cricketing jumper. For some reason he finished off his ensemble with a sprig of celery in his buttonhole. She was working her way up to asking why. All things considered she privately acknowledged that he was somebody she might find it very easy to fall for in a big way – except that she knew instinctively that was not going to happen. The usual rules didn't apply to the Doctor. For all his outward appearance, there was something mysterious and, well, alien about him. Perhaps that was part of his appeal

Chocky's Inn was only half full at this hour, which was why Hok had chosen it.

The moment he entered he saw his two customers already seated at a corner table nursing drinks. Humanoids, as he had suspected. One thin and elegant by human standards, neatly dressed and well groomed; the other stockier and slightly crumpled, looking around him with sharp impatient eyes. An interesting and rather ill-assorted pair, Hok thought. What chance had thrown them together? Still, as long as they had the money, it was no business of his.

'I am the seller,' he announced, sliding into the spare seat beside them. 'You have the payment?'

The crumpled man produced a small heavy case from an inner pocket, placed it on the table and raised the lid. Hok saw a metallic glitter within.

'Twenty bars, as agreed,' he said. 'You have the document?'

Hok produced a data capsule. The thin man took it and slipped it into a portable reader. Hok saw his eyes glint eagerly as he scanned the text, then nodded to his companion, who pushed the case across the table to Hok.

'Thank you, gentlemen,' Hok said, slipping the case into his belt pouch. 'I wish you luck. Perhaps you would be so good as to finish your drinks before leaving – discretion, you understand.' And he was away through the bar doors before they could reply.

When the two left five minutes later there was no sign of Hok. Not that either man took any trouble to look for him. There was a barely repressed eagerness in their steps as they headed in the direction of the main docking boom elevators. Neither noticed the floating camera drone that had been hovering unobtrusively in the shadows of the corridor ceiling. As they set off it dropped down and glided silently after them.

Astroville Seven served the recreational and administrative needs of a stellar nebula and its associated swarm of asteroids and minor planets. It more than satisfied Peri's expectations of what a futuristic space city should be like. As she had exclaimed when she first arrived, 'Oh, wow! This is really some place, Doctor.'

Astroville resembled a merger between a couple of Houston astrodomes, several skyscrapers and the Eiffel Tower, producing a central core bristling with residential towers and docking trees. Spacecraft from star yachts to liners berthed at its many airlock bays. Its huge open central concourse was ringed with descending concentric tiers of walkways and shops, while crossing above them were transparent freefall elevator tubes carrying passengers and cargo like floating thistledown. Viewing windows the size of tennis courts were let into the outer walls, revealing a glowing nebula of multicoloured gas illuminated by a dozen stars shining like diamonds in chiffon.

And populating this megastructure were things that walked on two legs, four legs, more legs that she could count. Blue skins, green skins, iridescent skins, scales. Crawling things, rolling things, flying things. Things of odd shapes she couldn't begin to describe hidden within pressure suits. There were even a few things she wasn't sure were alive or not, except that they moved about. Like the United Nations but cubed. And she must think of them all, the Doctor had gently explained, as people.

Suddenly, amid the riot of shapes and colours, the need came upon her to buy a souvenir.

'Peri,' the Doctor chided gently upon hearing her desire, 'isn't the experience itself enough for you?'

'But it's traditional,' she protested. 'I've got to have something tangible to show for being here, or else I'll never believe it really happened. I've got my cultural heritage to uphold, you know.'

'I thought all those clothes might suffice.'

'Clothes aren't souvenirs!'

'Aren't they?' he wondered with mild surprise. 'Well, I'm sure there's somewhere we can buy a model of the station in a glass globe, which produces a miniature snowstorm when you shake it.'

'Not quite so tacky, Doctor,' Peri said, consulting her electronic guidebook. 'It says the lower levels of Blue section are good for that sort of thing. That's down this way. Come on.'

The Doctor followed her to the nearest grav chute, an amused and indulgent smile on his lips.

Hok returned to his shop by the back door that opened off a small service passage. He was elated by his first transaction. The final sale of the data original to Alpha would be the trickiest, of course, but by then he would have nothing left to hide. It had been impossible to arrange the purchase of such an important item without Alpha's knowing, but he had been able to mislead him over the day of delivery. Those precious few hours so gained he planned to use very profitably indeed.

He passed through the storeroom, switching off the alarm

and master locking system on the way, and entered the front shop. As he was about to turn on the lights he realised he was not alone.

Three figures emerged from amid the jumble of bric-a-brac and curios. Two were human – one compact the other tall and thin – while the third was probably a Cantarite: bulky, slab-sided and horned. Their features were blurred by glimmer masks, but even with this distortion and the gloom of the shop's interior he knew immediately who they were, and a chill seemed to penetrate his carapace.

'Now where have you been all this time, Hok?' said the smaller human, his expression impossible to read behind his intimidating mask and his words oddly distorted by its diffraction effect.

'Nowhere special, Qwaid,' Hok said quickly, trying to keep his voice level. 'Just business... buying some new stock.'

'Just business, is it?' Qwaid said. 'Well that's fine, because we're here on Mr Alpha's business. About that special item of merchandise, remember?'

'But I arranged to meet him tomorrow.'

'Ah, well, Mr Alpha gets these strange fancies, you see, doesn't he lads?'

Gribbs, the thin human, clicked his tongue: 'That he does.' Drorgon the Cantarite merely grunted agreement, like a rumble of distant thunder.

'His fancy was,' Qwaid continued, 'that you might take it into your head to sell on a copy of the merchandise to somebody else before him, and he wouldn't like that. He wants to be the sole owner, like. I told him: Hok wouldn't cross you, Mr Alpha, he respects you too much. But he was very insistent, and when Mr Alpha insists on something it gets done. So we've come to collect the goods a little early, just to be on the safe side.'

'But, but... I haven't got it here.'

There was a crash and rattle of pottery shards. The remains of a third-period Tabaron vase lay about Drorgon's heavy horn-toed feet.

'Now see what you've gone and done,' Qwaid said regretfully. 'You've annoyed Drorgon. And when he gets annoyed he gets clumsy and breaks things: vases, doors... bones.' He looked about the shop and shook his head sadly. 'And there's an awful lot he could break here, so I'd think carefully about what I just asked you.'

Hok had never been particularly brave, and such resolve as he had crumbled under Qwaid's mocking tones. Why had he ever believed he could deceive Alpha? Instinctively a couple of tentacles clutched at his belt pouch.

'Oh, there it is,' Qwaid said.

Hok struggled feebly as Gribbs held his neck and Qwaid emptied the contents of his pouch out on to a table. The money-bar case fell with a thud. Qwaid opened it up and whistled.

'Now ain't that strange. You say you've just been out buying goods, yet you come back with a full twenty-bar case. I wonder what you sold to earn it. I'm disappointed in you, Hok, really disappointed. And Mr Alpha's going to be disappointed in you too. And you know what happens to people he's disappointed in...'

Hok was trembling and squirming in utter terror. He managed to insinuate one tentacle down the side of the pouch. 'The money's an advance! I've still got the merchandise... see, here it is!' he gibbered, withdrawing a duplicate data capsule from a concealed pocket in his pouch and thrusting it at Qwaid.

Qwaid took the capsule. 'There, you see, that wasn't so hard, was it? Now about payment –'

'A gift!' Hok choked out wretchedly. 'Tell Mr Alpha it's a gift.'

'Well that's very generous, isn't it lads?' said Qwaid with hollow sincerity. 'But what I meant was payment for trying to cheat Mr Alpha.'

It took a couple of seconds for Hok to realise the true meaning of Qwaid's words, and by that time Drorgon's massive hands were already settling about his neck.

Then the shop door opened with a jangle of its antique brass bell and two strangers walked in.

Because of the relative gloom inside the curio shop, Peri and the Doctor were actually several steps inside, with the door swinging closed behind them, before they properly took in the strange tableau of figures within. A creature about seven feet tall, vaguely reminiscent of a bipedal rhinoceros, had it hands clamped murderously about the neck of a much smaller and inoffensive-looking alien, resembling the mock turtle from *Alice in Wonderland*, but with bunches of tentacles instead of flippers. Watching them were two humans wearing anonymous utility coveralls. Disconcertingly Peri realised their faces were misty and blurred, almost as though they were out of focus, so she could see no details of their features.

'Uh, I think maybe we've come at a bad moment,' Peri said faintly, stepping backward so quickly that her heel came down on the Doctor's foot.

It seemed to her that, incredibly, the Doctor had noticed nothing amiss. Extracting his toecap from under her heel he beamed brightly at the oddly assorted figures and said cheerfully, 'Hello. We were just looking for some early Etruscan miniatures. Not the Wedgewood blues of course, but the Van Gough originals, with perhaps just a touch of Ming around the chasing…'

As he babbled this nonsense, he sauntered without any apparent haste over to a basket of assorted coloured-glass globes. He selected a fist-sized one, weighed it thoughtfully, then spun about and threw it very hard and very precisely at the pseudo-rhino's head. It could have shattered the skull of a lesser being. As it was, the impact merely stunned the creature sufficiently for the little turtle-backed alien to wriggle free of its grasp.

13

The taller of the two humans drew a wicked little snub-nosed pistol as Peri and the Doctor dived for cover behind a massive couch built of wooden baulks the size of railway sleepers. The gun hissed and some sort of explosive projectile blew a large chunk of wood to splinters. Another shot dislodged a stack of shelves and a small avalanche of oddments cascaded to the floor. The basket of glass balls was upset and tumbled at their feet. Snatching up the ornaments the Doctor started pitching them at the gunman and his accomplices. Peri followed his example and began hurling every throwable object she could lay her hands on. In moments the other side of the shop was being showered with fragments of bursting glass and china. Shots hissed and cracked in the return. The noise level was startling.

Then without warning a two-toned siren burst into life, adding to the din. Clouds of freezing vapour billowed out from ceiling vents, filling the air with a dense white fog. There were indistinct crashes and angry shouts from within the opacity. A final shot rang out, then came the sound of running feet disappearing into the back of the shop, and a distant door banged.

The siren cut off as abruptly as it had begun and the fog began to disperse. Coughing, the Doctor and Peri cautiously rose from behind their refuge. As they did so an amazing figure emerged out of the thinning mist from an alcove at the back of the shop.

He was a rotund barrel of a man with a white beard and moustache decorating his chubby pink jowls. He wore a wide-brimmed black hat with a red plume, a ruff collar, a scarlet doublet with slashed sleeves and breeches. A scabbard hung from the wide, silver-buckled, leather belt that encompassed his vast waist, while the naked blade itself was being brandished by its owner in flicks and slashes at the air, as though he was still spoiling for a fight. When it became apparent the intruders had fled, he lowered his

14

sword with evident regret.

'Hah! Eluded me in the fog – a plague upon them! Doubtless the scurvy knaves feared my steel!'

'Did you turn on the fire alarm?' the Doctor asked.

'I did indeed, sir. It seemed a little distraction was called for.'

By this time Peri had recovered her voice. 'Sorry, but just who are you?'

The man resheathed his sword and made a bow as low as his bulk allowed, doffing his cap with a flourish. 'Sir John Falstaff at your service, mistress.'

Peri found herself temporarily speechless once more. The Doctor filled in the gap.

'Really. And how did you arrive so conveniently... Sir John?'

'Why, I had entered surreptitiously through the rear portal after the proprietor some time previous, having certain confidential matters I wished to discuss with him, but found the premises already infested with the three varlets you have already encountered. I was preparing to set about them when you made your own entrance. Naturally I could not risk a confrontation with a lady present, so conceived a strategy involving the alarm panel situated in the passage here. But, I pray, stay further expositions for the nonce. What of Hok? Did he depart with the others?'

Peri looked about at the shambles of the shop interior. 'I guess he must have – oh...'

A tentacle protruded from under an overturned cabinet.

They rapidly heaved the debris aside, but it was clearly too late for the little alien. There was a bullet hole in the middle of the chest segment of his body shell – the plastron, as Peri remembered the analogous part was called on Earth animals. Hok's tentacles were twitching feebly, and the eyes in his wrinkled parody of a human face were beginning to lose their focus. From the Doctor's look of sad resignation she knew there was nothing they could do for him.

Overcoming her queasiness, she took one of the outstretched tentacles in her hand, offering what comfort she could. It felt cold and already lifeless.

With a wheeze, Falstaff knelt beside Hok. 'Did they get it, Hok, did they get it? It is I, Falstaff. Is there a duplicate? Tell me and I shall be your avenger... Speak man...'

'Leave him alone!' Peri protested.

But Hok was struggling to speak. A hoarse whisper forced its way out with the last breath in his body, his words broken and barely comprehensible: '... ovans... reasure... 385.06 by 946.573 by 157.67 positive; 385.06 by 946.573 by...' The figures became less audible and gradually trailed away as Hok lay still.

Falstaff was scribbling on the back of his shirt cuff with a pen. Peri looked at the Doctor in dismay and confusion. Suddenly they became aware of a chatter of voices and shadows at the windows.

Falstaff rose with a grunt. 'Please stay by the poor fellow. I shall secure the rear door.' And he disappeared into the back of the shop, moving very quietly for such a big man.

A head peered cautiously in through the half-open door.

'Can you call the police, please,' the Doctor asked its owner crisply. 'There's been a murder.'

Within ten minutes the broad walkway outside Hok's premises was cordoned off and ringed by emergency-service vehicles, its shadows starkly illuminated by coloured flashing lights. The interior of the shop was being examined and Hok's body photographed prior to removal. Astroville Seven's police, Peri discovered, were as varied in form as the throng in the main concourse. While something resembling a small mobile fir tree with eye stalks took statements from passersby, a creature with a sticklike body and a head as smooth and almost as featureless as an egg questioned them. All the two had in common were badges pinned to silver-and-green sashes, and a certain world-weariness that Peri decided must accompany police the universe over.

'So you cannot add any more to your descriptions of the three intruders,' the egg-headed constable said.

'The place was pretty dark and they had some sort of smoky masks on,' Peri pointed out. 'Anyway we only saw them for a few seconds before the rumpus started.'

'Did they call each other by name?'

'As my friend says, there was hardly time,' the Doctor said.

'Perhaps Falstaff knows who they were. He obviously knew the victim.'

'Ah, yes, the third human who turned on the shop's alarm.'

Peri was looking about her. 'Say, Doctor, where's he got to anyway?'

'He went to secure the back door...' the Doctor trailed off with a frown, then added, 'Oh dear.'

'He's dumped us, hasn't he, Doctor?'

'I'm afraid it looks that way.'

'Which leaves nobody else to substantiate your version of events within the shop,' the constable pointed out meaningfully.

'But you can't think we had anything to do with the actual murder!' Peri said. 'We only came here to buy a souvenir. We never saw this Hok person before in our lives.'

'That we shall have to determine, madam. Meanwhile I'll have to ask you to accompany me to headquarters.'

'Are we under arrest?' the Doctor asked.

'Not at all, sir. Merely helping with the ongoing investigation. This way please,' he indicated one of the police cars.

'Has this sort of thing happened to you very often?' Peri inquired grumpily, as they took their seats in the back of the police car and the door had closed with an ominously solid thud.

'From time to time,' the Doctor admitted.

17

'But things always work out OK in the end?'
'Oh, always… well, almost always.'
'Terrific!' said Peri heavily.

CHAPTER 3
DEPARTURES

Arnella Marri Jossena te Rosscarrino was bored.

She had been bored with her cabin on the *Newton*, which was cramped and utilitarian. She had moved to the ship's small common lounge until she had become bored with that. Finally she had taken to pacing the ship's main corridors with a scowl disfiguring her fine features, until it seemed she reached a state of total dissatisfaction with every deckplate and bulkhead door.

Arnella was intelligent enough not to be board if she put her mind to it. The ship's microlibrary alone was sufficient to provide a lifetime's entertainment and diversion, and she was only trying to fill a few hours. But her mind was not at rest. Everything about her surroundings only reminded her that she should be staying at the Stellar Grande, Astroville's five-star hotel, in between shopping for a new wardrobe, jewellery, and perfumes. Instead of which, after a single brief excursion into Astroville proper, her uncle had ordered her to remain on board the *Newton*. Partly, this was for security, and partly for more practical considerations that, currently, she did not care to dwell on.

And so she continued to pace the corridors, determinedly encouraging boredom to mask the deeper, darker despair that lurked within. On perhaps her twenty-fifth circuit she almost ran into Willis Brockwell.

As usual, his tall gangling form was ill-concealed behind his multipocketed utility smock, slightly frayed at the edges. He was carrying a complicated piece of machinery trailing several loose wires. His hair was awry and there was a smudge of grease across one cheek.

'Oh… Ms Rosscarrino… sorry.' He shuffled awkwardly aside to let her pass.

'Ms Rosscarrino' wasn't the correct form of address, but her uncle had suggested they shouldn't encourage use of her proper title for the moment. Besides, it would have sounded false coming from Brockwell's lips. Brockwell, she had decided some time back, disliked rank and titles and all that went with them. He betrayed it by the way he flushed and stammered and then retreated into a sullen silence in her presence. Well she couldn't help his common origins. She might like him better if he had the courage to speak his mind.

Arnella flashed him a look of mild contempt and started to stride past him. Just then the indicator over the main airlock, which was situated a little way down the corridor, blinked, and the inner pressure door swung open.

Her uncle and Professor Thorrin stepped inside. She saw the look on their faces and knew they had been successful. Her uncle's careworn eyes were sparkling and his mouth twitched with the effort of containing an unseemly grin of delight. Thorrin was beaming openly, his normally distracted and impatient manner temporarily masked behind an upsurge of benevolent good humour.

'Congratulate us, Will,' he said heartily, holding a data capsule aloft like a trophy. 'At last, we have it!'

'That's wonderful, Professor,' said Brockwell.

'But… you're sure it's genuine?' Arnella asked her uncle.

The Marquis te Rosscarrino recovered his composure. 'I am certain of it, my dear,' he said with calm authority. 'All the details I expected were there. With a little work we shall finally learn the truth!' And he caught and squeezed her hand in a rare display of emotion.

'To the navigation table!' Thorrin said eagerly.

And the two men strode off down the corridor to the control room, leaving Arnella and Brockwell alone once more. Brockwell mumbled something about getting the ship ready and set off in the other direction, his long legs moving with their usual jerky gait.

Arnella felt light-headed, hope and apprehension mingling within her. Was there really a chance to regain what they had lost? The future promised relief from the fate she dreaded, yet there would undoubtedly be risks, perhaps danger. After all they had already suffered, was it worth further sacrifice? She put down the thought as unworthy. She had a duty to fulfil. Yet she was also acutely aware of her own helplessness in the face of destiny. There would be no time for boredom now. Would she find herself missing it in the days to come?

The flying eye found a niche in the shadowy angle of a stanchion and attached itself to the metal with suction pads. It had followed Rosscarrino and Thorrin all the way from Chocky's Inn, merging easily with the other maintenance bots that constantly flitted about the station engaged upon their single-minded mechanical business. Unseen, it had ridden the same passenger tube as its targets up the docking tower until they had disembarked at the bay in which the *Newton* was berthed. It had hovered silently while they passed within. Now it had a vantage point from which it could observe anybody entering or leaving the *Newton*'s airlock, and it settled down to wait.

Qwaid hesitated before the expensive real-wood door of Mr Alpha's penthouse office apartment. Though they had what he had sent them for, they were late returning and had left behind potential witnesses to their disposal of Hok. It was an untidy piece of work and Mr Alpha hated untidiness. Steeling himself, Qwaid knocked. The door slid aside, and he and Drorgon and Gribbs stepped cautiously inside.

Beyond was a room only slightly smaller than a power tennis court. The distant walls were hung with precisely lit original tri-dees and actual brush paintings. Between them were sculpted forms on pedestals and environmentally controlled cabinets of tinted glass that held books bound with both paper and animal skin over a thousand years old. The far wall was taken up with a panoramic window, which framed the glowing streamers of the local nebula. This spectacle only served as a backdrop to a massive matching chair and desk, constructed of leather and more richly grained real wood, both carefully polished until they seemed to glow with an inner life. Alpha himself sat facing away from the window, as if to say: I can not only afford such a luxury, but I can afford to turn my back on it. This position, combined with the room's angled lighting, had the effect of placing him in silhouette to anybody who stood before the desk. This was not chance. Very little around Mr Alpha ever happened by chance.

Qwaid could see Alpha's distinctive outline behind his desk even as the three of them crossed the silent, thickly carpeted floor. The nebula light glinted off a hairless dome of a head as he bent over a document laid out before him, powerful square shoulders hunched forward, a carefully manicured hamlike hand with a suggestion of purple in its flesh reaching out to a key panel inset in the desktop, thick square-tipped fingers tapping the contacts with surprising delicacy. Except for the tint of his skin and a certain peculiarity about his eyes, Alpha seemed outwardly human. Qwaid had never learnt where he actually came from and suspected it would be unwise to inquire.

Alpha did not look up as they halted before the desk, but merely said, 'I trust you have the item, Qwaid?' His words were precise, his voice its usual level grate – the tones of an erudite but self-educated man.

'Uh, yes, boss.' Qwaid handed the capsule over and Alpha inserted it in a viewer. As he scanned the information, Qwaid thought he heard his breath quicken, and he saw one powerful hand clench as it rested on the desk, then slowly relax. For Alpha that was the equivalent of a shout of wild elation.

After a minute Alpha nodded ponderously. 'Yes, this is the

genuine article, Qwaid. Most… satisfactory.' Again Qwaid sensed that Alpha was controlling himself. Whatever the capsule contained, Qwaid realised, it had to be something important. 'And Hok?'

'He was trying to double-cross you like you guessed, boss. So we had to snuff him.'

'I see. Were there any problems?'

Qwaid swallowed uncomfortably. He didn't like to admit what had gone wrong, but it was always safer to tell Alpha everything – well, almost everything.

'A couple of tourists crashed the party, boss,' he explained. 'Hok had been going to open up and must have pulled the lock remotely and they just walked in. They started a ruck, but we could have taken them out too, only then somebody set off the fire alarm. I knew we couldn't hang around then, so we finished Hok and got out before we drew a crowd. I'm sure nobody saw us, boss. We kept the place eyeballed after we got clear, and saw some big stooge slip out the back way. Gribbs thinks he's seen him before up in the docking tower while he was working on the *Falcon* – he must have a ship there, too. Then the cops started arriving and we faded out. But I'm sure Hok's out of it, and we had our masks on all the time, so the gads couldn't have got much of a look at us.'

'Apparently not,' Alpha said. 'I have been monitoring the police bands, and there have been no descriptions circulated as yet. You have been lucky, Qwaid, but that does not excuse your ineptitude. You should have ensured you would not be disturbed.'

For the first time Alpha raised his head so the light caught his eyes. They were totally black, without any iris or surrounding paler ball, and their unblinking gaze had the same terrible hypnotic quality as that of a snake. They transfixed Qwaid now.

'I picked you and your friends out of the dross of the lower levels because I believed you had some slight potential. Do not give me cause to regret my decision...'

Alpha continued speaking for almost a minute without repeating himself, raising his voice, using expletives or gross threats. Yet somehow this measured dissection of Qwaid's character and ability shamed him far more than any such crudities ever could. It was at such times that Qwaid most hated Alpha, even as he envied the ruthless mentality that shaped the scathing words. He only wished that Gribbs and Drorgon were not present to witness the reprimand. Their continued respect mattered deeply to Qwaid, because, although he needed Alpha for the moment, one day he planned to be sitting behind the magnificent desk with the stars at his back.

Then it was over, and Qwaid said meekly, 'Sorry, boss. It won't happen again.'

'I trust not, Qwaid. Now prepare the *Falcon* for departure.' Alpha's cold eyes turned to Gribbs, who shivered involuntarily. 'Meanwhile, you will identify the ship belonging to the man you saw leaving Hok's premises. There are certain precautions to be taken before we leave.'

Inspector Myra Jaharnus, of the Astroville Police Department, frowned at the Doctor and Peri across the interview-room table. Peri stared defiantly back into her yellow slitted eyes while the Doctor smiled with dreamy amiability. The inspector was a Tritonite, a humanoid reptile, with lightly scaled green skin and a short, bony-frilled crocodile tail which swished impatiently as it hung over the back of her chair – a gesture Peri found both intriguing and irritating. Jaharnus leaned forward and, with a clawed forefinger, tapped the desk screen displaying the scene-of-crime report.

'And you can give no more details about the three persons you saw in the shop, or this "Sir John Falstaff" you say intervened?' she asked.

'For the tenth time,' Peri replied wearily, 'their faces were blurred – and this guy Falstaff did too intervene!'

'The problem is his name does not appear on our records either as a resident or visitor to Astroville.'

'Then isn't it possible he may have given us a false name?' the Doctor suggested gently.

'That had occurred to us' – Jaharnus glanced again at the unpronounceable symbols on the Doctor's identity card and evidently decided not to attempt them – '...Doctor. However, another possibility is that there is no such person. In fact you stated earlier that he was indeed a fictional creation.'

Peri gave another exasperated sigh and wished she had never tried to explain to people, who had evidently never heard of the Bard of Stratford-upon-Avon, about Falstaff's mythical namesake.

'We mean he looked like a famous fictional character. He even spoke like a bad copy of him. But I didn't mean we made him up! Why don't you put out a description? With his build and costume he should stand out like a sore thumb...' An image of the multitude of alien fashions and body forms she had seen in the main concourse caused her to pause. She reminded herself where she was and to stop thinking parochially. 'Uh, I guess maybe around here he isn't so unusual as all that,' she conceded.

'Inspector,' the Doctor said evenly, 'Hok was killed by a gunshot, yet neither I nor my companion have a gun, nor was any found on the premises, so logically there must have been some third party present to have removed it.'

Jaharnus appeared unimpressed. 'And perhaps you're giving a false description of him, or them, to help cover their trails.'

'Look,' said Peri impatiently, 'didn't anybody else see anything that backs up our story?'

Jaharnus flashed the scene-of-crime interviews up on the screen and glanced over them once again. 'Several passers-by and occupants of adjacent shops were alerted by the sounds of items being broken inside Hok's establishment and then the fire alarm, but it was too dark inside to see any details through the window. Nobody else entered the shop until the extinguisher vapour had cleared, where they found only you two and the victim.'

'I suppose nobody was watching the back door while all this was going on?' said Peri.

'Unfortunately, no.'

'You don't really believe we're killers, do you, Inspector?' the Doctor asked. 'What motive could we possibly have?'

'We know Hok occasionally dealt with goods of, shall we say, dubious origins. And I don't just mean antiques. He'd trade anything for a profit. Now you stated earlier that he spoke just before he died: a few garbled words and a string of figures. The combination for something, a set of coordinates or a code possibly? They must have been important for him to use literally his dying breath on them. Perhaps that's the motive.' She looked at the Doctor and Peri narrowly. 'I don't suppose you remember what the numbers were?'

'We could hardly be expected to in the circumstances,' said the Doctor reasonably.

'No, I suppose not. Nevertheless, we'll have to keep you here until we've completed our investigations. Meanwhile, Doctor, I understand you have a ship berthed here.'

'Yes, well, sort of.'

'Sort of?'

'Its not a regular model,' Peri said helpfully.

'Well, whatever it is, I'll have to look it over. Purely routine, you understand.' Her slitted pupils widened. 'Unless you've got something to hide.'

'If I did, you'd have a job finding it on my ship,' the Doctor remarked idly.

'He means it's surprisingly spacious for a compact,' Peri added quickly.

'I'm sure they'll be room for one more.'

'Oh there's plenty of room,' said Peri. 'That's what you've got to be prepared for.'

Thorrin and Rosscarrino had been hunched over the navigation table and its inbuilt computer for an hour, calling up star charts and plotting complex curves in its pseudo-three-dimensional depths. Eventually the lines intersected at a particular glowing dot among the millions within the machine's memory. Thorrin read the short string of numbers and symbols that tagged the pinpoint and beamed at the Marquis, who nodded solemnly in return. Arnella, who had been unobtrusively watching from the back of the control room, felt the breath catch in her throat.

'Will!' Thorrin called out loudly.

His assistant appeared. 'Yes, Professor?'

'Prepare to take us out of here. I'll give you a precise course once we've cleared local traffic space.'

Brockwell took his seat at the flight controls and opened a communications channel. 'Tower control, this is the ESS *Newton*, bay 37. We request a departure vector and clearance for undocking.'

The inner airlock doors of bay 37's docking tube closed automatically. Through the observation window the securing clamps could be seen retracting as the compact dumbbell form of the *Newton* edged away, impelled by short bursts of its manoeuvring thrusters. As it did so, the flying eye silently detached itself from its place of concealment and glided up the docking tower. At bay 53 it slipped into the open airlock of a compact grey ship, which closed immediately behind it.

Two minutes later the grey ship departed from Astroville on a course almost identical to that taken by the *Newton*.

Qwaid was waiting impatiently by the *Falcon*'s secondary airlock as it cycled and filled. The inner door opened and Gribbs emerged, unsnapping his helmet.

'OK? Nobody saw you?'

'Kept to the shadows. Set it just like the boss wanted.'

'It'd better be, unless you want him to give you the eye as well. We can't have another duff-up on this job.'

'It's as good as done,' Gribbs insisted indignantly, as though his competence was being called into question.

'OK, let's get going.'

The *Falcon*'s main airlock closed and the docking tube retracted. Shortly after, the *Falcon*, too, had left Astroville's traffic space.

Casting many anxious looks about him, sword and sheath collapsed and coat reversed to display a sober black, Falstaff approached the docking-tower passenger tubes. He had made his way from the service passage at the back of Hok's shop by a circuitous route, just in case he was being followed. With a final apprehensive glance around he practically leapt into a clear slot in the tube traffic and let the paragravity fields waft him up the shaft. He disembarked at bay 86 and hurried for the lock of his own ship. Only once its hatch had closed solidly behind him did he draw in a deep shuddering breath and let it slowly out in relief.

For a minute he rested against the inside of the hatch, recovering his composure and dabbing the sweat from his forehead with a fine lace-edged handkerchief. Then he hauled his impressive bulk upright and made for the control cabin. Once seated in the pilot's seat, he slid down his shirt cuff, and began entering the figures he had scrawled upon it into the ship's autopilot.

Myra Jaharnus looked about at the spacious console room of the Doctor's craft in disbelief. Shaking her head, she walked back out through its open doorway, across the short docking tube and into the docking bay itself. The constable who had accompanied them looked at her curiously as she peered out of the bay's observation port. The end of the docking tube still appeared to connect with a battered rectangular blue box not exceeding three metres in any dimension. It could have been an oddly designed station shuttle or escape pod. At the most it might have held four people. She re-entered the craft's impossible interior where Peri and the Doctor waited patiently.

'What did you say it was called again?'

'A TARDIS,' the Doctor said brightly.

'And how does it all...' She waved a hand uncertainly at her unlikely surroundings.

'Ah, well according to hyperdimensional engineering theory, space-time continua can be folded by the application of –'

'Enough – I shouldn't have asked.'

'I did say it was spacious, didn't I?' said Peri with a grin. 'Nothing illegal about having a spaceship that's bigger inside than out, is there?'

'No... I just haven't seen anything quite like it before.'

'You're welcome to search for anything linking us to Hok or his killers,' said the Doctor, waving a genial hand at the doorway that led to the rest of the ship. 'Any antiques you find are mine.'

'Can you prove that?'

'Inspector,' the Doctor said with quiet dignity, 'I've had some of them since they were new.'

Myra couldn't tell whether he was joking or not. 'You two stay right there,' she said firmly, and disappeared through the doorway.

While Jaharnus was making her inspection, Peri turned anxiously to the Doctor.

'Is that identity card of mine you gave the cops OK? I didn't even know I had one for here and now until you handed it over. Suppose they check back with Earth and find I was born over a thousand years ago?'

'Don't worry, Peri. Both it and the data on Earth will show your real place of birth and all the other necessary details, but simply with appropriately adjusted dates.'

'But where did you get it made up? And how did you fix the records back on... oh. Dumb question. Did you drop in there while I was asleep?'

The Doctor smiled. 'The details are unimportant. For now let's just say there are certain optional benefits to travelling in time of which I have decided to take advantage.'

A new thought struck Peri. 'But what about your documents? You're not from Earth.'

'No, but I did live there for a while in your century – as a resident alien, you might say – when I was provided with official identity papers. I've simply ensured they've been kept up to date over the intervening years. You never know when the right references may come in useful.'

'Did you ever think of the killing you could make on Wall Street with tricks like that?'

The Doctor looked appalled. 'Really, Peri. That wouldn't be cricket.'

Inspector Jaharnus returned to the console room.

'Just how many rooms are there in this ship?' she demanded.

'Well it varies,' admitted the Doctor. 'I had to shed a few thousand tonnes a while ago, but the TARDIS has regenerated most of the lost mass, I think –'

'Forget I asked. You can lock off the controls if you want, but I'll have to ask you to hand over the main hatch key. Just in case, may the gods forbid, we have to search this ship properly.'

'But the key is sensitised to my body pattern.'

'Very security conscious, Doctor – now desensitise it.'

The Doctor sighed, pressed the key to his forehead and closed his eyes for a moment, then handed it over to Jaharnus.

'We're going to have to check both of you out properly,' Jaharnus said. 'That means putting a request through to Earth for your records.'

'Well why don't you get on with it?' Peri said lightly. 'We've got nothing to hide.'

'Don't be impatient, Ms Brown. This far from Earth it takes six days to receive a reply, even via hyper relay.'

'Six days!'

'You'll stay in Astroville in reasonable comfort at the city's expense, but not aboard this ship.'

'Don't you trust us?' asked the Doctor.

'A suspicious mind goes with the job, Doctor. I have this picture of you suddenly remembering those numbers of Hok's, and trying to leave here without telling me first.'

Falstaff's shipboard synthesiser had a cordon bleu culinary program, so his meal had been excellent. Now he was reclining in a form-fitting massage chair in the ship's compact lounge, sipping a goblet of wine and listening to a recording of the Astroville local newsnet broadcasts he had made before his ship had slipped into hyperspace. He had long ago determined his priorities in such matters, and refused to allow bad news to spoil his appreciation of good food.

'Now, ballasted with capon and sack, I can face whatever slings and arrows outrageous fortune may hurl my way,' he soliloquised.

To his relief, thanks to a late-breaking political scandal, Hok's death was relegated to fourth place in the hourly summary. A man and woman were said to be helping with inquiries, but there was no mention of his part in the proceedings. Of course, the authorities might still be searching for him, but it was definitely encouraging. The longer it took them to make a positive identification the farther he and his ship would be from their jurisdiction; though he felt a slight pang of regret that his actions might have left those two tourists in a compromising position.

'However, for the nonce, discretion must be the better part of valour.' He raised his goblet again. 'To good fortune!' he toasted loudly.

Then an explosion jerked the goblet from his hand and split his ship open from stem to stern.

CHAPTER 4
HISTORY LESSONS

The *Falcon* had been under way for six hours when Qwaid knocked on the door of Alpha's stateroom. When he was bidden to enter he found his employer hunched over a compact duplicate of his office desk computer.

'What is is, Qwaid?'

'Thought you'd like to know, boss. We just picked up a hyperspace distress-beacon signal from behind us. Very weak, like it's going to die at any moment. The call sign matches the ship you had Gribbs fit his little present to.'

'Then I may assume our interfering friend will no longer be giving us any trouble. Is the signal likely to be detected in Astroville?'

'Shouldn't think so, boss. We're only picking it up because he's close by.'

Alpha stiffened slightly, and a new edge entered his words. 'Therefore he was either following us or on a similar course.'

A cold sweat broke out on Qwaid's brow. He hadn't thought of that implication. 'Uh, I guess so, boss.'

'So we may conclude that either he obtained the course information while he was in Hok's shop, presumably from a duplicate data capsule you overlooked in the confusion, or else Hok had already passed on a duplicate of the information.' Alpha's cold eyes lifted to transfix him. 'It had better not be the latter, Qwaid. Ever since he mooted the deal, I expressly ordered you to watch him and prevent that very eventuality –'

'He must have picked it up in the shop, boss,' Qwaid assured him, gulping desperately. 'We were watching Hok night and day like you said. We moved in as soon as we were sure he'd picked up the original capsule from the courier. He must have made a copy just before we arrived.'

It seemed an eternity before the cold depthless eyes left him.

'I trust that is the case. It would not do to disappoint me so soon after my last lecture on your competence.'

'No, boss.' Qwaid took a relieved breath, then hesitated. Despite a sinking feeling that was growing steadily in the pit of his stomach, his curiosity demanded an answer on another matter. 'Uh, there is another thing, boss.'

'Well?'

'Just so we can be ready to move quickly, for efficiency like, can you tell us what we're after? I mean is there a lot of it and is it going to take any special gear to shift?'

For a moment he thought he'd been presumptuous, but then Alpha nodded. 'That is a reasonable question. Perhaps you are learning to think ahead at last. Very well. If we find what I expect, you must be prepared to move a variety of items of different sizes. Ensure there are suitable containers ready in the hold.'

'And any other equipment, boss? Is there a vault to crack, or any guards that'll need taking care of?'

'Perhaps, Qwaid, you had better prepare for all eventualities. But the reward will be worth it.'

'Is this the big one, boss?' Qwaid ventured, intrigued by Alpha's palpable sense of barely concealed anticipation.

'Quaintly put, but an apposite description. Yes, this is "the big one".' Alpha allowed himself a low chuckle. 'But I doubt if you will appreciate the true value of what we may find.'

'I've got a good eye for valuables, boss,' Qwaid replied defensively.

'But this is more than mere monetary wealth, Qwaid. This will be a piece of history!'

Astroville's freefall dome was filled with darting, swooping figures beating their brightly coloured strap-on wings. Peri watched them grumpily from the observation gallery, her arms still aching from her own recent session. It had been fun, but she knew she was not in the right mood to fully appreciate flying like a bird.

'Why the long face?' the Doctor asked, after she had been silent for a long while. 'I thought the other day you said Astroville was a splendid place to be.'

'That was before we were put under house arrest... well, city arrest,' she pointed out tersely.

'I'm afraid you'll simply have to be patient, Peri.'

'I guess I'm not as good at it as you are.'

'No. You come from an impatient species, and you have youth against you as well.' He patted her hand. 'Don't worry, you'll learn in time.'

She looked at him curiously, suspecting he was hiding his resentment at their situation for her sake. If that was so, she couldn't penetrate his mask. Meanwhile, there was something she had been meaning to find out, and this seemed as a good a time as any. 'Uh, Doctor. Can I ask, just how old are you?'

'In your years, about eight hundred and fifty,' he replied easily.

She decided he wasn't putting her on. She took a deep breath and tried not to show too much surprise. 'Oh. I see. I suppose you would learn a lot about being patient in that time.'

He smiled. 'That among other things.'

There was another long silence, then Peri said with a sigh, 'I just wish there was something we could do to speed everything up.'

'Well it might help if we could fathom out Hok's last words.'

'Apart from those numbers, you mean? "Ovans reasure" it sounded like. Maybe it was in his own language?'

'You'd have understood it just as well if it had been. I told you, the TARDIS takes care of that sort of thing. No, I think it was some words the poor chap hadn't the strength to pronounce completely.'

'It meant something to Falstaff.'

'Yes, but he evidently already understood the context.'

'Then took off leaving us to face the music. Must have been something important.'

'Or valuable.'

'You mean like buried treasure or something? That would be too much!'

The Doctor had gone very still. 'Peri,' he said softly. 'I think you may have hit the nail on the head. Come on!' He leapt from his seat and headed briskly towards the exit.

'Where are we going?' Peri demanded, running after him.

'To find a library,' he said, suddenly sounding breathless with excitement. There's something I want to look up.'

Qwaid was talking to Gribbs and Drorgon in the *Falcon*'s control room. Every so often they cast anxious glances back down the corridor to Alpha's stateroom.

'Remember that full money case Hok had with him in the shop?' Qwaid said, licking dry lips.

'What about it?' said Gribbs.

'Suppose he really did get it for selling a copy of the capsule on to somebody – I mean somebody else, not the fat man.'

'But we watched Hok for last five days,' Drorgon rumbled. 'Just like the boss said.'

'Yeah, but we lost him a couple of times, didn't we?' Qwaid reminded him. 'Only we didn't mention it to the boss, did we?'

'Wasn't for long,' Gribbs said, with a dismissive sniff.

'Maybe long enough for him to pick up the original capsule earlier than we thought and make copies. How do we know how many he might have sold before we got to him? Who else might be coming after us?'

'Can't be very many.'

'That's right,' said Drorgon, clenching his massive fists enthusiastically. 'And we'll take care of them, you'll see.'

'But suppose even one turns up. The boss'll know then, won't he? And he'll kill us!'

'Urr, no,' said Drorgon, with a rare flash of perception. 'Kill you maybe, Qwaid. He'll still need us to do work for him.'

* * *

In an age of electronic data storage and transfer, Peri wondered if libraries as distinct entities still existed. However, inquires soon led them to Astroville's Central Archive. Perhaps there was some herd instinct that still ensured scholars preferred to congregate in lofty rooms with airs of slightly dusty, hushed silence. And though what she thought of as real books were kept in closed cabinets and were accessible only to licensed users, the information the Doctor needed was all on computer file, and readily accessible for a modest fee. The Doctor's lean fingers danced over the keyboard, and text was soon flashing across the screen within their study cubicle.

Rovan Hathcorl Clemont Delermain Cartovall.
Born 608,432.93 (Galactic Time Index) (1973 bc Terrestrial Calendar) on planet Centros, capital of Cartovallian stellar empire; comprising some fifty systems and 2.8×10^{11} subjects. First son of Emperor Dorrian III and Empress Kalia of Cartovall. Became Emperor in 608,465.04 GTI. Disappeared 608,469.29 GTI during voyage to vacation world of Serenity, when he ordered all crew to leave his private yacht at a remote Imperial outpost and took the vessel on alone to an unknown destination. It was later discovered that he had secretly arranged for the contents of the palace treasury (estimated value in current terms 6.4×10^{12} stellar credits) to be loaded aboard his yacht before departure from Centros. Despite a multi-system search by the Imperial forces, neither Rovan nor his treasure was ever found. As Rovan had no offspring he was eventually succeeded to the throne by his younger brother Athren in 608,472.63 GTI. This event is often said to mark the beginnings of the disintegration of the Cartovallian Empire.
For further biographical information see...

'And all that was five thousand years ago,' Peri said, looking up from the viewer. 'And nobody's found out what happened to Rovan since then?'

'Not as far as I know.'

Peri's eyes sparkled. '"Rovan's Treasure". You think that's what Hok was trying to say?'

'It's a strong possibility. Such a fortune would explain the ruthlessness of those three thugs we met and Falstaff's behaviour.'

'And the numbers were some sort of map reference for it – X marks the spot and so on?'

'Perhaps,' the Doctor said.

'But after all this time, what sort of line can they have got on any treasure, assuming it's still around?'

'I don't know,' admitted the Doctor, a smile creasing his smooth features, 'but it might be interesting to find out.'

Commissioner Vorland of the Astroville Police Department shook his head regretfully.

'I'm sorry, Inspector. Your section chief passed on your request but I can't spare the personnel or equipment to mount any sort of close surveillance at the moment. In any case I certainly wouldn't sanction any search of Alpha's home or business premises on the strength of this.' He tapped the crime file displayed on his office screen.

Myra Jaharnus looked at him uncomprehendingly. 'The word on the lower levels is that Hok was expecting the delivery of something important, and that he'd also contacted Alpha recently. Qwaid, Gribbs, and Drorgon have been seen in the area close to Hok's shop several times in the last few days. Based on all known factors, the computer assessed them as the most probable suspects.'

'Only a seventy-three-per-cent probability,' Vorland reminded her, consulting the case file again. 'You say here that the perpetrators wore glimmer masks. Perhaps two were human and one Cantarite. There are no usable bio traces to tie them in with the scene of crime. The murder weapon is still

38

missing. Then there's this character out of a storybook who may or may not be connected with the first three, and who may not actually exist. And all this on the word of two tourists you obviously suspect yourself, yet who have no apparent link with Alpha. Have you changed your mind about them?'

'I'm beginning to believe they might just be innocent bystanders like they say, sir, though I still think there's something odd about them. I'll know more when the reports come through from Earth.'

'And this "Falstaff"?'

'No trace yet.'

Vorland sighed. 'It's a mess. You daren't proceed further against Alpha until you've sorted out these other loose ends, and by the time you do the trail will have gone cold.'

'Which is why I want to put Alpha under close surveillance right now.'

'Forget it, Inspector. The waters are already too muddy on this one. I want Alpha put away as badly as you do, but I never underestimate him. If we touch his men he'll have alibis arranged for them within the hour. Make one move directly against him without solid evidence to justify it, and he'll be calling down the civil rights charter on us and talking about police harassment, which will simply make it harder to make a move if and when we ever have something stronger to use against him.'

'But a citizen of Astroville has been murdered!'

Vorland shrugged almost indifferently. 'Old Hok? You pulled him in a few times yourself, didn't you?'

Jaharnus stiffened. 'Minor import infringements, selling suspect antiques to tourists, that sort of thing. An old alien who lived close to the edge as best he could. Maybe he stepped over the line a couple of times.' She got up to leave. 'But he never harmed anyone in any way that mattered – and he still didn't deserve to die like that!'

She strode out of Vorland's office, managing to scrape her

tail across the door as it closed behind her and hoping it left a mark.

The first thing she found when she got back to her desk was a belated message from traffic control informing her that Alpha's ship had left the city several hours earlier, destination unknown. Had he run to avoid answering awkward questions, or was there some other reason for his departure? She felt the yoke of depression settle more heavily on her shoulders. By now, Alpha was probably out of their jurisdiction. And if Vorland wouldn't fund a standard surveillance operation, he certainly wouldn't stand for the cost of sending a police interceptor after him. In any case, Alpha probably had a perfectly legitimate reason for his sudden departure all highly polished and ready to wheel out should it be needed.

Still feeling dispirited, she checked on the activities of Peri Brown and the Doctor. At least she had been able to arrange standard monitoring on them without any problems, as they were still the nearest things they had so far to either witnesses or suspects.

A minute later she was frowning over the reports. What had possessed them to make for the Central Archive so suddenly? Still frowning, she called up the directory for the number of the chief archivist.

The first thing Qwaid noticed as he entered Alpha's stateroom was a glass and a half-empty decanter on the desk beside the computer screen. Then he realised Alpha's skin seemed a shade darker than usual.

'Here they are, Qwaid,' Alpha said almost mildly, holding out a data chip. 'Final course details. Enter them in the autopilot and confirm our ETA.'

Qwaid accepted the chip mutely, trying to cover his confusion. He'd never seen Alpha like this before. Even when he'd pulled off some really major filch in the past he'd stayed ice-cold sober and simply started planning the next one.

'What's the matter, Qwaid?'

'Nothing, boss. It's just… well, you never usually… er, celebrate like this.'

'I was merely toasting the memory of a man long dead, Qwaid. Perhaps a fool, perhaps an adventurer. In either case our unwitting benefactor. To Rovan of Cartovall…'

'Who, boss?'

Alpha blinked, as though reviewing what he had just said. Then the familiar edge returned to his voice with a snap.

'Don't trouble yourself with it. Leave the thinking to me and concentrate on providing the unskilled help. I'll tell you all you need to know when the time comes.' His eyes burnt coldly, causing Qwaid to flinch. 'Well get on with it!'

Trembling, Qwaid scuttled back out of the door, head hung low.

Outside in the corridor, however, he straightened up again, letting his face show the anger and resentment he would never dare let Alpha see.

The boss shouldn't have spoken to him like that. He wasn't simply some dumb slab of hired muscle. It wasn't right to keep him in the dark about what they were getting into, either. Well he'd show the boss he could think for himself!

He strode resolutely along the corridor to the control cabin. Gribbs and Drorgon were in the crewroom, so for the moment he had the place to himself. He sat down before the auxiliary systems console and called up the general database history files.

It took a few minutes to sort through the wide parameters he had to set and the phonetic variants of the name Alpha had let slip, but soon his lips were moving as he read the information he was after. The database was basic and the entry was not a long one, but it was enough. Qwaid felt a shiver run up his spine and drew in his breath with a shudder. An emperor's treasury! What he couldn't do with a slice of that!

41

His reverie was interrupted by Alpha's voice coming out of the intercom. 'Have you entered the new course yet, Qwaid?'

'Just doing it, boss,' he called back guiltily, and rammed the data chip into the slot and started punching buttons.

As the autopilot digested the data and projected the new course, he brooded further. He had no idea what they'd meet when they got to wherever it was, but for the biggest snatch ever he'd risk anything. Well why not? He'd show the boss. He'd run the job himself given the chance. He didn't need Alpha looking over his shoulder all the time.

He didn't need him.

The thought hung in his mind, a weak and feeble thing at first, but slowly growing in strength as he considered the full implications of the simple statement.

He didn't need Alpha at all.

Suddenly he knew the last twenty years had just been a prelude to this moment. Twenty years before he'd stolen a box of jek fruit from a market stall in Dryden Dome back on Sirius Nine. It had been the initiation test to get into the Burke Cross Gang.

How he'd ducked and dived the length of the market tunnel to get away with it. Still breathless, knees scraped and bleeding, he'd presented his proud trophy to the rest of the gang. They'd eaten all the fruit, leaving none for him. Ten minutes later the stallholder had caught up with him and given him the sort of hiding his father had regularly delivered when he'd still been around.

Well now it was his turn. He could learn from the past as well as the boss. Maybe better.

But how could he do it? Not to his face. He could never defy those eyes for long enough, as Alpha was arrogantly aware. But there were other means. Yes, the method was obvious now he thought of it. The boss had already shown how to deal with somebody who was in your way. Accidents could happen, and space was awfully unforgiving.

But when?

Right now, before the flush of anger that fuelled his courage died. No time to talk it over with Gribbs and Drorgon. In any case they'd never have the guts. But he had. He'd show them all just what Crelly Qwaid could do.

He took a toolkit from the service locker and went out into the corridor, feeling numb and oddly detached from his actions. He unlatched an inspection panel, exposing a service conduit, and calmly traced cables from the main airlock and Alpha's cabin door. A few snips with the cutters, two cross connections and it was done.

Qwaid returned to the control room, quietly closed its airtight hatch, went over to the engineer's station, and strapped himself into the chair. He opened a cover plate on the panel and pulled out a circuit board, disengaging the secondary safety system. Then, with a deep breath, he released the cover guard on a sliding toggle and pulled it down to the bottom of its slot.

With a feeling as though the floor had dropped from under his feet, the *Falcon*'s paragravity faded away.

He swallowed hard to keep his stomach under control, and resolutely started punching buttons. Safety doors slid closed, isolating the main corridor and the sleeping compartments. Alarms sounded and distant thumps came from the crewroom as Gribbs and Drorgon pounded on the hatch. The control-room intercom monitor came to life, showing the image of Alpha floating in his cabin like some misshapen balloon, his face enlarged as he pulled himself towards the console pickup.

'Qwaid!' he bellowed. 'What's happening? Qwaid!'

Qwaid kept his eyes firmly fixed on the controls and hit the last button.

With a faint whirr both doors of the main airlock opened simultaneously, followed immediately by the hiss and roar of escaping air. The whole ship trembled and the port in the control-room door suddenly clouded with mist. The door of Alpha's stateroom, which normally should have sealed itself at the first sign of pressure loss, slid open smoothly.

Only then, when the irrevocable step had been taken, did Qwaid dare look directly at the monitor.

Alpha's bloated features filled the screen. Frighteningly, even at the last he showed no fear, only overpowering rage, his eyes as baleful as ever. His lips moved, and there came faintly to Qwaid over the roar of escaping air, 'You'll regret this...'

Then he was jerked backward as though by an invisible hand, rebounded from the door frame and spun out into the main corridor. The distorted starscape of hyperspace blazed beyond the gaping airlock. With the last gust of escaping air Alpha tumbled through it and into eternity.

CHAPTER 5
CELEBRATIONS

The transdimensional portal that opened into the space-time vortex flew towards the nebula, which still glowed hotly after its ejection from the stellar furnace that gave it birth. A heterogeneous elemental plasma flowed through the portal and into the black marble chamber, held in check by the mental fields of Shalvis and the others of the Seventh Circle. Then the portal was allowed to collapse until it was a microscopic point of warped space at the core of the softly glowing amorphous form that pulsated before them.

The lights came on, and the Seers sank their heads in exhausted relief.

'We have done well,' Shalvis said softly. 'It is stabilised for as long as we require. Now we can only wait.'

Arnella Rosscarrino sprawled on the narrow bunk in her cabin on the *Newton*. Resting before her was a portable reader screen displaying a copy of the text contained within the data capsule her uncle and Thorrin had bought on Astroville. She ran it through for what must have been the twentieth time, though she practically knew it word for word now. It held a terrible fascination, yet she also thought she hated it. In the fruitless quest for a document such as this, her father had dissipated the family fortune and broken his heart.

Her uncle, now the only other surviving member of her family, had been infected with the same passion. Since he had become her guardian she had seen him consume his own wealth in the same futile quest; houses, servants and possessions had been stripped away until they had nothing but a name and honour left. Then, with bitter irony, when they no longer had the means, the word came to them that an

45

obscure trader on Astroville Seven was offering what they had been looking for. Cautiously, her uncle had moved outside his normal circles to find the backer they needed. And he had found Alex Thorrin, one of that rare breed of financially successful and acute scientist-inventors. He had piqued his curiosity about the underlying reasons for Rovan's disappearance almost as much as with the promise of raw wealth, and soon had a convert and partner almost as fervent as himself. Thorrin agreed to support them until a division of the spoils could be arranged.

Rosscarrinos living on charity! The thought sickened her. And all for what? Simply an extract translated from a spacecraft log written almost five thousand standard years before. Its author could hardly have imagined that one day it might change the course of history.

He had been the master of a vessel crewed by Ymerl, a race of methane-breathers who lived at supercold temperatures. The account told of how their hyperdrive motors had developed a fault, forcing them to drop back into normal interstellar space. While there they had encountered another spacecraft drifting past them at extreme detector range. Curious as to what a vessel would be doing in interstellar space and getting no response to their hails, they pursued and boarded it. They found it was quite empty of both people and artefacts. However, from the description of its markings, it could only have been Rovan's yacht. There was no clue as to why it had been abandoned, but the evacuation appeared to have been orderly and there was no sign of any damage. Only one lifeboat was missing. As the ship was designed for the use of warm-blooded oxygen-breathers it was of no use to the Ymerl, so they left it to go on its way, merely noting its current course and speed.

In those few figures rested the hopes and dreams of the House of Rosscarrino.

Because the Ymerl had little contact with the rest of the galactic community of the time, they had no idea of the significance of their find. It took many years for this information to filter through to other races, by which time the Cartovallian empire had already begun to disintegrate. And so for thousands of years the curious discovery had been ignored, until somebody came across it who recognised its potential value. Because, converting from the Ymerl's reference system and allowing for stellar drift over time, it was possible to project the yacht's course backwards to its point of origin. But this was not the system where Rovan had abandoned his crew, so presumably it was the point at which he had emptied the ship of its treasure.

This innocent document might be the clue to almost unimaginable wealth – and perhaps something more.

She flicked a key to replace the text with an even more familiar image, one that she had known since she was a small girl. It was a scarred and much-reproduced picture of an ancient book, a massive folio bound with golden strapwork and studded with rare gemstones. And once more the unworthy thought rose within her that she never dared admit to her uncle. Had it all been worthwhile?

'There's… there's something we've forgotten…' Gribbs said blearily to Qwaid, who was cradling his head on his hands in an attempt to keep it firmly fixed to his shoulders. Drorgon was slumped in his oversize chair in one corner. His snores made the forest of bottles on the crewroom table rattle. The drinking session had now lasted three days. Fortunately the *Falcon*'s autopilot was steering the ship.

They were drunk on what had been the select contents of Alpha's cabinet. For Gribbs and Drorgon it had been to steady their nerves after the shock of Alpha's demise. For Qwaid it had been an attempt to blot out the memory of Alpha's eyes staring out of the monitor in those final seconds. Gradually it had turned into a shared celebration of a sort of new-found freedom. Then they had continued because, though they would not admit it, they were all frightened of waking up sober in a world that no longer contained Alpha. He may have ruled them partly through fear, but at least he'd always known what to do next. Now all the decisions were up to them, or rather, as Gribbs and Drorgon realised, up to Qwaid. For the moment they were in awe of him. But could he really take the boss's place?

Qwaid attempted to focus on Gribbs. It wasn't easy, as there seemed to be two of him. 'What've we forgotten then?'

Gribbs frowned with the mental effort. 'Inna hold... Alpha's strongbox...'

The strongbox was the size of a large wardrobe, and Alpha took it with him on every journey. Privately they guessed it contained assorted gems and precious metals, plus a few select items from Alpha's collection, stored ready should he ever have had to leave Astroville in a hurry. Through the alcoholic mists, Qwaid recalled that Alpha had gone to the hold an hour or so after they had left port, just after he had made his initial course calculations. Was there a connection? Perhaps the strongbox also held files Alpha had not wanted to commit to his shipboard desk computer, maybe information about wherever it was they were going. Whatever it was, didn't it all belong to him now, as Alpha's successor?

Qwaid struggled to his feet. 'C'mon,' he said to Gribbs, 'get your toolkit.' He stumbled across the room and kicked Drorgon into wakefulness. 'We're going to have a look inside old Alpha's box.'

Five minutes later they stood, rather unsteadily, in the hold before the strongbox. It stood upright and as tall as Drorgon, secured to a bulkhead by bolted flanges. It was made of some dull grey synthetic material, no doubt specially formulated to be resistant to drill bits, thermal cutters, and corrosives. The close-fitting lid was featureless, save for a single black disc in its very centre.

Gribbs blinked at it through bloodshot eyes and tried to

assess it professionally. 'Yeah, well it's a Brody and Yang Executive Model 18,' he announced, clicking his tongue. 'Obdurite body, tuned molecular pattern lock. It's going to take some cracking.'

He opened his specialised toolkit, flexed his fingers to loosen them, then began taking out small sensor receptor units and placing them carefully around the lock and rim of the lid. Despite his inebriation, his hands moved swiftly and surely. Once the sensors were in place he put on a pair of slim headphones and began delicately adjusting the controls built into his toolkit lid.

Then he stiffened, the colour draining from his face.

'What?' Qwaid demanded.

Gribbs's eyes had widened and he suddenly looked uncomfortably sober. Very carefully he took off his headset. 'Something inside there is in the middle of a countdown sequence. It sounds like... like the timer circuit for a bomb.'

'How big?' Drorgon demanded, also apparently sobering rapidly. 'Just enough to take out the box... or the ship?'

'How should I know!' Gribbs snapped back.

'Well how long's it got left to run?' Qwaid asked.

'I don't know!' Gribbs shouted wretchedly, clutching his aching head. 'Probably something he had to keep resetting. It could blow any time! Krek it, Qwaid! Why did you have to get rid of the boss while we were out here?'

For a moment Qwaid looked at them blankly, and Alpha's last words echoed mockingly through his confusion. Then his brain seemed to jerk into life. 'Find the cutters and get it loose – tear out the hull plates if you have to. When it's free we'll cut the hold grav field and blow it out the cargo lock. Move!'

It was twelve heartstopping, sweat-filled minutes before the *Falcon*'s cargo hatch swung open. In a billow of air and crystallising water vapour, the grey strongbox tumbled away – following its former owner into the void.

Qwaid watched it go on the external monitor with a sigh of

relief. Then he took a deep breath and turned to the others. 'OK, so we lost Alpha's stash. But we're still on to something better – remember that. We'll be there in a couple of days and we'll need to be sharp, so go and sleep it off, and no more juice from now on, understand? This is going to be the big one!'

'I propose a toast,' said the Marquis, smiling at Arnella, then at the others seated round the dining table in the *Newton*'s lounge. They raised their glasses.

'In a few hours we shall reach our destination,' he continued. 'So I give you: luck and destiny. May neither let us down!'

As they drank, Arnella noticed that Brockwell, who was seated opposite her, was wearing a troubled expression. Professor Thorrin apparently noticed it as well.

'Why the long face, Will?' he asked benevolently.

Brockwell looked uncomfortable. 'Uh, sorry, Professor. It's just that I can't help wondering… about the treasure.'

'Well?'

Brockwell was obviously unhappy about appearing to contradict his employer, but he spoke up. 'Well for one thing, we're acting as though it'll be lying around just waiting to be picked up.'

Thorrin chuckled tolerantly. 'Hardly. We're prepared for a long search, if need be, but we can already narrow down its scope. From all the evidence, Rovan abandoned his ship voluntarily. Therefore, it must have been on a habitable world. But the system is listed as being uninhabited, at least by any intelligent life. We have equipment aboard that can detect traces of any artificial structures or a quantity of refined metal at considerable distances. Rovan did not have the means to conceal it from any such detailed search, but then why should he? The only clue to where he unloaded his hoard was his ship, and it was a remarkable chance that it was ever discovered.'

Surprisingly, Brockwell raised another question. 'Well, after five thousand years, what chance is there that it'll still be where he left it. Suppose somebody else has already taken it? According to the Ymerl log a lifeboat was missing. Suppose Rovan used it later to move his hoard.'

Unexpectedly Arnella found herself agreeing with Brockwell. 'Yes. Sometimes I've wondered that myself,' she added, almost timidly.

The Marquis flashed a disappointed glance at her, but said confidently, 'A lifeboat would be far too small to transport anything but a fraction of the treasure. Remember, the search continued for years and huge rewards were offered for any clue leading to Rovan or the recovery of the missing treasure. If any item had turned up, whoever had traded it would have immediately been questioned. There is no evidence Rovan ever used his stolen wealth, and every reason to suppose the bulk of it is still waiting to be discovered.'

'And we shall find it,' Thorrin said, raising his glass once more, then leaning back in his chair easily. 'Now, enough of negativism. At the risk of tempting fate, have you any more thoughts on what you plan to do with your share, Rosscarrino?'

'Only to restore my family's proper rank and position,' the Marquis replied automatically. 'I shall be able to reclaim our ancestral estates once more, and ensure they are managed as they should be.'

'What about you, Professor?' Arnella said quickly. 'Have you any special plans?'

Thorrin blinked, as though surprised by the direct question, but responded smoothly: 'Why, it's always been my dream to found an institute for pure scientific research. There must be thousands of worthy projects currently denied funding because of commercial or governmental shortsightedness. Think what tremendous advances and discoveries might be made by turning those baubles of Rovan's to practical use.'

'I trust you do not deny the value of the craftsmanship that went into shaping those "baubles", Professor,' said her uncle.

'As long as you do not deny the beauty in science, Marquis,' Thorrin countered.

Arnella frowned as their conversation fell into good-humoured and inconsequential banter. She saw Brockwell's eyes meet hers across the table, and for a moment she saw the same concern mirrored in them, before he looked away in his usual awkward manner. But the brief contact had confirmed her suspicion. She knew her uncle had not told the whole truth just then – but what was Thorrin concealing from them?

The *Newton* drove smoothly on though hyperspace. Behind it, just out of detector range and quite unsuspected, the nondescript grey ship followed along the same course.

CHAPTER 6
RESCUE

Peri made the best of their enforced confinement on Astroville by spending further instructive and educational time in the archives. She was curious to find pictures showing the Cartovallian royal family looking quite human, even though they had been taken some four thousand years before Earth developed interstellar travel. The Doctor explained that the humanoid form was already widespread throughout the galaxy long before then, adding vaguely that 'my people' were partly responsible. That was obviously another story in itself, but for the moment it was the mystery of Rovan that intrigued Peri. One question still remained unanswered after five thousand years. What could possibly induce a man who apparently had everything to give it all up?

Then, after a week, came a summons to police headquarters.

It was Jaharnus's sergeant who informed them that the report from Earth has been satisfactory. They were no longer suspected of any involvement in the death of Hok and were free to leave Astroville. The TARDIS key was returned to the Doctor, who signed a receipt for it without comment, though his quiet relief was evident. Peri was less restrained.

'So the inspector didn't want to apologise face to face for keeping us here all this time, huh?' she said bitterly.

'I'm sure she was only doing her job,' the Doctor said, with what Peri considered infuriating forbearance.

'The inspector is involved in another aspect of the case,' the sergeant explained. 'She sends her apologies for any inconvenience – and hopes you have enjoyed your stay on Astroville.'

The Doctor hustled Peri out before she could say another word.

'Even allowing for the circumstances, you seem very impatient to leave,' he observed, as they glided down the tower's thousand-metre-long passenger shaft.

Peri looked at him hopefully. 'Well, I was sort of wondering if we could use the TARDIS to go back in time and, maybe find out where Rovan leaves his treasure and –'

'Collect it for ourselves?'

'Sure, why not? It wouldn't do any harm, if it's been lost all this time anyway.'

'Wouldn't it? If Rovan's treasure was discovered before its proper time, how do we know what effect it would have on the last five thousand years? The information in the archives that you've been studying might never have been written, which means a segment of your own timeline would have to change as well. Perhaps Hok would never have obtained whatever information it was those three thugs were after, and so we wouldn't have disturbed them and the last few days would never have happened as they did, and we wouldn't be here now. It would create a temporal paradox and I try to avoid them if possible. Besides, spying on Rovan to see where he hid the treasure wouldn't be –'

'I know: it wouldn't be cricket.' She was silent for a moment, then added thoughtfully: 'Still, there's no reason why we couldn't try to find it now, is there, since we've gotten mixed up in it anyway, I mean? That's what everybody else seems to be trying to do.' She frowned. 'I just wish I could remember those numbers Hok said. They must have something to do with where the treasure is hidden.'

'You mean 385.06 by 946.573 by 157.67 positive? Yes, I suspect they're galactic navigation coordinates.'

She looked at him in amazement, which rapidly turned to annoyance. 'Doctor! Why didn't you tell me you remembered? Do you know how long I've been racking my brains over them? And why didn't you tell Inspector Jaharnus?'

'I thought it might cloud the issue. Priorities tend to get

misplaced where large sums of money are involved. It shouldn't matter why Hok was murdered, just the fact that it was an unnecessary death.'

'But we're going to use them ourselves now, right? Because that guy calling himself Falstaff wrote them down, so we can get on to his trail. And he might know who the actual killers were.'

'And finding Rovan's treasure doesn't come into it?' the Doctor asked, his eyebrows raised in mild interrogation.

'Well… can't we try to do both?'

'It might be dangerous.'

'Doctor, I'll kick myself for the rest of my life if I pass up a chance to go on an honest-to-goodness treasure hunt.'

He smiled tolerantly. 'All right, then. But there's something I want to check up on first.'

Half an hour at Astroville traffic control and some honeyed words had produced a list of all the craft that left Astroville during the twenty-four-hour period following Hok's murder.

'If we encounter any of these where we're going,' the Doctor said, scanning the list rapidly, 'we shall know who to watch out for. Ah, and here's our pseudo-Falstaff's vessel I suspect.'

Peri looked at the name he was indicating. '*The Merry Wife*? Oh, I get it: from *The Merry Wives of Windsor*, right?'

'Yes. A jolly little play, but Bill dashed it off too quickly, I always thought. I told him it could do with another revision, but the Queen wanted to see it performed as soon as possible and… well, never mind.'

'Sometime, Doctor,' Peri said sincerely, 'you are going to tell me all about meeting W. Shakespeare. Meantime, can we get going?'

The official police seal had gone from the TARDIS door. Peri was glad to be back inside the familiar console room, with its

55

dimpled walls and subdued hum of power. Even though she had known it only a few days, she felt there was something strangely homely about the TARDIS, almost as though it cared for her. Seeing the way the Doctor beamed paternally as he circled the hexagonal main console, checking the systems and feeding Hok's coordinates into the navigational unit, it was certainly easy to believe it was alive.

'I just wish Falstaff hadn't got such a big lead on us,' Peri said anxiously. 'Those crooks might also be out there by now. We don't know what they got out of Hok before we butted in.'

'Remember,' said the Doctor, 'a journey that may take them days we can make in a few minutes of our time.'

'Will that get us there first?'

'By a few hours, I should think.'

'Can't we go back a few days and get a proper head start?'

'No. Crossing your own timeline puts the fabric of time and space under great strain. It can be dangerous.'

'Uh, how dangerous, exactly?'

'Terminally.'

'Oh, well I guess we'll give that a miss.'

The Doctor called local traffic control and informed them they were ready to leave, closed the airlock and checked that the docking tube had retracted. He smiled as they were given a spacial departure corridor to follow, and let his fingers flicker across a series of contacts. Peri felt a little thrill of anticipation. She'd consciously experienced this moment only once before.

The transparent cylinder containing a complex glittering mechanism mounted at the centre of the console began to rise and fall. At the same time a deep pulsing whirr reverberated throughout the ship, gradually rising in tone and frequency. As it faded out into a shrill note beyond human hearing, the incongruous blue box, whose external appearance had so puzzled Inspector Jaharnus, vanished from the vicinity of the Astroville docking tower.

The TARDIS was on its way.

'How long will we be in flight, or whatever you call it?' she asked the Doctor as he studied the displays with a satisfied expression.

'About eight minutes, relatively speaking.'

'Just time to freshen up then.'

Bag slung over her shoulder, she had taken a dozen steps down the corridor towards her room, when a sudden urgent beeping sound emanating from the console brought her running back.

'What is it? Something wrong?'

The Doctor was working the controls rapidly, his face set and intent. The beeping faded and died in a burst of static, then grew stronger again. 'A hyperspace distress beacon on minimal power. Somebody's in trouble. Interestingly enough it seems to be in normal space on a line between Astroville and our destination. I'm trying to get an exact fix on it… ah.' He touched another sequence of switches and the descending tones of rematerialisation sounded.

The scanner screen, which had a moment before been filled with the grey of the deep interdimensional void, now swirled with colour that resolved into a hard image. It was the interior of a spacecraft cabin, dimly lit by green-tinted emergency lights. Trailing wires were strung about the walls, and several gaping splits in the bulkhead were patched over with strips of glistening transparent plastic. In one corner was a discarded pile of emergency-ration-pack wrappers and several oxygen cylinders, while in the other was a large chair. Looking up in astonishment from it, a section of disassembled control panel resting across his knees, was the man who called himself Sir John Falstaff.

'A remarkable contrivance you have here, Doctor,' Falstaff said five minutes later, after they had taken him and his few salvageable belongings on board. He had recovered his composure with remarkable speed.

''T'was most fortunate that you heard my hails, for I was beginning to give up hope of salvation, and commend my soul to God and beg his understanding for any trifling transgressions I may have committed over the years. But now I can rest easy once more. Have you any decent food aboard? I am a shadow of my former self. Bad enough to be so disabled by a device planted in such a knavish manner, but the blast destroyed my source of fresh victuals, since when I have had to survive on morsels that would not keep a church mouse alive.'

Peri, however, was in no mood to play along with his fantasy. 'You can drop the act. We know you're a phoney,' she said scathingly.

Falstaff looked affronted and hitched his belt a little higher over his massive belly. 'You accuse Falstaff of being an imposter, Mistress Brown? What, old Jack? Never.'

'I think you should know, we are familiar with the work of William Shakespeare,' the Doctor said helpfully. 'Even if he is currently out of fashion in this part of the galaxy.'

To their surprise this did not appear to trouble Falstaff. 'Ah, so you have heard of my chronicler.'

'Chronicler?' Peri exclaimed.

'Certainly. Thou didst not think such a man as Jack Falstaff could be conjured out of nothing by some pen scratcher? The fellow used some licence with my adventures, I grant you, but Falstaff was cut from whole cloth.'

'Falstaff was a fictional character,' Peri insisted.

'No, you have it turned about. The fiction came after the fact.'

'Well if you are the real Falstaff, that would make you about fifteen hundred years old. Unless you've also got a –'

'Another means of travel,' the Doctor cut in. He looked at Falstaff narrowly for a moment, then said a few words in a flowing tongue, to which their guest stared back at him blankly. 'No, I didn't think you were Gallifreyan. So how do you claim to have lived so long?'

'Now, sweet wag,' Falstaff admonished. 'I do not inquire of

your origins. Pray allow a man to call himself by whatever name he chooses, unless you can produce another to contest his right. Besides, it is not mannerly to tax your guest so, especially when he is fainting away from lack of sustenance.'

Peri gave an audible 'Huh!' of disbelief at the claim. The Doctor tried a more direct approach.

'Tell us how Hok came to be selling the location of Rovan's treasure.'

For the first time, Falstaff seemed taken aback. 'Ah, the secret is out, I see. Poor Hok. It would have been his most profitable venture.'

'And how did you find out what was on offer?' Peri asked.

'I had dealt with Hok before in the matter of some rare folios of my chronicler's work, and learnt then that he occasionally dabbled in darker dealings. I received word, as one of his more discerning clients, that he had something of value to offer, namely the transcript of an ancient ship's log from which the true resting place of Rovan's hoard could be deduced. My offer for the item was accepted and I was attempting to meet with him to conclude the deal, a little earlier than planned I admit, when we had our memorable encounter.'

'After which you bugged out, leaving us to explain everything to the police without anybody to back up our story,' Peri reminded him.

'Do I get no thanks for so masterfully saving your lives first? Ingratitude, thou art truly marble-hearted! Besides, I was sure the matter was in capable hands, and I had to pursue those whoreson cutthroats to ensure they did not profit from their villainy.'

'Really?' said Peri dubiously.

'Verily so. I was hard upon their tails when they turned like cornered rats. What a battle it was! Two of their craft dived upon me, their lasers spitting fire –'

'You didn't say anything about a battle,' Peri protested. 'I thought they planted a bomb on your ship?'

'Nay, you misheard. 'T'was a battle royal that laid me low. There were these four ships, armed like men o' war –'

'I thought there were two ships.'

'Pray do not interrupt or I'll lose the thread of the tale. Now, six ships bore down upon me –'

'Sir John, would you like something to eat?' said the Doctor brightly, stemming the flow. 'Peri, please show our guest how to use the food synthesiser.'

Leaving Falstaff in a corner happily stuffing himself, Peri and the Doctor conferred quietly.

'Just who is this guy really?' Peri wondered.

'I don't know,' the Doctor admitted, 'but he seems determined to stay in character.'

'You don't think he believes himself that he actually is Falstaff?'

'Perhaps. It can't do any harm to humour him for the time being, as long as we don't rely on him for anything important. Remember, Falstaff was a liar, cheat, and pragmatic coward.'

'Well, anyhow, now we know what happened at Hok's. I guess he had a copy of this data on Rovan's treasure and those crooks got hold of it before we came in.'

'Yes. Hok must have examined the data first and worked out the vital coordinates, which was what he passed on to us. He probably planned to sell it on in another form to other interested customers. Or perhaps he had already done so,' the Doctor added thoughtfully.

'You mean there might be others heading for the same place?'

'Well, there's only one way to find out.' The Doctor turned to the controls and the TARDIS dematerialised. 'We'll be there in a couple of minutes.'

'No you won't, Doctor,' said an unexpected voice.

Falstaff froze with a fork halfway to his mouth as Peri and the Doctor twisted round.

Myra Jaharnus was standing in the doorway leading to

the rest of the ship. She was holding a dull black pistol-like object in her hand in a very assured manner. Suddenly Peri realised why the inspector had not returned the TARDIS key to them in person.

'Ah,' said the Doctor, recovering his voice first, 'I see we have a stowaway on board. I don't think you've met our other guest. May I present Sir John Falstaff? Sir John, this is Inspector Myra Jaharnus of the Astroville police force.'

Falstaff recovered himself, rose to his feet and made a sweeping bow, doffing his cap with a flourish. 'Your servant, madam.'

'He's the man you never believed existed,' Peri explained helpfully.

'So I understand from what I've already heard.'

'May I add,' Falstaff continued smoothly, 'that it is a great comfort to know the forces of law and order are ever vigilant? I know I can leave it to your capable hands to apprehend the villains responsible for the murder of dear old Hok. If the Doctor would be kind enough to set me down on some convenient planet, I won't take up any more of your –'

'Sit down and be quiet,' Jaharnus snapped. Falstaff sat. 'Now, Doctor, you will pilot this... this craft back to Astroville.'

'Oh, why? For that matter, why the gun? We're really not dangerous you know.'

'I'm not sure what you are, Doctor, but I do know you're all under arrest. He's guilty of leaving the scene of a crime and you two are guilty of withholding evidence, namely the figures Hok revealed, which you claimed earlier you could not recall.'

'Evidently you believed otherwise.'

'As I said then, a suspicious nature goes with the job. It also caused me to check up on your researches in the archives. Rovan's treasure would be motivation for anything, and that's reason enough to take you into custody until we find out the truth.'

'I think you may be out of your jurisdiction, here,' the Doctor pointed out.

'Perhaps, Doctor. But I do have the gun, which like possession, is said to be nine points of the law. Now turn this thing around.'

'But we're almost at the place given in Hok's coordinates,' Peri exclaimed. 'Those men you're after will be coming here as well.'

'One thing at a time. With a new witness and further evidence a proper squad can be sent out here, but for the moment we return to Headquarters.'

The Doctor shrugged, turned back to the controls and reached out a hand to reset the coordinates. Peri saw a strange look come over his face as his hand froze over the row of buttons. His jaw tightened but his hand did not move. He took a step back, flexing his fingers.

'Peri,' he said in a slightly strained tone. 'I seem to have a slight problem. Could you press the black, green, and blue buttons on that row in order?'

Frowning, Peri reached forward. The muscles of her hand and arm locked. She knew what she wanted to do, but she simply could not make it happen. She pulled back with a little gasp of alarm.

'What's happening?'

'I think some extremely powerful mental force is at work here.'

'Don't try any tricks with me,' Jaharnus warned him.

'I'm not, Inspector,' the Doctor said with a compelling intensity in his words. 'If you disbelieve me, try for yourself.'

Jaharnus reached forward, only to find her own hand refused to obey her.

'It would seem somebody is determined that we finish our journey,' said the Doctor matter-of-factly. 'Whether we want to or not.'

CHAPTER 7
THE SPEAKER OF GELSANDOR

The materialisation pulse faded away into a solid thump of reality.

Cautiously the occupants of the TARDIS unbent their knees and stood upright once more.

'Well, we've arrived,' the Doctor announced. He tried to reset the coordinates, but his hand refused to obey him once again. 'Sorry, Inspector. We'll have to postpone our return to headquarters. Somebody would seem to have other plans for us.'

'Can't you send a distress call? Hasn't this thing got a hyperwave transmitter?'

The Doctor looked pained at the slur on his TARDIS and moved to a different section of the controls. 'I'm afraid I can't operate this either. Whoever is responsible obviously doesn't want anybody else to know where we are.'

Jaharnus looked at him intently for a moment, then apparently decided he was telling the truth. 'Remember, you're all still under arrest,' she said, holstering her gun. 'Now, can we at least find out where we are?'

Nothing prevented the Doctor activating the scanner, and they all peered intently at the image.

It showed a grassy glade, ringed by tall trees bearing large heart-shaped leaves. Fingers of golden sunlight slotted between the interlaced branches and made dappled patterns on the close-cropped grass, which was itself speckled with clumps of small purple and white flowers. The Doctor panned the camera and more of the same type of scenery rolled across the screen. Peri, prepared for something more alarming, began to relax. Then the Doctor stopped the camera. A man in a long yellow robe was standing on the grass watching them, his hands folded before him inside his voluminous sleeves. His costume and placid stance reminded Peri somewhat of an oriental priest.

'I guess that's the welcoming committee,' she said aloud.

Even as they looked at him, the man withdrew one arm from his robe and beckoned gracefully to them.

'There seems to be no point in staying inside,' said the Doctor, reaching for the plunger lever that controlled the doors.

'I'll do the talking, Doctor. Understand?' Jaharnus said.

Falstaff managed to be the last to leave the TARDIS by bowing Peri and Jaharnus through in front of him in a show of apparent gallantry. 'After you, ladies,' he said. Peri grinned ruefully.

Outside the air was mild and flower-scented and the grass springy underfoot. A light breeze rustled the leaves of the trees, accompanying the twitter and shrill of what Peri presumed was birdsong. All in all it was very tranquil, and she felt a sense of overwhelming calm descending upon her. Surely there could be nothing to fear in a place like this. She saw the Doctor looking round him intently, his deep eyes glittering, his lips pursed. Then a look of understanding crossed his face and he smiled slightly.

'This place has the flavour of Merrie England about it,' Falstaff remarked. 'It lacks only the Boar's Head Inn nestling through yonder trees to be a veritable paradise.'

'And do you like it as well, Peri?' the Doctor inquired.

'It's beautiful – though it reminds me more of parts of the States.'

'Yes, of course it would. That's due to a very subtle mental field being cast over us. Somebody wants us to feel untroubled and peaceful. We've already had one demonstration of their power, so don't necessarily believe everything you see.'

Jaharnus alone seemed unmoved by their surroundings. After a quick glance about her, she strode determinedly up to the robed figure, her tail tip flicking from side to side, and held up her official identity badge.

'I'm Inspector Myra Jaharnus of the Astroville Police Department. I want to talk to somebody in authority.'

The robed man was already extending his arm, indicating a path winding away through the trees. 'Please follow me. Shalvis is expecting you.'

'Who's Shalvis?'

'She is the Speaker of Gelsandor. She will explain everything in due course.'

'Gelsandor? Is that the name of your people, or this world?'

But the man had already set off down the path at a steady even pace, and they all had to run a few steps to get level with him. Close to, Peri saw the man was not quite as human as he first appeared. His skin was unwrinkled but parchment thin, with a distinct bluish tint to it. Growing out of his forehead and curving up and back over his hair were five wire-thin silver tendrils that bobbed slightly as he walked.

Through the trees on either side of the path they saw occasional low domelike buildings. Several other paths crossed theirs, and they caught glimpses of other robed figures, both male and female, making their way along them in the same purposeful but unhurried manner as their own guide. The atmosphere of meditative calm grew stronger.

'What is this place?' Peri wondered. 'Some sort of religious retreat?'

'Something far more complex than that, I think,' the Doctor replied.

Then ahead of them a more substantial structure rose out of a clearing, topping all the trees around it. It was a pyramid faced with what appeared to be white marble, perhaps a hundred metres high at its apex, its surface pierced by many slotted windows. In the centre of each base side was an entrance at the top of a flight of shallow steps, overhung with a single cantilevered slab of stone. They climbed the nearest of these and entered a long, cool, stone-floored passageway, lit by softly glowing panels set in the walls. At the end of the passage was a set of heavy but undecorated double doors, which swung open of their own accord as they approached and closed silently behind them, leaving their guide on the other side.

They were in a large, plain, square room surfaced in polished blue-veined marble, lit by more of the glowing panels. A semicircle of twelve simple chairs had been set out, with a slightly larger high-backed chair at their focus. Seated in this was a woman in white robes tied with a red sash. She also had tendrils, and skin as delicately smooth and unlined as their guide's, but her hair was silver blue. Peri wondered how old she was, and suspected it was probably much more than she looked.

'I am Shalvis, Speaker of Gelsandor,' she said. He voice was clear and perfectly controlled. 'Please be seated Myra Jaharnus, Sir John Falstaff, Perpugilliam Brown, Doctor.'

Hesitantly they took their seats, Falstaff first bowing to Shalvis. The Doctor, however, looked at her more quizzically.

'I must say you're very well informed about the complement of our party,' he observed, 'considering that we only picked up our third member less than half an hour ago, and the fourth was a stowaway who only revealed her presence since then. Unless of course you simply read our identities from our minds.'

'We might have done, Doctor,' Shalvis conceded easily. 'We do have certain mental powers, nurtured and honed over many generations.'

'So we've already discovered,' he remarked dryly. Then his eyes narrowed. 'And do you also delve the time winds?

'You are perceptive, Doctor. Yes, as do you Time Lords with your mechanical devices, so do we with our minds. It was in this manner that your coming was foreseen, as was that of the other seekers.'

'Seekers?' Peri asked.

'The name we give those who come to Gelsandor on the quest for Rovan's treasure.'

There was a surprised silence at the open manner in which Shalvis delivered the words. Falstaff spoke first.

'Mistress Shalvis, you would not tease a poor man. Do you truly affirm that Rovan's treasure may be found on this fair world of yours?'

'I do. But I will tell you no more until the other seekers have taken their places.'

'Now hold it,' said Jaharnus sharply. 'We're not "seekers", nor are we engaged in any kind of quest. These people are in my custody, and it's my duty to return them to Astroville. If you're responsible for holding us here, then I demand you release us immediately!'

'They are each in their own way seekers, and by our law must be allowed the opportunity to complete their quest. Until then you will not be permitted to interfere with their activities. Afterwards you may petition for their extradition if you wish, but you must understand you have no jurisdiction on Gelsandor. And you are also in error stating that you yourself are not a seeker. Think on it.'

As Jaharnus hesitated, unsure of how to respond, Shalvis held up a hand. 'The next party of seekers is here.'

Peri twisted in her seat as the doors swung silently open and four people walked uncertainly in. Two were older men, the others a tall thin younger man and an attractive woman. All wore practical-looking safari suits, with sturdy high boots, backpacks, and pistols holstered on their belts.

'I am Shalvis, Speaker of Gelsandor,' Shalvis said to the newcomers. 'Please be seated Professor Alex Thorrin, Marquis te Rosscarrino, Arnella te Rosscarrino, Willis Brockwell.'

Looking understandably bemused by their welcome, the four cautiously took their seats at the opposite end of the row from the TARDIS party. The oldest man recovered himself and looked sternly at Shalvis.

'I don't know what's going on here, but we're on a peaceful scientific research mission. Something… er, forced us down from orbit before we were ready.'

'We apologise for any distress caused to you, Professor Thorrin. We guided your hands so you might set down on a convenient landing ground at the appropriate time. And we know you are not on a scientific mission. You are here because you wish to find Rovan's treasure, as do these others beside you. I will explain how this may be accomplished shortly, when all the seekers are assembled.'

The four exchanged uncertain glances and low words between themselves, then looked about them at the chamber. The two older men seemed angry. For a moment Peri caught the eye of the young woman Shalvis had called Arnella and gave a friendly smile. She returned it uncertainly, but before Peri could open a conversation she turned aside to whisper urgently to the aristocratic Marquis. Peri realised the thin young man was looking at her.

'Hello. I'm Will Brockwell,' he said.

'Peri Brown.'

'Do you know what's going on here?' he asked frankly.

'No, not really,' Peri admitted with a shrug.

He grinned back. 'I suppose we'll find out soon enough. They seem to have everything pretty well arranged. We detected a couple of other ships as we came down. That must be who we're waiting for.'

'Will, be quiet,' Thorrin commanded sharply.

'Hey, he was only being friendly,' Peri protested, but Thorrin ignored her.

'The next group of seekers approaches,' Shalvis announced.

Peri turned to look as the doors opened again and three figures cautiously entered, glancing about them with every sign of suspicion and deep distrust, despite the calming mental field that Peri could still sense about her. Two were human, the other a larger bipedal alien slightly resembling an upright rhinoceros. They wore utility suits and had stubby weapons like oddly shaped sub-machine-guns slung from shoulder straps. She was just trying to work out what it was that seemed vaguely familiar about them, when she realised the taller of the two humans was staring directly at her and the Doctor.

'Qwaid – it's the tourists from Hok's shop!' he blurted out.

Even as he spoke, Jaharnus had sprung to her feet with her pistol drawn. 'Crelly Qwaid, I'm arresting you on suspicion of murder...'

The criminals' guns swung about towards her and the Marquis drew his own pistol. Brockwell threw an arm about Arnella and pulled her to the ground as, with a grunt, Falstaff also hit the floor. Peri followed their lead, wishing there was more cover in the room.

There was a surprising silence.

Peri looked up cautiously.

The Doctor had not moved from his chair, a knowing smile on his face. The three criminals, the Marquis, and Jaharnus were all wrestling with their weapons in a desperate attempt to fire them. But for some reason it seemed they could not make their fingers close on the triggers. Finally they let their guns hang limply by their sides as they realised the futility of their efforts, and looked in bewilderment and not a little fear at each other and their companions.

'There will be no violence here,' Shalvis said calmly. 'While you are on Gelsandor you will find the use of weapons is strictly limited. You will learn why shortly. Now please take your seats Crelly Qwaid, George Erasmas Gribbs, Drorgon Ves.'

It was an impressive display of power and in a hushed silence the three obeyed. Arnella shook off Brockwell's protective arm and scrambled to her feet, leaving him looking hurt and angry. The Marquis holstered his gun stoically,

Jaharnus with an angry lashing of her tail. Falstaff hauled himself upright clasping the handle of his sword as though having to restrain himself.

''T'was fortunate for those gorebellied knaves that Mistress Shalvis intervened,' he hissed, 'or else I would have set about them and laid them open from orifice to orifice.'

'From the floor?' Peri inquired, as the Doctor gave her a hand up.

'A mere stratagem to lure them into a false sense of security, allowing me to get within their guard.'

'Oh yeah?'

'It deceived you, lady, did it not?' he countered swiftly, leaving Peri too astounded to respond.

Jaharnus was still glaring at Qwaid. 'Where's Alpha? He never lets you three far off the leash.'

'He had an accident on the way here,' Qwaid said with a slight swagger. 'Anything you want you come to me now, cop.'

Jaharnus looked surprised and fell silent.

'Your past deeds are no concern of ours,' Shalvis said to Qwaid and his companions. 'Whatever disputes you may have with Inspector Jaharnus or anyone else will be settled away from Gelsandor. Now you are embarked on the quest for Rovan's treasure you shall take your chances equally with all the rest.'

The three started at her words. Qwaid looked about him like a hungry rat before asking, 'It's really here then?'

'It is, and soon you will learn how you may claim it.'

'But we've got one more place left to fill first, haven't we?' said the Doctor, nodding at the remaining vacant chair.

'And he comes now,' said Shalvis.

In through the doors strode a single figure. He appeared to be a slender human male, wearing what might have been a classically styled trench coat and fedora from nineteen thirties Earth, except that they were raven black and trimmed with white piping. He was accompanied by an object floating at head height which reminded Peri of an oversized Frisbee. It moved with a barely audible hum, and carried on its rim binocular camera lenses and what she guessed were compact directional microphones. It immediately began to drift about the chamber as though seeking different angles to film from, at the same time capturing close-up shots of everybody present.

The man took one look about him, as though rapidly assessing his surroundings, then strode up to Shalvis, pulling out a card from his pocket. 'Dexel Dynes, Interstellar News Agency,' he announced crisply. 'In accordance with the Galactic Declaration of Freedom of Investigation, I claim the right of free and unrestricted access to witness, record, or otherwise report all newsworthy events on this planet in any way related to or concerning Professor Alexander Thorrin and the Marquis te Rosscarrino and their associates or families, whom I declare to be figures of public prominence and therefore exempt from the protection of parts one and two of the Privacy of Sentient Beings Act, 2830.

'And,' he added righteously, 'something closed down my live feed to the INA net before I landed. Interference with press communications is –'

'Welcome, Dexel Dynes,' Shalvis said calmly. 'You may record whatever you wish without interference from us while you are on Gelsandor, and you are free to leave our world at any time. Those are the only concessions we grant you.'

There was something very final about her tone that Dynes wisely did not challenge, and he took the vacant seat, scanning the rest of them with intense unblinking eyes. Qwaid, Gribbs, and Drorgon shuffled their feet and turned their heads away. Jaharnus looked disgusted. Falstaff brushed of the front of his ruff collar, fluffed up his beard and beamed.

'A reporter!' Thorrin exclaimed. 'This is absurd.'

'Why? Do you have something to hide, Professor?' Dynes asked, slipping easily into interviewing mode. The floating camera dropped down to point over Dynes's shoulder, catching Thorrin full face.

'It is permitted,' Shalvis said solemnly. 'In his way, he too is a seeker. Besides, he is only here because you are, Professor. He planted a tracking device in your ship while you were on Astroville.'

Dynes showed surprise but no shame at the revelation. Thorrin flushed angrily. 'What do you mean by spying on us?'

'Just doing my job, Professor,' said Dynes. 'Followed you all the way from Altor. When two oddly matched characters like yourself and the Marquis get together and start acting secretly, there has to be a story in it somewhere. Remember, the public has a right to know.'

The flying camera glided away from Dynes and resumed its steady circling of the chamber. It flew close to Peri and she saw Drone Audio Visual Equipment #1 stencilled on the side. Its lenses focused on her and she felt herself begin to grin at it in a foolish rictus of embarrassment.

'Now you are all gathered, I will tell you how you may seek for Rovan's treasure.' Shalvis said. Suddenly she had their undivided attention.

'Five thousand standard years ago, Rovan came to Gelsandor with our contrivance. He had secretly negotiated with us to aid his disappearance, and we fulfilled our part of the bargain. I shall not speak of the exact details of our agreement, nor of the reasons why Rovan made his choice, but in compensation we became the guardians of his treasure. The careful use of a tiny portion of its total enabled us to maintain our independence and continue our studies into the science of the mind, some of the consequences of which you have already experienced.

'But Rovan knew there would be those, through the ages, who would come after him and his treasure, and so we agreed how they should be received. We could quite simply erase all knowledge of the last few hours and send you away unaware that any such place as Gelsandor exists. But we chose not to. Rovan believed that courage and determination should reap their just rewards – as should greed and deceit. So his treasure lies at the end of a difficult, perhaps to some of you, a deadly road. But any who survive may leave Gelsandor enriched, as was Rovan's intent.'

There was a deep silence broken by whispers and uncertain glances. Dexel Dynes alone showed no trace of bafflement or incomprehension.

'I publicly state that this situation and all participants here present constitute an item of exceptional newsworthiness, and claim the right to record it in its entirety,' he said excitedly. 'Please note your changed status as individuals in the eyes of the press. This declaration has been recorded. Remunerations on the standard scale will be offered to individuals for exclusive rights to their stories, should they survive.'

Peri felt slightly dizzy. The situation was strange enough without fanatical reporters. Only the Doctor still seemed calm and incisive. 'What else do you get out of this agreement?' he asked Shalvis.

'We do not claim to be altruists. Seekers of many races have come here over thousands of years. The study of their minds under stress allows us to extend our knowledge of mental phenomena.'

'How can we believe you?' the Marquis said sharply. 'You seem to have turned the quest for the most wonderful prize in history into an amusement... a game!' He scowled at Dynes. 'If you were serious in your claims you would not allow this creature to record it for the entertainment of the masses.'

'How do we know it's possible to find the treasure at all?' Thorrin said suspiciously. 'Perhaps you're keeping it to yourself.'

'We abide strictly to our covenant with Rovan,' Shalvis replied gravely. 'Telepathy also makes us by nature truth speakers. We may withhold information, but we will not tell a direct lie.'

73

'You say there have been many seekers over the years,' the Doctor continued. 'Did any of them ever make it through to the end? If so, why hasn't the treasure been seriously depleted by now?'

Shalvis looked about her at the assembly, catching and holding their gaze one by one. Peri felt the presence of a powerful mind behind those clear eyes. 'I see some of you believe there is some deception involved. I shall say this: any that win through to the end will have to opportunity to receive exactly what they desire and what their conduct merits, no more, no less. I promise that the bulk of Rovan's treasure still remains, even though many have come before you and found the ultimate prize. Tomorrow the quest shall begin, and you will be shown the path that may lead some of you to the same goal. Until then I advise you to return to your craft and rest.'

'The Quest For The Ultimate Treasure,' Dynes said huskily. 'What a title!'

Back in the *Newton* an hour later, Arnella faced her uncle angrily.

'I will come with you. We don't know how long it's going to take, and I won't stay shut up in this ship any longer.'

'But Nell, it might be dangerous.'

'Well with all these strange people about it might be just as dangerous to stay here. You can't stop me coming, so you might as well let me.'

The Marquis shook his head in bemused defeat. 'You have your father's stubbornness and courage. Perhaps it is best. You above all must prove yourself worthy.'

Arnella could not admit to her uncle her true reason for wanting to accompany the expedition. It was because she was afraid it would be the last taste of real freedom she would ever know.

Alpha's strongbox tumbled through interstellar space.

Inside an electronic countdown sequence reached zero.

For some minutes nothing outwardly changed, then several slender antennae emerged from in its hard grey shell. After a further pause, concealed panels opened to reveal hyperdrive emitter nodes. With a surge of power the box blurred and distorted, then vanished into hyperspace.

CHAPTER 8
THE WOOD OF LIES

Peri found it hard to sleep that night.

Of course there was no problem about accommodation room on board the TARDIS, but she was still conscious of their two unexpected guests and the unknown quantities they represented. Just who really was Falstaff and why did he maintain the charade so relentlessly? Would Jaharnus really arrest them once the quest was over? For that matter, would she accompany them or stay to keep watch on the ships? And then of course there was the treasure hunt itself. The very idea that she was actually going on one the next day seemed incredible, and passages from Stevenson's *Treasure Island* kept insinuating themselves into her confused thoughts, until eventually they became part of her uneasy dreams.

She woke in the early hours, local time, feeling as though she had hardly slept at all. It took five minutes under an alternately hot and cold shower before she felt reasonably alert. Then she went to choose some clothes for the forthcoming expedition. Nothing she had bought in Astroville would be suitable, and, besides, it was all too good to risk spoiling.

The wardrobe room was vast, fading away into dark shadows on all sides, and filled with row upon row of costumes representing every age and style Earth had ever produced, plus some whose origins she could only guess at. Bearing in mind Gelsandor's mild climate, she chose a loose cord shirt and thigh-length shorts, knee-high woollen socks, and stout but supple walking boots. To this she added a hooded cape in case the weather turned. She then dialled up a coffee and sandwich from the food synthesiser and went along to the console room.

The Doctor, who she was not sure ever slept, had four

backpacks complete with bedrolls and walkers' staffs already lined up along one wall. He himself had made no obvious concessions in his own costume to their forthcoming venture, apart from changing into walking boots similar to hers.

'Do you think it's going to take us that long?' she asked, examining the well-stocked packs.

'Shalvis has been careful not to specify any likely duration for the journey, but I'd be most surprised if Rovan's treasure was less than a day's march from here. Reaching it's meant to be a challenge after all.'

'I see we're going to have company along the way.'

'Inspector Jaharnus will be accompanying us,' the Doctor confirmed. 'I believe she's decided that way she can best keep an eye on both us and Qwaid and company.'

'You don't reckon she's interested in the treasure?'

'No, I think her sense of duty is far too strong for that. At least, at the moment.'

'Why should it change?'

'Your own country helped make the expression "gold fever" famous in the nineteenth century. The prospect of suddenly acquiring vast wealth can do strange things to otherwise normal and well-balanced beings.'

'You reckon some of us are going to start gibbering, do you Doctor? I hope you don't think it's going to happen to me.'

'I trust not, Peri,' he said with altogether too much gravity. She changed the subject.

'And how's Falstaff making out? I see he's coming to.'

'Yes. He's spent half the night regaling us with his heroic deeds in what he claims are similar circumstances.'

'But underneath he's really scared sick, isn't he?'

'I should say that was an accurate assessment of his state of mind, but for some reason he's decided to try to live up to his boasts this time, which is not really in character. Well, we shall see.' He looked at her sombrely. 'Are you sure you still want to come yourself? Despite the circumstances, this is not a game.

You might get hurt.'

'For that matter, Doctor, why are you going? You sure don't need the money.'

A distant look came into his eyes, as though he was staring out into infinity. 'Perhaps somewhere it's expected of me,' he replied obliquely. 'And of course, I do have this insatiable sense of curiosity.'

The other spacecraft were parked – if that was the appropriate expression, Peri thought – in three separate clearings in the parklike wood within half a mile of the TARDIS. The various parties rendezvoused at a confluence of pathways approximately midway between them, just as the morning sun caught the higher branches of the trees and the dew was still on the grass. Each party exchanged uncertain glances encompassing varying degrees of hostility. Brockwell smiled at her but his companions seemed almost aloof. The three crooks, she noticed, were laden down with backpacks, multipocketed belts, bush knives and side arms. The rhinoceros-like one, Drorgon, also carried something resembling a slender missile launcher slung across his back.

Shalvis was waiting for them, with Dynes by her side. As they approached three identical DAVE drones swooped towards them to record their arrival, while one hovered expectantly over Dynes's shoulder. Drorgon growled and took a swipe at a DAVE that ventured too close to him, but the tiny device bobbed agilely out of his reach.

Shalvis spoke. 'I must ask you all to confirm you are doing this of your own free will, knowing that the way ahead is dangerous and your lives are at risk. Are you all resolved to go on?'

They all nodded. 'Yes, yes, get on with it,' Thorrin said impatiently.

'Then you must begin by choosing the best route through these woods. There are signs you can follow but they will *always* lie. If you meet any of our people you can ask them for guidance, but they *may* not speak the truth about which direction to take, though they will remain truthful about everything else.'

'Excuse me,' said Willis Brockwell diffidently, 'but I thought you told us yesterday that your kind never lied?'

'But I have just told you that you may be misinformed, so it is not a fundamental deception.'

'But that's not fair,' Peri exclaimed.

'We do not believe Rovan intended the way to be either fair or easy, Perpugilliam Brown,' she replied, making Peri feel as though she was about eight years old and had just said something foolish in school class. 'If you apply your reason you will be able to choose the quickest path through the woods.' She glanced at Qwaid's party. 'You may also win through to the next stage by simple perseverance, of course, but in any case you must all keep to the paths if you wish to remain safe.'

'Safe from what?' Jaharnus asked.

'That you will find out. Are there any further questions?'

'Can we use our ship?' Qwaid asked.

'You may operate it now, but not to aid your journey or avoid any obstacles until you have reached the treasure.'

Dynes cut into the thoughtful silence that followed. 'Has anyone any words for the viewing public before you set out on this historic quest?'

'If you publish anything scurrilous or defamatory about myself or my niece I shall sue,' the Marquis said simply.

'Keep those things away from us,' Qwaid warned him, glowering at the camera drones, 'unless you want them turned into scrap.'

The Doctor tipped his hat politely but said nothing.

Peri shook her head, unable to cope with mad reporters at that moment and just wishing they could get started.

Falstaff swelled proudly. 'I do not embark upon this perilous way for personal gain, but to raise funds for a good and noble cause in a far-off land I may not mention…'

As he continued in the same manner, Peri shrugged helplessly at the Doctor, who smiled back.

'Be quiet you fool, and let us get started,' Thorrin snapped, interrupting Falstaff's fantasy.

'Do not let your words run so shrill, sir,' Falstaff replied easily, 'lest by their tone you reveal your fears and alarm the womenfolk.'

As Thorrin gaped back at him incredulously, Shalvis pointed a slender hand down a particular path leading off through the trees that was a little broader than the others. 'That is the beginning of the trail that leads to Rovan's treasure.'

They set off, each party trying not to mingle with the others, followed by a flock of DAVEs that glided after them at a discreet distance.

The woods on either side of the path grew thickly, with many broad-leaved bushes, trailing wisps of moss, and hanging vines filling in the spaces between the lower tree branches and the ground. It reduced visibility to a few yards on either side, making them feel uncomfortably enclosed. Peri shivered. The peaceful beauty of the woods around the TARDIS's landing site seemed to have evaporated within the space of a few paces. Was this natural, or more of the Gelsandorans' mind tricks?

The first junction they came to was unmarked by any sign. Four paths diverged from it, curving gently away into the woods. Almost gratefully the three parties separated, each taking a different path by unspoken consent. Dynes's drones followed them, one to each party.

The TARDIS party had walked perhaps a hundred yards, when the new path forked. At the apex of the fork was a neat white-painted post bearing two wooden boards with arrow-tapered ends. Peri thought they wouldn't have looked out of place on a country road, apart from the legends they bore. The one indicating left said WHITE PYRAMID, while the other to the right was ROVAN'S TREASURE.

'Ah, this is one of the lying signs of which Mistress Shalvis warned us,' said Falstaff.

'I didn't think she meant it literally,' said Jaharnus.

The Doctor was smiling. 'Well, at least it's a simple problem to start with, assuming we take the deception at face value, and there are no genuine signs among the false ones to further confuse matters.'

'That was too easy,' said Peri, as they took the left path.

'I doubt if they'll remain that way,' the Doctor warned her.

Thorrin's party had arrived at a fork in the path as well. Their sign showed that the treasure lay to the left, but the other path was unmarked. Arnella saw Thorrin glance at it for a moment almost contemptuously, then stride ahead down the right-hand path.

Qwaid, Gribbs, and Drorgon had arrived at a T-junction. On either side the paths curved rapidly away out of sight. Both paths, according to the sign, led to the treasure.

'So, if they're both false, that means neither way is the right one,' said Gribbs.

'Yeah, well maybe that's what they want us to think,' said Qwaid. 'Suppose it's a double-cross? Come on.'

Both paths terminated in dead ends. They had to retrace their footsteps to the original unmarked divergence of the main track and set off down a fresh path.

'Right, so I've got the idea of how it works now,' said Qwaid, trying to sound easy as they hurried along. 'I had to find out, you see, so we don't go really wrong later.'

Gribbs and Drorgon said nothing.

After negotiating several simple junctions without difficulty, the TARDIS party came to a point where four paths met. Here the sign informed them that the pyramid was to the left, and the woods were to the right. The way ahead was unmarked. 'The woods!' Peri exclaimed. But we're in the woods already. And where's the unmarked path lead to?'

'Yes, the choices have become more complex,' agreed the Doctor. 'All we can be certain of, according to Shalvis, is that each sign cannot indicate the thing it purports to. Therefore the pyramid cannot be to the left, the woods alone are not to the right, and anything might be straight ahead – at least as far as the next junction. The correct path might be any of them, since none mention the treasure and so can definitely be excluded. There is no simple answer. But logically the unmarked path should at least lead to another signpost, since it cannot actually lead to nothing. Let's try that.'

Soon they reached another junction with just two paths leading from it. However, the sign was of a different kind. To the left it said NOT THIS WAY, while to the right it said DON'T FOLLOW THE OTHER SIGN.

'What is this – something from *Alice in Wonderland?*' Peri said.

'The two cancel each other out,' Jaharnus observed, becoming interested in the puzzle despite her professional preoccupations. 'They don't tell us anything.'

'Not quite,' said the Doctor. 'The right-hand sign does not mention a direction but merely the other half of the sign, so it's actually self-referential. I think we should treat it as a double negative.'

They proceeded to the left.

'What if the next sign says "Ignore last sign"?' Peri asked.

Arnella stared at a sign that said THIS WAY to the left, and FOLLOW THE OTHER SIGN to the right.

Thorrin fumed. 'We cannot even be sure of the solution. How deep should we assume the deception runs? Childish puzzles!'

'But you're not going to let that stop you from solving them?' Rosscarrino asked mildly.

'What? No, no... of course not. But they are most trying.'

'Exactly. Perhaps that's the point. A lesson that we have to abide by Rovan's rules.'

Brockwell spoke up, and Arnella realised he was trying to soothe his irritable employer's ego.

'They might be deliberately insulting our intelligence and trying to get us angry in the hope that we'll make a foolish mistake. But you're not going to fall for that sort of trick, are you, Professor?' He lowered his voice. 'And remember, all this is being recorded.' He tilted his head at the DAVE drone hovering a few metres away.

Thorrin scowled, but then recovered himself and sniffed thoughtfully. 'Yes, you could be right, Will.' He looked at the sign again. 'Well, clearly, taken as a whole, it indicates we should go right.'

'I agree,' said the Marquis with a smile.

Arnella knew her uncle was also trying to keep Thorrin in a tolerable humour. They still needed him until they reached the treasure. After that, of course, they would need no one's charity ever again.

Eventually Qwaid called them to a halt. They were back at the junction of four paths, which they had left ten minutes before.

It had seemed to say that the central path had been the right one... or perhaps the wrong one, looked at another way. He was getting sick of neatly painted signposts.

'I've had enough of this. I don't care what that woman said, we're going to take a short cut.' He took out a miniature inertial compass and looked at the sun as it sparkled through the branches.

Then he pointed between two of the paths. 'Right, that's the same line as the first path that led in here, so we'll stay on that. If we keep going straight ahead we're bound to come out somewhere soon enough.'

'But she said it was dangerous to leave the paths,' Gribbs reminded him, peering anxiously at the tangle of lush greenery ahead of them.

'How do we know that?' Qwaid retorted. 'Maybe that was a lie as well, just to get us running around like rats in a maze while they laugh at us. Perhaps working it out is part of the test, and this is how you're meant to go.' Gribbs still looked unhappy. Drorgon shrugged his massive shoulders. 'Anyway were all kitted up for trouble, aren't we? Maybe we can't use our guns on the others, but nobody said we couldn't use 'em on anything else that gets in our way. Go to it, Dro.'

Drorgon's huge machete with its ultra-fine diamond slick coating hissed effortlessly through a hanging tangle of creepers, and they marched forward off the path and into the green-tinted shadows. Gribbs held his own blade ready and hacked nervously at an innocent bush. In two minutes they had passed through the spur of wood and came to a path that crossed their line of travel. Unhesitatingly Qwaid led them across it to the next wall of green.

Down at the end of the path they saw the figures of Thorrin's party clustered round another signpost.

'Hah. Let 'em run around in circles,' Qwaid said contemptuously.'This is the way the really smart types go.'

They had taken perhaps twenty steps from the path when there was a sharp snap. Drorgon gave a howl of pain, dropped his machete, and crouched down clutching at his ankle. The heavy spiked jaws of a plant head that had been inconspicuously spread open flat on the ground had closed about it like a man trap.

Gribbs flinched away from Drorgon even as the Cantarite tore his leg free, looking about him wildly for any new danger. There was a sudden rustle and swish in the grass at Gribbs's feet and a tall slender sapling that had been bowed over a few metres away from him suddenly sprang upright.With a yell he was jerked off his feet and up into the air, a thin noose of

85

wirelike ivy tight about his left ankle connecting him with the top of the sapling.

His frantic struggles subsided as he realised nothing worse was going to happen, and he hung upside down swaying gently to and fro. Then he saw that the DAVE drone hovering a little way off was recording his undignified elevation. 'I don't think this was such a good idea, Qwaid,' he said faintly.

Inside his ship the *Stop Press,* Dynes beamed in satisfaction at the monitor image of Gribbs. Good knockabout stuff and just what the social class Ds and Es lapped up, along with the rest of their predigested newspap. Actually, everybody secretly liked seeing other people's misfortunes, especially if they were known criminals. Could he play the ambivalent card there and slant the angles to make them into the comic element of the story? Blundering crooks getting what they deserve, but struggling bravely on, so that they subconsciously inspired a touch of sympathy for being such hopeless foul-ups? Yes, it was a distinct possibility.

He checked the monitors that were following the other two parties. Now these were more for his prospective A and B audience to relate to. They were going about the business of solving the sign problem methodically. If he could record enough of their chatter they could feature it as a brainteaser for the viewers over a station break, or something.

That oversized man, Falstaff, was obviously an eccentric. You didn't see many body styles like that nowadays. Maybe he'd come up with something interesting. At least he could be relied upon to fall over amusingly or get stuck in something somewhere along the way.

And of course these groups also had the two attractive human women with them, one from an aristocratic family, and also Inspector Jaharnus, who was quite a slick-looking Tritonite if he was any judge. They should please the humanoid male audience, and a few related species besides.

He remotely adjusted the bias of the DAVEs following them to hold them in shot more often. He hoped as they went along they might pick up a few suggestive tears in their costumes and some tasteful smudges of dirt here and there. After all, there was nothing like seeing pretty women a little dishevelled to boost the ratings.

Dynes had long ago renounced personal scruples and passing judgment on anything he reported. Priorities to him were exemplified by the fact that there were fewer mutual agreements between planetary law enforcement agencies than between rival news organisations. People wanted gossip and entertainment in preference to law and order, and his job was to deliver what the market wanted with single-minded efficiency. Which was why he was the best in the business. And he had a feeling that this story would shape up into one of the hottest items of the year.

Peri realised that the two-way junction ahead of them was not marked with a signpost. Instead, one of the native Gelsandorans stood there waiting impassively, his hands folded into the sleeves of his robe. While they considered their next move, Falstaff sat down heavily on a convenient boulder by the side of the path and massaged his knees.

'I must catch my wind. I am not suited to this means of travel. Eight yards of uneven ground is threescore and ten miles afoot with me.'

Peri had some sympathy for him. They seemed to have been wandering up and down woodland paths for hours. Falstaff had several times complained about the soreness of his feet and wiped his brow regularly, but for a man of his size he'd actually kept up the pace quite well. She suspected he didn't want to get left behind in these rather sinister woods. She looked at the silent native again, then at the Doctor. 'Now, he might tell us the truth or he might lie, right?'

'Yes,' said the Doctor, 'but only about which path to take, according to Shalvis, so we can't catch him out with a question about the sky being pink, or anything on those lines.'

'Then how shall we know whether he speaks true or false?' Falstaff wondered.

'This is going to be worse than the signs,' said Jaharnus. 'I don't want us to fall behind Qwaid and his friends.'

The Doctor smiled. 'Fortunately there is a solution. On Earth it was originated in the mid-twentieth century by a philosopher called Goodman, though of course it's been independently discovered many times on many other worlds. We'll see if it works here.'

The Doctor walked over to the Gelsandoran. 'I believe you may or may not tell the truth if I asked you specifically which path leads to Rovan's treasure?'

'That is correct, Doctor.'

'And have you already determined whether you will be one kind or another, that is either a liar or a truth-teller, in this matter?'

'I have.'

'Then tell me if you're the kind who would tell me that the right-hand path leads to Rovan's treasure?'

'No, I am not.'

The Doctor raised his hat politely and turned to the others. 'We'll take the left pathway,' he said.

When they had gone round the next corner, Peri asked, 'Now how did you work that out?'

'Well, if he was telling the truth when he said no, he wasn't the kind who would tell me the right-hand path was the correct one, then the right-hand path would be wrong, since only a liar would say otherwise. If he had intended to lie, then he would say the right-hand path was the correct one in an effort to deceive me, therefore it would still be the wrong choice. If he'd said yes, meaning he was the kind who would tell me the right path led to the treasure, and he was telling the truth, then the right-hand path would have been the correct one. If he had said yes and was lying, then he was actually not the kind who would say the right-hand path was the correct one, since only a truth-teller would say that, and so again the right path would have been correct, whether answering "yes" was true or not.

'Either way, if he'd said yes I would choose right, and left if he'd said no. I came across something similar on Mars, once. It's very simple, really.'

Peri shook her head and shrugged. 'I'll take your word for it. But you still don't know if he was lying or not?'

'No, but it doesn't really matter, does it?'

'Uh, I guess not.'

They trudged on. The path no longer branched. Perhaps they were getting somewhere at last. In the near silence she became aware of the slight hum of the DAVE unit that still trailed after them. She'd almost forgotten it was there during the last few hours.

Back inside the *Stop Press* Dynes checked his monitors. The Doctor's party seemed slightly ahead of Thorrin's, who had just encountered a native in a different part of the wood and were going through a similar logical debate. Both were well clear of Qwaid's group. The three criminals had given up any attempt to force a way through the woodland between the pathways, and had settled on following a compass course as closely as they could, notching signposts and blazing marks in pathside trees to help them keep their bearings.

There were two other monitors presently active in the bank before Dynes. They relayed images from a couple of DAVEs he'd sent out to pick up establishing shots around the white pyramid and the Gelsandorans' settlement. He also hoped they might catch any newsworthy local customs or practices, of course. Regrettably, so far, they seemed entirely too civilised, but he maintained a watch just in case. You could never tell with these quiet types.

The trees thinned and suddenly they were out in the open. Peri looked about her. The edge of the woodland stretched away on either side in a line that could hardly have been natural; while lying before them, already shimmering under the near midday sun, was the most unusual plain she had ever seen.

Inexplicably, Dynes's cameras failed to record Shalvis and the other Seers emerging from the pyramid. They moved in a ring at the centre of which was the plasma cloud. Carefully maintaining their formation they set off towards the landing fields.

CHAPTER 9
THE TILED PLAIN

By eliminating every path through the woods that seemed to lead back towards the white pyramid or the landing grounds, Qwaid felt they were at last making some progress. At any sign he couldn't make sense of he simply chose a direction at random. The important thing was to look decisive. That had been Alpha's secret, he decided: always act as though you know what you're doing.

Whatever happened, he mustn't lose any more face before Gribbs and Drorgon. Not that they'd have the guts to do to him what he'd done to Alpha, but they might just give up, which would be nearly as bad. He'd already caught some reproachful glances as they limped along beside him. That hurt because what he wanted, perhaps even more than Rovan's treasure, was to hear them call him 'boss' to his face, and mean it.

Qwaid knew he had it in him. Hadn't he jiggered the *Falcon*'s systems neatly enough to dispose of Alpha, for all his brains? But he simply didn't have the sort of mind to untangle word games and such abstract problems. And suppose there were more obstacles of the same sort ahead. OK, so they could get through in the end by blood and sweat, but by that time the rest would have lifted the treasure. There had to be a way to even things up. There just had to be.

When they finally came upon a native waiting patiently at an otherwise unmarked junction he didn't waste any time in futile debate, but pointedly drew a coin from his pocket and flipped it to decide their route. He'd show them all that Crelly Qwaid played by nobody else's rules but his own.

The plain stretched away into the distance before them, into the shimmering heat haze, where it was just possible to make out a line of green that suggested another wood might lie on the far side. Peri estimated it was five miles across, perhaps more. To left and right the plain extended at least as far as the point at which it was lost in the haze, out of which rose two parallel walls of rock, apparently the sheer sides of a very wide, flat-bedded valley. It was the largest level surface she had ever seen, rivalling the monotonous expanses of those dry desert lake beds where they held land-speed record attempts. But none of them had ever been paved.

She could think of no better description of the neatly jointed pale-grey, hexagonal slabs, about ten or twelve feet across their flat sides, which covered the plain for as far as the eye could see. She saw that Jaharnus was equally surprised by the spectacle, which had left even Falstaff momentarily speechless. The Doctor crossed to where the straggling turf and weeds of the wood gave way to the first of the tiles, and touched the hard surface.

'Hmm. Stone, or some very fine concrete, I think.'

They all moved to his side. Peri noticed that finer grooves divided up the tile into six equilateral triangular segments.

'Why does it have a red dot in its centre?' Jaharnus asked.

It was a small circle, perhaps six or eight inches across, apparently painted on. From where Peri stood every slab in sight seemed to have one, though the colours differed.

'I've no idea,' the Doctor admitted.

'Well at least we can see where were going,' Peri said. 'I suppose we've got to cross to the other side. I wonder how long it'll take.' And she walked out a few yards.

As she put her weight on the third tile it soundlessly split open into its component segments under her feet and she dropped into darkness. Then there was a splash and green-scummed water closed about her head with a roar of bubbles.

She kicked upward frantically and surfaced coughing and spluttering and drawing in a deep breath. But immediately she felt the weight of her backpack pulling her under again. She flailed about but there was nothing to catch hold of. The sides of the hexagonal well shaft were smooth and sheer, and the segments of its cap lay flat against them. She tore in panic at the pack's straps, trying to wriggle free, but it was taking in water and growing heavier every second.

The Doctor's head and shoulders appeared over the lip of the shaft some eight feet above the surface of the water as he threw himself flat on the ground and stretched out his staff to her, handle first.

'Grab hold, Peri,' he shouted.

As the water was closing over her head again, her fingers closed about the end of the staff, and she pulled herself back into the air again, trembling with fright. Jaharnus was lying beside the Doctor, reaching down with her staff.

'Peri,' the Doctor said, his words crisp and steady and very reassuring. 'We can't lift you and your pack if it's full of water. Take it off and hook it over the inspector's staff.'

Numbly Peri obeyed, struggling one handed with the straps, but managing to remove it and twist them about the staff's handle. The pack was lifted clear, then the second staff reached down again and she was able to grip both handles. In a few seconds she was sprawled on the hard stone on the edge of the well.

'It had to happen to me!' she panted miserably.

'Well what do you expect if you will start off without thinking?' the Doctor scolded, but she read genuine concern behind his eyes.

They retreated carefully to the edge of the wood, stepping only on those slabs they had already used. While they considered how to proceed, Peri emptied her pack and spread out the contents to dry. She hadn't brought a change of clothes, so she settled for taking off her boots and wringing her socks out as well as she could. With the midday heat, everything else would soon dry.

'I suppose it could have been worse,' she said, trying to make light of her misfortune. 'I only lost my staff.'

'Yes, it could have been much, much worse,' said the Doctor coolly. 'Even if you'd been able to remove your pack quickly enough, how long would you have survived if we hadn't been here to pull you out?'

The full enormity of it struck her, and she felt giddy for a moment. She had been thinking that there could have been more dangerous things waiting for her at the bottom of the shaft than water, but now she realised it might only have prolonged the inevitable if she'd been alone. 'I guess I really could have died down there.'

'Let that be a lesson to us all,' the Doctor said, his stern gaze passing over Jaharnus and Falstaff. 'However artificial and contrived all this seems, it's not a game. If you want to go back I suggest you do it now, while we've only the wood to contend with.'

Falstaff puffed himself up. 'John Falstaff retreat from danger? Never!'

'We go on,' said Jaharnus. 'I'm not letting you three out of my sight. Besides, if there is any treasure I want to be sitting on it ready and waiting for Qwaid and his friends. As soon as this ridiculous quest thing is over and the locals remove their protection, I'm going to arrest them.'

'Well one dunking's not going to make me give up,' Peri said, hoping her voice sounded steady.

The Doctor shrugged. 'Very well. But we must take some sensible precautions, until we work out which slabs are safe and which aren't. At least we now know why they're colour-coded.'

'Oh,' said Peri, 'you mean there's a pattern to it. What colour was the one I dropped through?'

'Green,' said Jaharnus.

'For a start, we'll avoid those,' the Doctor said, rummaging in his pack. 'Sir John, you will have the honour –'

'I pray you, good Doctor, do not deny yourself the satisfaction of being the leader of our brave band on my account. I crave not the glory –'

'– of going last,' the Doctor continued, pulling out a coil of climbing rope from his pack. 'We need a solid anchor man, and you are eminently the most qualified.'

Five minutes later they set out, roped together, the Doctor leading, Jaharnus second, Peri third, and Falstaff bringing up the rear. The Doctor used his staff to probe each slab ahead of him. It took a significant weight to trigger a slab, and he had to lean heavily on it to be sure it was safe. Twice he almost fell into concealed pits, one of which had been dry, the other floored with spikes. Fortunately, there were no remains of a previous seeker in the bottom. It was slow going. After an hour they had hardly covered a mile, which was probably as fast as conditions would allow, Peri decided. They stopped for a drink from their canteens and to eat food bars provided by the TARDIS's synthesiser. The sun was high in the sky. Peri took her cape and hood out of her pack and draped it over her head and shoulders for some protection from its rays. The Doctor and Falstaff both had hats, while Jaharnus was bareheaded. Perhaps, with her tough skin, the sun didn't bother her, but Peri noticed she had been walking with her mouth agape, flicking out her red pointed tongue, rather like a dog panting.

The Doctor, who had been looking around him thoughtfully, suddenly asked, 'How many different-coloured slab spots have you seen?'

They looked around them. 'They are of all colours,' said Jaharnus.

'Really? Have you seen a brown or pink, black or white?'

'Surely that is a black over there?' said Falstaff pointing, then mopping his brow with a large handkerchief he had pulled from his sleeve.

'I would say that's violet,' said the Doctor. 'You see, it's a little darker than that one over there, which is indigo.'

'Does it matter?' asked Jaharnus.

'Doctor,' said Peri, 'what are you getting at?'

'I should have noticed. There are only seven spot colours: indigo and violet, plus green, blue, red, orange and yellow.'

'The colours of the rainbow!' said Peri.

'Yes, and that suggests a sequence.'

'Well fillip me with a three-man beetle!' said Falstaff. 'I believe you have the key to the safe path over this interminable plain, Doctor.'

'Perhaps. There's only one way to find out.' He looked about for the next red-spot tile that had an orange adjacent to it in the direction they were travelling. He tested it and stepped forward. It was sound. So was the orange. They followed after him across yellow, green, blue, indigo, and violet. It meant travelling by a snaking course, but it was much faster than they had been going. Sure enough, there was a red tile adjacent to the violet. They began to move with more confidence.

The Doctor's party were just visible as dots out on the shimmering plain, when Arnella followed her uncle through the last of the trees and stood on the edge of the great expanse. Thorrin quickly had his binoculars focused on their rival seekers.

'They are apparently picking their way carefully and watching where they step,' he reported after a minute. He put the binoculars away and cautiously examined the nearest of the hexagonal slabs. From his pack he took a small device like a hand torch and played it across the first row. The fourth slab he tested triggered a sharp beeping. At his direction Willis found a large rock and dropped it on to the slab, which split open, precipitating the rock into a deep chamber below.

Thorrin chuckled. 'I think this is going to be perfectly straightforward, provided you step only where I do.'

Holding the scanner before him, he led the way out on to the tiled plain.

* * *

Red, orange, yellow, green, blue, indigo…

The grooves between the slabs going past underfoot, endless clusters of triangles building into endless hexagons.

Red orange, yellow, green, blue…

Left, right, left, right. Angles and lines, all the same…

Red, orange, yellow, green…

In a vague and remote way Peri wished she had brought sunglasses. The glare off the pale slabs was brilliant and it was getting hard to see the spots of colour on the tiles.

Red, orange, yellow…

The reflected heat washed over her as though it was the open door of an oven, but she plodded on.

Red, orange…

A part of her knew her feet were burning, but there didn't seem to be anything she could do about it.

Red…

Her legs gave way and she fell on to her hands and knees. The line around her waist jerked as Jaharnus carried on marching. Falstaff nearly trod on her. Her skin was burning where it touched the stone slabs! With a yell of pain she scrambled to her feet again, feeling dangerously light-headed. The others kept on walking, pulling her along with them. The Doctor hadn't even noticed she'd fallen. What was the matter with them all?

Then she realised to her dismay that the entire horizon was lost in the quicksilver ripples of the heat haze. The sun seemed to be hovering directly overhead, blazing down out of a brassy sky and giving no clue as to their orientation. She couldn't see the sides of the valley or the woods. Their line of march had zigzagged as they followed the safe path. How did they know they hadn't gone off course? Their eyes had all been on the ground watching where they put their feet. She tried to shout to the others to stop but it came out as a croak through her parched throat. How long since she'd taken a drink? Desperately she jerked hard on the line. Jaharnus and the Doctor stopped and Falstaff cannoned into her.

Falstaff and Jaharnus stood swaying slightly and even the Doctor seemed unsteady. They were blinking and frowning, looking about them as though waking from a dream. Peri suddenly remembered that her feet were scorching even through the thick soles of her boots, and began hopping from one to the other. She must have been sweating profusely, yet the air was so dry and hot it evaporated right off her skin.

The Doctor took a long draught from his canteen, splashed a little over his face, then looked at them bleakly. 'It's a trap,' he said, his voice cracking as he spoke. 'A subtle one. Partly the Gelsandorans' doing perhaps, together with line hypnosis.'

'What?' asked Peri.

'A repetition of regular patterns going past the eye. It can induce a sort of trancelike state.'

'We must find some shade, at least until the sun starts down,' Jaharnus said, her long tongue flicking out between words. 'We daren't walk any further like this.'

'Shade!' exclaimed Falstaff, swaying dangerously. 'Out here? Surely you jest, mistress. A pox on Rovan! Old Jack is done for!'

'The sleeping rolls,' said the Doctor. 'It's better than nothing.'

They had to sit on their packs to insulate themselves from the ground. Putting the bedrolls over their heads to form a crude awning relieved some of the sting of the sun, but most of the heat was reflected up from the ground around them and they began to stifle in the dead, motionless air under the covers. Peri knew they had to last at least another couple of hours before they could expect any drop in temperature, but she was beginning to wonder what condition they would be in by then. They sat and suffered. Their water, which had seemed like an ample supply when they set out, judging from the temperate woodland where they had landed, ran out. How could they have anticipated finding desert conditions within a few miles of them? Peri thought dizzily. It wasn't natural. No, of course it wasn't.

Jaharnus tried to laugh, but her voice sounded terribly hoarse. 'We are like my ancestors caught in the cracked mud at the bottom of a dried-up lake. We find their fossils from time to time.'

Peri was aware of the Doctor muttering, 'There must be an answer, there must be…'

Peri felt herself slipping away. Dimly she realised Dynes's drone was still hovering a little way off, its gleaming lenses focused upon them. Surely it wasn't going to sit there and watch them die! The last thing she remembered was the Doctor on his hands and knees crawling out from under the bedroll awning, and trying to haul himself upright with his staff.

In the *Stop Press*, Dynes hunched forward over the monitor, staring intently at the figures huddled beneath their makeshift sunshades. This was good stuff. What was the Doctor doing? One last futile effort? Chasing after a mirage, perhaps?

'DAVE 2, move in for a close-up,' he directed.

He just hoped he was going to die artistically.

Arnella began to feel dizzy, even with her power-cooled sun helmet and protective neck flap. Thorrin had called a halt, so she took another mouthful of water. She'd never known such heat. Thorrin stared at the compass in his hand, then he flipped up the tinted visor of his own helmet and peered about him. Arnella followed his gaze, as did Brockwell and her uncle.

It was as though they were in the middle of a glassy bowl, paved with the interminable hexagon slabs and roofed with blazing sky. They turned about, but there was no sign of any horizon.

'What's the matter?' her uncle asked Thorrin. Mutely he held out the compass. Arnella saw it was spinning wildly and felt a little twinge of fear.

'I'm afraid we're lost,' Thorrin said.

'Perhaps we can use the orientation of the paving grid as a guide?' Brockwell suggested quietly. 'I noticed we were going perpendicular to their faces.

Thorrin chuckled. 'Of course we can. Keeping your head, Will. That's good,' he commended absently, glancing at the slabs before him and setting off once more.

'Wait, Professor. Were we not facing that way?' said the Marquis, pointing sixty degrees to the left of Thorrin's proposed line of march.

'No, it's to the right, isn't it?' Brockwell said.

They looked at each other, then at Arnella, who shrugged hopelessly.

'We must have turned ourselves around scanning the horizon,' Thorrin said. 'We'd better stop here until the sun is lower and we can orientate ourselves again. We cannot go much further in this heat anyway.'

Brockwell was carrying a self-assembly tent in his pack. It was a surprisingly small package that he placed on the ground, then pulled a cord in the side. Pneumatic ribs, inflated by a tiny high-compression gas cylinder, writhed and popped open. In half a minute the dome-shaped structure was fully erected and they climbed inside gratefully. The foil-lined, double-thickness floor helped insulate them from the scorching ground. They threw open the side panels to encourage any through draft, but even so it was only the cooling helmets that made it bearable, though hardly pleasant.

'This is another test,' Thorrin stated, his jaw set resolutely. 'Fair enough, I should have anticipated something like it in the circumstances. But we shall survive, and won't let it slow us down for long. We should still be able to reach the far side by nightfall.'

The Marquis nodded in agreement, but seemed suddenly too exhausted to speak. Arnella looked at him in concern. He had driven himself through so many years of despair that she sometimes worried what effect it had had on his health. The trouble was he would never admit to any weakness.

'I wonder how the Doctor's party is doing,' Brockwell said.

Arnella found herself frowning. She had noticed the interest Brockwell had shown in the other party, especially that girl with the curiously dated hairstyle and odd accent. Well, it was not unreasonable that he should show some concern, she decided. The girl was more likely his type.

Thorrin used his binoculars and peered out through the open sides of the tent. Methodically he quartered the horizon, then lowered them again. 'It may be the atmospheric disturbance, of course, but I can't see them anywhere.'

Peri was floating somewhere cool and wet. Somehow the heat had gone. Even the terrible glare was muted. She opened her eyes. The Doctor was beside her, his arm gently holding her upright. Falstaff and Jaharnus were opposite them. They were all chest deep in greenish water, holding on to ropes at the bottom of a six-sided shaft. It took her addled mind a moment to realise why it seemed so familiar, then she gave a rasping laugh.

'Pretty smart,' she croaked. 'Hardly needed to dry off, did I?'

Looking up, she saw that the ropes were tied to the middle of each of the remaining staffs, which had been laid across the angled corners at the lip of the shaft. Over these had been draped their bedrolls, shading all but the centre of the well beneath. Insulated from the surface, the water and the stone around them had remained surprisingly cool.

''T'was the only shade around, though I do not relish the climb out,' said Falstaff. 'I may need some small assistance to ascend.'

'We'll solve that problem when we must,' said Jaharnus. 'I for one have no desire to move anywhere for the moment. I couldn't have lasted much longer up there.'

'We must remember to refill our canteens before we leave,'

said the Doctor. 'They have integral purifiers so the water shouldn't do us any harm.'

Peri felt as though she was thinking clearly for the first time in hours. She squinted up the shaft at the glare from the sky, noting the camera drone peering down at them over the edge. Better luck next time, she thought, then frowned. 'How can it be so hot out there? The sun is right overhead, but the woods around the white pyramid seemed pretty temperate. For that matter, who built all these traps and the plain? It must have taken years.'

'Well, by Shalvis's own admission, the Gelsandorans have had thousands of years to construct and refine the quest,' the Doctor pointed out. 'I think they are more materially advanced than they appear superficially. The engineering that maintains them is probably hidden well out of sight.' He grimaced, betraying a momentary flash of anger. 'Assuming of course that all this isn't simply an illusion.'

The others looked at him in surprise and disbelief.

'Blocking the nerve impulses to a finger to prevent a gun being fired I can just about believe,' Jaharnus said, 'but creating an illusion as perfect as this? Never.'

'I only said it was a possibility.'

It was afternoon when Qwaid, Gribbs, and Drorgon finally emerged from the wood. Qwaid could not make out the other two groups, but it seemed likely they were ahead of them. With the worst of the midday heat abating, the paved plain looked open and inviting, but Qwaid's natural distrust of anything that looked like a sucker bet made him hesitate before stepping straight out after them.

'Dro, get some rocks. Let's check this out.'

On the fifth try, a hexagonal slab fell inward. There were spikes at the bottom of the pit beneath, together with a few unidentifiable bones.

Drorgon scratched his massive head, squinted into the hazy

distance then at the thousands of slabs that lay between them and it. 'Throwing rocks ahead of us is going to take forever,' he pointed out practically.

Qwaid said nothing. That much had been immediately apparent. There had to be a trick to getting across, of course, but how long would it take to figure out?

Gribbs was muttering something.

'Spit it out,' Qwaid said automatically.

'Well, I was just thinking… If these slabs are all pressure-triggered, but hinged at the sides…'

'Yes?'

'Maybe, if we walked on the cracks to spread our weight, they wouldn't drop, and even if they did we'd only have to step to one side to get clear.'

'Now I was waiting to see which one of you would think of that,' said Qwaid.

As they got closer, the straggling green line that marked the edge of the plain resolved itself into tall grasses, fern bushes, and the more distant tops of trees, rising from what was presumably a valley that lay beyond. The last few slabs were speckled by moss and lichen, then replaced by a carpet of thick lush grass. It felt like walking on foam rubber after the hours of hard stone underfoot. Peri, still slightly damp from their time in the well, dropped gratefully to her knees and sprawled full length upon it, luxuriating in its soft coolness.

'Oh, wow, this is good. I'll never forget to water a lawn again!'

The others shed their packs and joined her.

After a few minutes she sat up, removed her boots and began massaging her feet. Still a little way out on the plain and about half a mile to their right she saw Thorrin's party also making for the strip of greenery.

'Think we should say hello?' she wondered.

'Their manner was a little standoffish this morning,' the Doctor observed. 'Somehow I don't think we'd be that welcome. In a sense we are rivals, after all.'

From the valley ahead of them came, faint but clear, a low moaning roar, which reverberated through the still air for several seconds. This was followed by a series of rapid guttural yelps, as though produced by several animals.

They all sprang to their feet, Falstaff's hand resting nervously on the pommel of his sword, while Jaharnus had drawn her gun. The sounds continued for some minutes, then faded away, although Peri now became aware of occasional muted chattering cries.

The Doctor looked at the lowering sun and made a decision. 'I propose we make camp here. I think we've had enough challenges for one day.'

They all agreed. As Falstaff succinctly put it: 'Tomorrow is sufficient unto the day thereof. In any case, we cannot face unknown perils on an empty stomach.'

Night had fallen by the time Qwaid, Gribbs, and Drorgon finally stumbled on to the green strip of land that fringed the far side of the plain. They had travelled the last part of the way by the light of hand torches. Some distance along to their right was the firefly glimmer of the camp lights of one of the other questing parties, and Qwaid stared at it with intense interest.

He had a plan.

As they had trudged across the plain he had realised he couldn't rely on Gribbs coming up with dodges like that again. Besides, he had to show that it was Crelly Qwaid who was making the smart decisions if he ever wanted to truly be the boss. They also needed some sort of advance notice of what was ahead of them so as not to be caught by surprise. The solution to both problems, when it dawned on him, was wonderfully simple.

'Get a couple of hours' sleep, boys,' he said confidently. 'We've got a busy night ahead of us.'

CHAPTER 10
NIGHT MOVES

Myra Jaharnus woke with a start, trying to place the dull thump that had roused her.

Overhead the stars were being obscured by a grey cloud, and for a moment she thought a bank of mist was rolling across the camp. Then the first tendrils touched her and she smelled a distinctive chemical tang. Blackout gas! She drew her gun even as her nostrils pinched tight and she clamped her lips shut. She could hold her breath for twenty minutes if need be. But despite the protective nictating membranes that instantly closed over her eyes, the gas burnt and stung, setting them watering. She heard the others shouting and a torch sprang into life, no more than a blurred fuzz of light through the tears and smoky haze.

From somewhere Falstaff was yelling at the top of his voice, 'Cowards! Whoreson caterpillars! Fight like men! Take that, and that!' The camp was being attacked, but even if her firing reflex had not been inhibited by the Gelsandorans, she dare not risk a shot in these conditions.

She had an impression of a menacing figure, bulkier even than Falstaff, looming out of the murk towards her. Instinctively she twisted about, letting her bone-fringed tail cut an arc through the air at knee height. There was a cry of pain, a heavy body crashed into her, sending her sprawling, then it was gone. She heard a yell that sounded like Peri's voice being stifled. The torchlight vanished and with it a scramble of footsteps that faded away into the night. The veil of blackout gas slowly dispersed, allowing the stars to illuminate the camp once more.

Wiping her eyes, Myra got to her feet, felt around for her own torch, and snapped it on. In the middle of a patch of trampled grass and scattered bedrolls was Falstaff, still coughing and yelling curses. He had a hand over his eyes and was blindly charging about, swinging his sword in great wild sweeps, turning and running away a few steps in another direction at a half-crouch, then futilely hacking the air again.

'They've gone,' she said sharply, 'so you can cut the act now.'

He paused in mid-swing. 'Is that you, my good Inspector?'

'Who else?'

Cautiously he removed his hand from over his eyes, red-rimmed and streaming, and peered about him into the darkness. Seeing no danger, he straightened up. 'Hah! So, the horde dared not stand against me, the pie-faced cowards!'

'Horde? It was Qwaid, Gribbs, and Drorgon. It had to be.'

'Nay, 't'was a dozen or perhaps a score, no less. But they cared not to taste my steel.'

'Somebody did,' Myra pointed out. 'There's blood on the blade. I hope it doesn't belong to the Doctor or Peri Brown.'

Falstaff looked at the glistening dark streaks on his sword with apparent astonishment, and Myra wondered if, for all his boasting, he'd ever actually drawn blood in combat before. Then his normal expression of bumptious self-confidence returned. 'There, what did I tell you? You have nought to fear with Falstaff here. Now, we must set about to rescue our comrades. Perhaps I should remain to hold the camp while you make a reconnaissance –'

'Maybe, but let's look around here first.'

A quick search of the camp revealed that both the Doctor's and Peri's packs, were missing. They had been using them as pillows, as they all had, so the packs wouldn't have been hard for their abductors to snatch up in the confusion. This in itself was suggestive.

'Either they think they're going to need extra help at some point along the way, or they've taken them as hostages to use against me when this is all over,' Myra speculated. 'They'd probably have knocked us on the heads or slit our throats while they were at it if they'd had the chance, only we put up more of a fight than they were expecting.'

'But are we not going to attempt to rescue them?'

Myra did not comment on the 'we'. 'I doubt if blundering around in the dark would help, and I haven't got the right equipment anyway. They've had time to prepare this, and could be hiding anywhere along this boarder zone, or else already setting off down into the valley to get a head start. Besides, I don't think the Doctor and Peri are in any immediate danger. Unless we can catch them unawares along the way, the best thing we can do is find this treasure first and let them come to us. Then we'll have something to bargain with. Otherwise, if they get there first, they won't need hostages any more.'

She realised that the DAVE drone that had been relentlessly trailing after them had moved closer as she had been speaking. The cursed things were so easy to forget, and she wondered if the Gelsandoran influence would prevent her shooting it down. Wait a minute: surely it and its fellows must have seen everything.

'Dynes,' she said, addressing the flying camera, 'I am making an official request for press cooperation, with the usual benefits for a successful outcome. Have you still got a drone with Qwaid's party? What have they done with the Doctor and Ms Brown? Where have they taken them?'

Dynes's voice came back clearly from the device's speaker grille. 'Inspector, you know better than to ask that. You have no jurisdiction here, so any deal you offer is worthless. Besides I want my subjects to know they can act perfectly naturally without fear of any interference from me. The impartiality of the press is sacrosanct, you know.'

The drone fell silent again, leaving Myra swishing her tail angrily across the grass. Sometimes she felt the press valued its independence a little too highly. In ancient times it had been different, she understood. She turned back to Falstaff. 'It looks like we're going to have to do it the hard way after all.'

'Just the two of us?'

'Believe me, it's not my ideal partnership either, but there's no other choice. Why, are you scared?'

'Old Jack does not flinch from danger. It is only that the Doctor seemed to have a certain facility for overcoming the hazards of our journey. Without him we may not proceed fast enough to effect a rescue. Perhaps it would be better if I returned to –'

'Quiet! Listen…'

Footsteps were approaching along the edge of the plain. A dim figure came into view around one of the fern bushes, and a circle of torchlight danced across the ground towards them.

'Hello? Are you all right? We heard the noise and I thought I'd better come over,' said Willis Brockwell.

Arnella sat on her bedroll with her chin on her knees and arms folded across her shins, awaiting Brockwell's return. Her uncle and Thorrin sat with their backs to the camp portafire, which they had switched on to drive the chill of the night away. They each held their guns ready.

She knew the camp had to be guarded, but Brockwell shouldn't have had to go on his own. Actually, when they had been roused by the distant commotion from the Doctor's camp, neither her uncle nor Thorrin had wanted any of them to risk investigating the cause. But to her surprise Brockwell had insisted he at least should go, claiming that, if it was the result of some indigenous danger, they had better be forewarned. She had not expected such defiance from him, and had to admit that he had more courage than she had previously given him credit for. But why couldn't he speak to her as forthrightly?

She was still brooding over this half an hour later when Brockwell returned with Falstaff and Jaharnus. The inspector explained what had happened and her theory of the criminal's motivations, then announced that she and her companion would be joining them. Her uncle and Thorrin looked unhappily at each other.

'Ah, I'm not so sure that will be a good idea,' said Thorrin slowly.

'We really cannot afford to be delayed,' the Marquis added.

'Besides, this is not our responsibility,' Thorrin continued. 'Better if we do not get involved.'

'What have you against cooperating with the police?' Jaharnus asked.

'Nothing at all, but, as Speaker Shalvis pointed out, you have no authority here.'

'Look, I don't care about any treasure. I just want to reach it before those scum, so we certainly won't delay you. My sole interest is catching a gang of killers and the safety of witnesses in my charge. Don't innocent lives count for anything?'

'I'm sure you're just doing your job, and your impartiality is beyond question, Inspector,' allowed the Marquis, 'but what about him?' He looked at Falstaff. 'He claims a knighthood, yet I am dubious as to his entitlement.'

The big man replied haughtily: 'Doubt me, do you sir? Why, I am as valiant as Hercules – a lion among men. Any expedition should be proud to number Falstaff amongst its muster. It is not thirty minutes past since I was disputing with cold steel against those villains, and making them pay dearly for their impudence. Were it not for their rascally vapours that did half blind me I would have filleted them all there and then.'

Jaharnus sighed. 'I'll vouch for his conduct. Just remember: Qwaid's taken two hostages already. Do you want him to try for another?' Her gaze passed meaningfully over Arnella. 'One of you, perhaps? You need as much help as you can get, and leave arguing over who gets what shares in the treasure until after you've found it, assuming Qwaid's men don't get there first.'

'It would make sense,' Brockwell said. 'Safety in numbers, and so on.'

'Yes, let them come with us, Uncle.' Arnella said, trying not to sound too eager.

Thorrin and the Marquis looked thoughtful, then nodded.

'Good,' said the inspector. 'Now let's get some sleep. We'd better make an early start.'

Peri's gag and blindfold were not removed until she had been dragged for what seemed like miles through damp fern thickets and over ground studded with mounds of tussock grass. When at last she could see again through her smarting eyes, it was only to squint into the glare of a hand torch shone full in her face.

'Are you all right, Peri?' came the Doctor's voice, and her heart gave a little jump of relief. She had thought they had brought another prisoner with them, but hadn't been certain who. Most of the time she could only hear two of the thugs complaining about the minor injuries they'd received during their raid on the camp.

'Sure she's OK,' came a rough mocking voice, before she could answer for herself.

The torch beam swung away, and by its reflected light she began to make out dim forms. They were in a hollow surrounded on three sides by rounded boulders and roofed by overhanging branches of the heart-leaf tree she was becoming familiar with. Various items of camping gear were piled in one corner. The Doctor stood at her side, while before them were the three crooks, two of whom were fumbling in their camping packs for a first-aid box. Unconsciously, she tugged at the strap that bound her hands behind her back, but it remained fast.

'Now the question is,' continued the speaker, the smallest and apparently uninjured one of the three, whom she now recognised as Qwaid, 'do you want her to stay that way?'

'Can we take the usual threats as read?' the Doctor said coolly. 'Just tell me what you want.'

'That's very sensible of you, Doctor,' said Qwaid. 'It's very simple. You'll help us keep up with the others, solving any more of these skewheaded tricks we run into, until we're ready to get ahead at the best moment.'

'Letting them break the ground for you, in case there are any more unpleasant surprises in store for us? So that's why your attack on our camp was so restrained.'

'Didn't I tell you he was the smartest one of the lot, boys?' Qwaid asked his companions rhetorically as they treated their wounds. 'You got it right, Doc, that's just what we're going to do.'

'And what about Peri?'

'Your friend goes back to our ship with Gribbs, just in case you get any ideas about being a hero. He'll keep in touch with us over the comm link' – he tapped a device like a bulky wristwatch – 'and you'll be able to talk to your friend regular to see she's being looked after. But don't think of getting away from us or trying anything cleverer. If Gribbs gets the wrong word from me, or doesn't hear from me on time…' He gave Peri an unpleasant smile. 'Well, we may not be able to use guns on each other here, but there must be plenty of other ways to make things unpleasant for someone. And if your friend the Doctor here steps out of line, I'll give Gribbs the go-ahead to start trying a few of them out on you.'

Peri shivered and tried not to let her fear show.

CHAPTER 11
THE VALLEY OF MIST

They were up with the dawn, as Inspector Jaharnus had suggested, striking camp and setting off through the strip of fern forest before the sun had cleared the horizon. Arnella was still rubbing the sleep from her eyes as they went.

She had not slept well after their interrupted night. The newly realised menace of the three criminals had been one reason, the behaviour of her uncle and Professor Thorrin another. She had been a little surprised by their initial reluctance to investigate the disturbance at the Doctor's camp, then to allow the inspector and Falstaff to accompany them. Thorrin, she had already decided, could be thoughtlessly inconsiderate at times, but her uncle normally never let circumstances prevent him from showing the proper sensibilities. As she had learnt from her youngest days, it was the duty of those in positions of power and responsibility to aid those less fortunate than themselves. That their own circumstances were temporarily reduced should be no excuse for ignoring such obligations. Could the prospect of what lay ahead be influencing their judgment? In fact only Brockwell had behaved well, and that was probably due to his apparent liking for that Brown girl. Still, at least he'd made the effort.

The forest ended suddenly at the edge of a cliff, running away in a wavering line on either side. Before them, tinted pink by the low rays of the sun, was a sea of softly swirling mist, broken only close to by the crowns of a few high trees. On the far side of this

113

insubstantial mass, perhaps eight or ten kilometres away, was another ragged cliff face, cut through by the threads of several waterfalls.

Peering cautiously over the edge, they found there was a shelf of rock only a few metres below, with the dim outline of a second ledge beyond that, suggesting a series of terraces that faded away into the misty depths of the shrouded valley. They walked along the clifftop for a short distance and came to a narrow fault in the rock, which would make a workable stairway down to the next level. As they were examining this a muted snorting sound rose up out of the valley, accompanied by a medley of barking cries.

'Clearly there are creatures of some kind down there,' Thorrin stated, 'and we must assume they are dangerous, otherwise traversing the valley would not be a challenge.'

'Jack Falstaff is as loath to refuse a challenge as the next man,' said their new companion, 'but I have neither the horns nor legs of Pan. Might we not exercise a modicum of discretion and attempt to circumvent this obstacle rather than needlessly plumb unknown depths?'

Thorrin shook his head. 'This cleft seems to reach as far as the main valley walls. It might take days to find a way round, assuming any existed, and we can't risk the delay.' He took out his compass and examined it carefully. 'It seems to have settled down now,' he remarked, taking a bearing on the opposite cliff.

Arnella saw her uncle sneer at Falstaff, even as he slid his sporting rifle from his pack and checked its charge gauge. 'Perhaps you are afraid, Sir John? If you would rather stay behind after all, that is your privilege.'

'I merely counselled caution,' Falstaff replied. 'Knowing the difference between bravery and foolhardiness is no cause to gird at me.'

'We're going down,' Inspector Jaharnus said firmly. She checked her own side arm, then led the way down the sloping cleft to the first terrace.

'You can come last, if you wish,' said the Marquis to Falstaff. 'Just make sure you do not fall on top of us.'

As they started down, Arnella noticed the DAVE unit that had shadowed Jaharnus and Falstaff from their old camp suddenly turn and speed away, leaving their drone to continue following them alone. Briefly she wondered why Dynes had recalled it.

Gribbs returned to the camp in the hollow a little after dawn.

'They're all gone,' he reported to Qwaid. 'Set off for the valley, the cop and the fat one as well.'

'Good,' said Qwaid, finishing off a self-heating can of soup and tossing it aside. 'Now it's our turn.'

Drorgon pulled the Doctor and Peri, who had been sitting together on a boulder, to their feet. The Doctor's hands were released and he was given his pack.

'Don't worry about me, Doctor,' Peri said, trying to sound reassuring. 'I'm just sorry I talked you into all this. You just be careful out there.'

'I'll be all right, Peri. I'm sure these gentlemen don't intend to take any unnecessary risks,' he said lightly.

'That's right,' said Qwaid cheerfully, 'specially as we've got you along for insurance.' He turned to Gribbs, who was gathering up his own pack. 'Now you get back to the *Falcon* as fast as you can and wait for my call if we need any reconnaissance. Once we find the stash, you bring her across so we can load up.' He nodded at Peri. 'And don't let her give you the slip.'

'No chance,' said Gribbs, taking hold of Peri's arm and twisting her about. The strap about her wrist was released so that she could put on her backpack, then replaced. Then she felt a rope being tied about the strap. 'A jerk on this'll soon teach her to behave.'

Her last sight of the Doctor was as he, Qwaid, and Drorgon

disappeared between the ferns. Then Gribbs gave her a shove and they set off back towards the tiled plain. As the grass gave way to stone, Gribbs said, 'You go first. Walk on the cracks between the big slabs.'

She did as she was bidden, wondering if she should reveal the colour-code sequence. Was there any advantage in keeping it safe? If she broke free of him could she move faster and perhaps get away? Probably not, as he'd soon see what slabs she touched. Could she somehow lure him into stepping on the wrong slab? If she did would he let go of her tether or pull her in after him?

As they set out across the plain, picking their way between the slabs, she saw a camera drone drift along the line of greenery, and then head after them. Was there no escape from Dynes's intrusions? Then a new thought struck her.

'Hey,' she called back to Gribbs. 'Don't you know you're on camera?'

He glanced behind them and waved. 'Yeah, that's Dexel Dynes's eye. I always wanted to be on one of his shows. So what?'

'But how can you do this when you know it's all being recorded?'

Gribbs laughed. 'Who cares? You aren't a citizen of Astroville and the locals don't seem to mind what we do here. Anyway, what does it matter now? This is going to be the big one. After this we can retire anywhere we like and nobody'll ask what we did to get there. So you'd better behave yourself. Now stop gabbing and watch where you put your feet. If you fall into something, don't reckon on me pulling you out any too quickly.'

The descent from terrace to terrace seemed endless, even though the climb was quite an easy one. The sun had vanished after the third level, and all about them was the cold grey mist. The cleft paths were steep in places but sound underfoot. The only vegetation were lichens, damp mosses, and low bushes bearing thick clusters of orange grapelike fruits. The sounds from below were louder and more frequent now, causing them to keep their hands near to their holsters. At Thorrin's direction, Brockwell had unpacked several egg-sized grenades, which they now wore clipped to their belts, all except Falstaff, who insisted a 'gentleman' would use cold steel in his defence. Arnella suspected he was simply scared of the devices, but she found his protestations an unexpected and welcome distraction from the unknown dangers ahead. She hoped her fear did not show, and wished she could be like Thorrin and her uncle, who simply looked defiant and eager to get on. But she knew she could no longer find the same enthusiasm for the undertaking.

And then the grey got darker as the shadowy forms of massive trees rose through the mist past them, and suddenly they were on the valley floor, which seemed to slope slightly down from the foot of the cliff. The ground was damp and covered with coarse grass, interspersed with clumps of the orange-grape bushes. Thick-boled trees topped with crowns of feathery fronds made strange shapes in the mist. The visibility was no better than thirty metres.

Thorrin took out his compass and checked it carefully. 'It's still steady. We should have no problem keeping to a direct course for the opposite side –'

There was a rustle and swish of branches from somewhere in the greyness. As they turned about trying to locate its source there came a panting snort, a monstrous snuffling, and then a huge form loomed out of the mist.

Qwaid, Drorgon, and the Doctor were halfway down the series of terraces when they heard the sounds of battle break out below them: the sharp echoing concussions of microgrenades exploding mingled with the multiple cracks of energy bolts. Rising and falling as though in ghastly accompaniment to this was a series of roars, snarling cries, and bellows of pain.

'Seems our rivals have run into a little trouble,' Qwaid said with a grin. 'We'll just wait here until they're finished – one way or the other.'

The Doctor's face was ashen, while his eyes blazed accusingly. 'They might be killed! Aren't you going to help them?'

Qwaid simply laughed. The Doctor made as if to start forward, but Drorgon's massive hand restrained him, and he could only wait and listen to the battle.

'They're putting up a good fight,' Qwaid observed. 'Least they had the sense to come prepared. Sounds like there's some good-sized meat down there.'

At this remark a questioning frown was added to the Doctor's expression of anger and dismay. He stared intently into the mist, then at the slopes about him.

The first creature they had killed had resembled a prehistoric terrestrial sauropod, standing five metres at the shoulder and perhaps twenty-five long, including its spiked tail – except that it had three pairs of limbs and a turtle-like shell on its back. Possibly it was only a herbivore and had simply been curious about them, but Thorrin had snapped off a shot from his pistol that had apparently annoyed it, and it had charged them. It had taken a dozen energy bolts and two grenades to kill it.

A pack of seven smaller four-legged beasts had appeared before the massive body had stopped twitching, as though summoned by the scent of spilled blood, forcing the seekers to retreat until they huddled with their backs to the bole of one of the massive trees whose tops broke the misty ceiling. The newcomers had powerful jaws filled with rows of dagger-like teeth and tore into the carcass with incredible savagery, making Arnella turn her head aside in disgust, trying not to be sick as the stench of the entrails reached them.

Those scavengers that were pushed aside by their more determined fellows started snapping at the quest party. The Marquis shot the nearest cleanly through the brain and it dropped in a flurry of wickedly clawed limbs. Falstaff waved his sword at the beasts as though engaged in a hand-to-claw duel with them and shouted defiance, without coming close to inflicting any actual injury.

Four more of the scavengers appeared and began circling the tree. They fired upon them, but they moved swiftly and were difficult targets. A grenade killed one and injured another, but gradually the beasts edged closer as they became used to the flash and crack of their weapons.

Then a massive horned lizard head emerged from the greyness, followed by a long scaled body supported on many pairs of short legs. Fanged jaws yawned wide, and a long tongue flickered, tasting the air. It vented a hissing roar that caused the scavengers momentarily to lose interest in the seekers as they turned to face a more deadly foe.

'Come on!' shouted the Marquis. 'While they're distracted!'

They ran for the next clump of trees, snapping shots to the left and right to discourage any pursuers. Even Falstaff maintained the frantic pace, puffing and wheezing like an ancient steam engine, until the mist had swallowed up all sight and sound of the primitive conflict. Only then did they sink down in the shelter of a thicket and catch their breath.

Peri stumbled and almost fell. Walking on the cracks was hard work, especially when you couldn't use your arms for balance. And to think when she was young she'd tried not to step on the cracks in the sidewalk. It was also very slow going. She looked at the morning sun and made a quick calculation, then said, 'Hey, I can tell you a quicker way to get across this…'

She explained about the rainbow tile sequence, and suggested it could be reversed for travelling in the opposite direction. Gribbs was suspicious.

'Are you trying something? Why didn't you tell me this earlier?'

'You expect me to make things easy for you? Look, I'll go first to show you it's safe, only please let's get a move on.'

She'd wanted to reach the cool of the wood before noon. Even Gribbs's company was preferable to the heat of the plain. She tried to convince herself, like Mr Micawber, that something would turn up when they got back to the ships.

The TARDIS stood in the glade, its door slightly ajar.

Through the crack between door and frame light flickered erratically, pulsating brightly with multicoloured flashes, then sinking almost to extinction. And accompanying the lights were noises, sometimes muffled and indistinct, then loud and shrill. Even without words they told of fear, confusion, and pain.

CHAPTER 12
STAIRWAY

Qwaid waited for ten minutes after the sound of gunfire ceased before letting them descend the rest of the way to the valley floor. It didn't take them long to find the scene of the conflict – the smell alone was sufficient to guide them. Carcasses littered the ground, being greedily consumed by a host of scavengers ranging in size from that of small dogs to rats. A trail of blood and flattened grass leading off through the trees suggested where one whole animal had been carried bodily away by something even larger. There was no sign of any humanoid remains among the carnage.

'Looks as though they were lucky,' Qwaid said. 'See if you can pick up their trail, Dro. We'll keep following on after them if we can.'

Drorgon began quartering the ground, all the time keeping his portable cannon at the ready. The Doctor walked around the carcasses and began examining the surrounding trees and bushes carefully. Qwaid watched him with a frown. After a minute he asked, 'What are you looking for, Doc?'

'I'm trying to establish what the indigenous life in this valley eats.'

'You, if you're not careful. If you want your friend to stay healthy, try not to get yourself killed.'

'I have no intention of risking that eventuality,' replied the Doctor absently, still peering intently at the vegetation. Apparently coming to some conclusion, he turned to Qwaid and launched into a rapid breathless explanation. 'I see evidence of chewed tree bark, split nuts, rooted ground, cropped grass and leaves. However, not one of the five bushes bearing orange berries in this immediate vicinity has been touched, yet the fruit seems soft and ripe. There aren't even any piles of droppings near them. It was the same on the terraces, which was what first brought them to my attention. Also, note, we haven't seen any form of flying predator yet, though you'd think all this carrion would have attracted a few by now.'

'So what?'

The Doctor picked a berry, split it open and sniffed cautiously. His nose wrinkled. 'It has a distinctive, not to say penetrating, smell. The creatures down here appear to avoid them, possibly because they're naturally poisonous, or because they have been conditioned to stay clear of them by the Gelsandorans. This would explain the absence of any flying creatures here, since I suspect the bushes are intended to serve as a sort of botanical barrier which would only work against ground-dwelling animals, preventing them leaving the valley. Therefore, if we apply some of their juice to our persons, and carry a few berries with us for the unforeseen, they should also avoid us.'

Qwaid realised he was gaping and shut his mouth quickly. 'Now that's smart thinking,' he acknowledged. The Doctor smiled back coolly.

'That is why, shall we say, you acquired my services.'

'Right, we've had long enough to rest,' said Thorrin, rising from the thicket.

'A little longer,' pleaded Arnella. 'I still feel sick.'

'My dear, we must keep going,' her uncle said.

'Surely a few minutes don't matter?'

'A modest boon that I too would dearly crave,' puffed Falstaff, still mopping his brow.

'We do seem to be safe here, Professor,' Brockwell said. 'If we're all properly rested we can move faster.'

'Oh, very well,' said Thorrin impatiently. 'Five minutes only.'

Arnella realised her uncle was looking at her with a troubled expression. 'You insisted on coming, my dear. Now you must keep up. We cannot go back or afford to waste any time now. What we are after is too important to let any personal weakness slow us down.'

'I know, Uncle. But let's not kill ourselves in the process,' she said with a weak smile, trying to lighten the mood.

He looked at her blankly. With a tiny shiver she saw he hadn't realised she'd been joking.

They set off exactly five minutes later. The mist had not lifted appreciably, and Arnella wondered if the valley was permanently shrouded all day. The diffuse unchanging light had a disorientating effect, and she kept checking her watch to see how much time had actually passed. The mist bleached the colour out of everything more than twenty metres away, and the drabness added to her sense of detachment. It was hard to believe they were moving, and that it was not the pale shadows of the distorted trees and bushes that were drifting past them. There seemed to be animal noises all round and they flinched at every one and each twitch of a leaf or rustle of undergrowth.

A creature like a four-metre-long turtle with a spiked shell shuffled out of the greyness towards them. The professor raised his gun but Brockwell said quickly, 'Look at its mouth – I think it's a herbivore.' The animal paused, sniffed, and peered at them with tiny stupid eyes, but then continued on past.

Two minutes later a slightly smaller version of the horned multilegged lizard they had seen earlier lunged at them from out of the bushes in a flurry of churning limbs, jaws agape. They all fired without thinking, blinding it and burning off its forelegs. Then they ran before the creature's death throes could attract another of the fleet-footed scavenger packs.

Arnella was desperately afraid, but she steeled herself not to show it. Exhaustion could be admitted to before strangers, but not fear. Perhaps her uncle had been right about every minute counting. What would it be like here at night?

The land continued to slope gently downward. After

covering what must have been five or six kilometres, she noticed that the ground was getting spongier underfoot. The tall trees that had loomed like grey spires on either side of them appeared less frequently and the mist, though not thinning, became slightly lighter. From ahead of them came a faint splashing. In a minute they were standing by the rushes that fringed the shore of a broad lake that stretched away into the white opacity. Out across the water they saw a dark swanlike neck rise into view and glide along serenely for several seconds before submerging again.

'So, our resolution is tested again as we have to face yet another change of terrain, no doubt with its own special dangers,' said Thorrin. 'Fortunately we came prepared. The inflatable, please, Will.'

Brockwell rummaged in his pack and pulled out a rectangular package almost as compact as the tent had been. Unravelling a thin cord from one end, he tossed the package into the water. With a hiss its thin but extraordinarily tough fabric expanded and unfolded. It was driven by ducted electrostatic panels set in its underside and powered by sheets of flexi-batteries. They climbed in, Thorrin at the front with his compass, Brockwell steering with the slender telescopic tiller and throttle control. The light craft settled alarmingly under Falstaff's weight but maintained an adequate freeboard. Silently they set off. The Marquis had his rifle ready, while Jaharnus held a primed grenade in her hand. Both stared intently at the slate-grey water as it rippled sluggishly past.

Qwaid had to admit that the Doctor's berry juice worked perfectly.

They strode slowly through the sombre valley, letting the aroma diffuse through the heavy air before them. Half-seen forms shuffled between the trees about them. They heard snorts and grunts, then heavy feet stomping away. Drorgon began to look annoyed that he had no opportunity to use his portable cannon.

Qwaid, however, began to feel a strange elation. So this was how you got things done, he thought. You found the right people to do a job and forced them to make it happen for you. It was good, it was… well, satisfying, in a way he had never expected. This was what Alpha must have enjoyed all those years. To be the one pulling the strings, to be in control, to shape the world around you to what you wanted it to be.

His new-found satisfaction was slightly shaken when they came to the lake. Muddy footprints gave evidence of where Thorrin's party had clearly embarked on some sort of boat. Unfortunately they had nothing similar with them. Then he reminded himself that now he had somebody to solve that sort of problem for him.

'Looks like we have to get across this, Doc. What do you know about building rafts?'

Even as the Doctor looked about him, there came drifting from the white expanse before them the dying echoes of grenades and gunfire.

'Sounds like Thorrin's lot are having some more fun,' Qwaid remarked cheerfully.

A second serpent head reared up high out of the water beside them, jaws agape. The Marquis shot it cleanly through the back of its mouth, and it fell back hissing and writhing into waters already foaming pink with the blood of its fellow. The inflatable bucked again as an unseen body brushed against its pliant underside, and Brockwell fought the tiller to keep it steady.

The water shivered and bubbled some twenty metres off their port bow, as though some huge form was rising from below. Thorrin tossed a microgrenade into the swirling vortex, and a fountain of foam laced with unidentifiable gobbets of flesh and scale burst forth, showering them with stinking spray.

A head crowned by a glistening spinney crest broke surface right beside them, and lunged forward over the side of the inflatable. Arnella screamed as the metre-wide jaws snapped at her, and threw herself aside. The fangs missed their mark, but the lower jaw caught her shoulder and with a gasp she toppled over backward and vanished beneath the heaving grey waters – Brockwell's hand reaching out after her just a fraction too late.

'Arnella – no!' the Marquis shouted.

Falstaff cut at the huge head blindly with his sword and actually opened a gaping wound across its snout, making it rear backward. Jaharnus thrust her pistol forward, fired three times virtually down its throat, then turned and dived in after Arnella, just ahead of Brockwell, who was about to do the same.

The serpent writhed and twisted in its death throes, throwing up waves that threatened to swamp the inflatable, before the convulsions gradually lessened until it lay still on the surface of the water. A strange silence descended as the mist, temporarily dispersed by the shockwaves from the grenade blasts, closed in about them again. Brockwell swung the inflatable around, circling the few surface bubbles that were all that marked the spot where Arnella and Jaharnus had disappeared. They peered over the sides, straining their eyes for any sign of victim and rescuer, guns still held at the ready.

There was nothing to be seen. Slowly the bubbles stopped rising. Brockwell made to dive over himself, but Falstaff unexpectedly stayed him.

'Steady, lad. If one of the inspector's kind cannot find her, no one can.'

'It's finished. It's all been for nothing,' the Marquis said almost inaudibly in a dead voice, causing Brockwell to flash him an angry, puzzled glance.

Then with a splash Jaharnus broke the surface, Arnella's limp form clasped to her.

As they hauled Arnella aboard she started choking and

retching, bringing up water. Jaharnus drew herself smoothly out of the water and back into the boat, hardly breathing deeply after her exertions.

'Get us away from here,' Thorrin commanded. Brockwell obeyed, sending the inflatable forward at maximum thrust, all the while casting anxious glances at Arnella.

'Thank you,' said the Marquis to Jaharnus with a curious intensity. 'You've no idea what this means.'

Falstaff patted Arnella helpfully on the back until she had finished coughing and sat pale and trembling on the floor of the inflatable. With a flourish he took off his short cloak and laid it about her shoulders. 'You see what valuable comrades you almost rejected when the inspector and I petitioned to join your company,' he said smugly.

Qwaid allowed the Doctor to lead them along the shoreline, examining the low trees and bushes that grew on the edge of the forest for suitable raft-building materials. He did not have to go very far.

'This tree here,' he said, indicating a straight slim-trunked growth with a feathery puffball on its crown, 'appears to be similar to balsa wood in density, and each one grows to remarkably uniform length and diameter. A dozen of those logs side by side will make an excellent raft. Note the handy creepers lying across the ground to serve as ready-made bindings. Those tall bamboos there will make bracings and punt poles, while this bush here with the broad, stiff, spatulate leaves, will provide serviceable paddles. It's all too easy!'

'What you mean, too easy?' growled Drorgon.

'I mean it's ready-made for building rafts. Probably carefully chosen and bred for the purpose.'

'So what?' said Qwaid. 'It's here and we're going to use it.'

'But don't you see what it means?'

'Why don't you tell me while you put the raft together?' Qwaid suggested, feeling he was getting the measure of executive decision-making.

Drorgon did the heavy work under the Doctor's directions. As they cut and tied, the Doctor explained. He had a way with words, Qwaid gave him that.

'This is more than a test of ingenuity and making use of natural resources. This is confirmation that they've had time enough to provide the means to help even those seekers who haven't come with a boat of any sort. That indicates they've had a lot of experience with them.'

'So?'

'It means there's a catch to it all somewhere, assuming we take what Shalvis told us at face value.'

Oddly enough Qwaid had. Some sixth sense told him so. He'd met so many liars and hustlers in his life that those speaking the truth stood out as though they were illuminated. 'She's on the level about the treasure,' he said simply.

'Yes, but that still isn't the whole story. The way is dangerous, but obviously they intend any reasonably determined and alert seekers to have at least a sporting chance to win through. There must have been hundreds, even thousands of them over the millennia. Yet Shalvis says almost all the treasure remains. How can that be?'

'Because there was a lot to start with. A shipful! The others could only take so much away with them.'

'Oh, so you intend only to take just enough with you for your immediate needs?' the Doctor inquired innocently. 'Only what you can carry in your own arms, perhaps – an amount sufficient for a modest retirement somewhere, charitably leaving plenty for those who will come after you?'

Qwaid glowered at him. 'Trying to talk me out of it, are you? So we'll give up and let you and your friend go just like that? What sort of a simp do you take me for?'

The Doctor shook his head sadly. 'No. I'm just trying to prepare you for a disappointment, so that you won't overreact when your beautiful dream comes crashing down.'

128

'Shut up and get this thing finished.'

In an hour the raft was complete. It was crude but sound and very light, floating well even under their combined weight. They made an incongruous crew, the Doctor's costume more appropriate for a boating party and contrasting strangely with Drorgon's inelegant bulk. They rubbed the remaining berries on to its blunt prow and sides for whatever additional protection they might give, then Drorgon and the Doctor took up the paddles and they pushed off from the shore.

Peri and Gribbs crossed the tiled plain without mishaps and before the unnatural heat of the day became oppressive. The cool of the wood still came as a welcome relief though. As they had trudged along, Peri had thought furiously, conjuring up a dozen plans to get free, and discarding just as many. Now they were walking the shaded paths, she began to wonder how the Gelsandorans would react when they saw she was Gribbs's prisoner.

Gribbs was cursing fluently. 'Can't trust anything around here!' he exclaimed with feeling.

Peri saw he was staring at the first of the signposts. Each arm was now completely blank.

'Which way?' he demanded of her.

'I haven't the faintest idea,' she said with as much dignity as she could muster. 'You're the one in charge.'

'Don't give me any lip, girl,' he warned her.

'I'm just saying it might be anything. A subtler kind of intelligence test, or maybe the signs are changed regularly – I'm from out of town so I don't know. But the Doctor might be able to work it out. Shall we go back for him?'

Gribbs guessed a path and headed back, hopefully, towards the landing ground. All of the signs they came across were blank. Did they show anything only when they needed to? she wondered. Had they ever shown anything at all? Then came the sound of soft, measured footsteps from along the curve of the path ahead. Immediately Gribbs pulled her a little way into the undergrowth by the side of the path, clearly nervous about where he put his feet, but evidently intent on smuggling her into his ship secretly. 'Don't say a word, or else!' he hissed in her ear.

Two robed Gelsandorans rounded the corner, proceeding on their own mysterious business.

Then Peri realised they'd both forgotten about Dynes's ubiquitous camera drone, which was patiently hovering over the path, pointing its lenses at them. The natives had to realise they were there, but what would they do? She tensed herself.

To her utter amazement and dismay the two natives paused by the drone, looked directly at them, nodded politely and continued on their way.

'Well how's about that?' Gribbs muttered, as they disappeared from sight. They returned to the path. As he led her on with a distinctly more relaxed swing to his stride, Peri's spirits sank.

What was she to make of the Gelsandorans behaviour? In their own way they were as bad as Dynes. Or was she the one out of step? Was this an alien thing or the way it was in the future? Didn't anybody, apart from the Doctor, really care here? With an effort, she tried to reason it out from their point of view and saw her mistake.

The Gelsandorans ran the whole treasure-trail process essentially for their own self-interest. They had apparently been quite willing to let them die out on the plain yesterday, as they would have if the Doctor hadn't been smart enough to find a refuge. Apart from the single restriction on the use of guns against each other, they must treat everything that happened while on the quest simply as another challenge for their subjects to overcome without their interference. Was that really what she was now: an experimental subject in the Gelsandorans researches? Were they prying into her mind at this instant? she wondered with a shudder. Were they dispassionately recording her reactions? Whatever was the case, she certainly couldn't rely on their help or sympathy.

She was very definitely on her own.

They had run parallel to the grey shadow in the mist for twenty minutes without finding any break. Now the nose of the inflatable scraped softly against the shelf of rock at its base. The Marquis scrambled ashore and held the line while the others disembarked, hauling ashore their packs. Arnella, still pale and shivering in her damp clothes, stepped on to solid ground with a sigh of relief. Falstaff alighted with a heave and a peculiar, quick, dainty step. Brockwell, the last one off, released the valve and with a hiss of air the craft deflated. He pulled the limp form from the water, shook it dry, then began to fold it. In a minute it was small enough to slip back into his pack.

The rocky shelf ranged between three and five metres wide. At its back the mist rolled against a sheer wall that turned the swirling vapour to a leaden grey. To their left they could hear the continuous rush and splatter of a waterfall discharging into the lake.

Thorrin checked his compass again and nodded. 'From our observations this formation seems continuous, therefore it must be the base of the cliffs we saw this morning. Clearly we must now ascend.'

'But how are we going to manage it?' Myra asked. 'That rock looks pretty smooth. Unless you've got a set of flight packs hidden away somewhere.'

'Just so,' Falstaff said. 'Old Jack is even less a fly than he is a mountain goat.'

'We have some compact climbing gear and lines, and I have done some rough rock work in the past,' Thorrin said impatiently, 'but I hope it will not come to that. There are still a few hours of daylight left and we must make use of them to examine the barrier more closely. If necessary we can camp here and continue in the morning.'

They made their way along the ledge, Arnella almost brushing the rock wall in an effort to keep as far away from the water as possible. The rock remained to all appearances sheer and virtually unclimbable, until Brockwell said, 'Hey, look at that.'

A section of the rock wall had been planed perfectly smooth. Projecting from it was an ascending series of horizontal flat stone slabs, each about a metre and a half long, forming a continuous stairway. Thorrin tested the bottom step. 'It seems sound enough. We should be able to reach the top well before the light goes. Come on.' He started up.

Soon they were climbing through the mist. There was no sign of the ground or sky, which perhaps made the climb more tolerable, since it was easy to believe it was comfortingly just out of sight below them, and not hundreds of metres. Falstaff protested every so often, and convinced Thorrin that they should take five minutes' break after fifteen minutes of climbing. They all sat on the steps and massaged their aching calves gratefully. However, it was evident that Thorrin and the Marquis begrudged every second they were not advancing towards their goal, and once again Thorrin started them upward precisely on time.

They climbed on and on. After another fifteen minutes they took a second break. There was no lightening of the mist to show they were nearing the top. Myra could see Thorrin and the Marquis, who were leading, trying to step faster. She looked at her watch, made a swift mental calculation, then called out, 'Hold it. Stop. There's something wrong.' They halted, strung out on the steps above and below her, and turned puzzled faces in her direction.

'What's the matter, Inspector?' Thorrin said briskly.

'You know what's the matter. We should have reached the top by now.'

'We shall any minute, as long as you do not delay us any further.'

'But we should've reached the top at least ten minutes ago.'

'Nonsense. It's just a little further.'

'Excuse me, Professor,' said Brockwell hesitantly, 'but I think the inspector's right. I was beginning to wonder myself.'

'You're just letting the conditions confuse you,' the Marquis interjected. 'It's this mist that's doing it.'

'No, Uncle,' said Arnella unhappily, 'it's more than that.'

The Marquis glowered at her as though disappointed. Thorrin said impatiently, 'We cannot be sure how long the ascent will take because we do not know for certain how high this cliff is.'

'But we can make a good estimate,' Myra insisted. 'When we looked across the valley from the other side the top seemed about level with us, right?'

'Agreed,' Thorrin said curtly.

'The terraces couldn't have been more than a hundred and fifty metres deep in all. From there the land sloped gently all the way down to the lake, so over that distance say it added another three hundred metres at the most. Even adding on another fifty for error, this cliff can't be more than five hundred high.'

'So. We have simply to go a little further.'

'I noted when we started up. Excluding the breaks, we've been climbing for almost forty-five minutes. I reckon there are about four steps to the vertical metre. At an average pace of one step per second, which is what we've been doing, we should have already climbed six hundred and seventy-five metres. So where's the top?'

Her calculations were unarguable, she knew, but logic and reason were not the only factors at work here. Thorrin and the Marquis simply didn't want to accept that there might be another obstacle in their way.

'We'll go on for another five minutes,' Thorrin said.

They climbed on. The mist grew no thinner, nor was there any sign of the interminable stairway ending. When the time was up, Thorrin stood with fists clenched, staring up at the ever-receding mist, the rock wall, and the stairs.

'This is intolerable,' exclaimed the Marquis, his frustration boiling over. 'What's happening, Thorrin?'

'Some trick of the natives, I imagine,' Thorrin said, evidently fighting to keep his voice level, then added an admission that must have cost him considerable self-esteem: 'I simply don't know.'

'It's like being in a dream, where you run and run but don't get anywhere. It's... a little frightening,' Arnella admitted with unexpected candour.

'I've had those sorts of dreams to,' Brockwell said quietly.

'Well I have a dream about wine and brace of capon, a warm fire to chase the ague from the bones, and a feather mattress,' grunted Falstaff. 'But I'll be content with rations and a rock bed so long as it is level. Let us descend while there is still light, lest we spend a night on this perilous perpendicularity. We may renew our assault on this bewitched mount on the morrow when we are rested.'

The suggestion was so sensible that even Thorrin and the Marquis did not object. So they turned about and set off back down the stairs.

Automatically Myra took note of their rate of descent. She estimated they were going a third faster than they had ascended. Thirty-five minutes to go, then. No one requested a break. All they wanted was to be off the stairs and to feel solid ground under them. Myra began to appreciate how vulnerable they were – exposed upon the narrow stair slanting up the unending cliff. Anything could be out there in the mist. They had seen no flying creatures in the valley, but how did then know there weren't any? Could they fight a battle in such a place? What if there was an avalanche? There was no shelter and they'd be swept away. She tried to go faster and almost fell, flicking her tail out to maintain her balance. Steady, steady, she told herself. You don't want to go down that quickly.

The stairs rolled up at them, materialising out of the mist. Down, down. She checked the time: thirty minutes. More stairs. Everybody must have been suffering terrible pains in their legs, but nobody complained. Down further. Surely they should be able to hear the waterfalls on the lake by now. Thirty five-minutes… forty… No, not again!

They stumbled to a stop and collapsed sprawling on the steps, panting to regain their breath, legs cramped and trembling. Myra saw their frightened, incredulous expressions, and heard Arnella sobbing aloud:

'We'll never get down, never! We're trapped!'

CHAPTER 13
WHAT THE PUBLIC WANTS

Dynes frowned at the image of Thorrin's party relayed from his drone, floating in the mist a few metres away from the cliff wall. What was going on there? He checked the DAVE's current telemetry readings, then called up its log and reviewed the inertial guidance chart. Gradually a smile began to spread across his face, then he chuckled. Now this had comic potential if presented properly. The D and E illits and vid-junkies would love seeing a party of their social betters making fools of themselves if the trick was carefully explained to them first.

He checked the other DAVE that was following Qwaid, Drorgon, and the Doctor across the lake. Their journey was entirely too easy, without any sign of a bloody attack by sea monsters. That Doctor was too clever by half. Still, maybe he'd get trapped like Thorrin to make up for it. And he had got some high-quality action shots earlier, especially Inspector Jaharnus's bit of lifesaving.

He checked another monitor and reached for his hat.

It was drawing in towards evening as they entered the open glade in which the *Falcon* had set down. Dynes was waiting for them, a DAVE unit hovering beside him. Of course, Gribbs thought, he knew exactly when we'd be arriving from the drone that had been trailing them. But why had he bothered to turn up in person? Didn't his drone cameras give him everything he needed? He recalled that they had recorded his humiliating misfortune in the wood the day before, and decided he was not going to make a fool of himself a second time, even for someone as famous as Dynes.

'Mr Gribbs, Ms Brown. I want exclusive interviews with both

of you,' said the pressman briskly, coming straight to the point. 'Naturally that means a bonus on top of the standard rate.'

The girl's expression changed to one of astonishment, as though she couldn't believe her ears, while Gribbs felt a thrill of excitement, which dispelled his earlier misgivings in an instant. Dexel Dynes wanted to interview him in person one to one!

'You mean like the one you did for Marrak Theel during the Cavandar Bank siege?' Gribbs asked hesitantly, just to be certain.

'Just that sort of thing,' Dynes said encouragingly. 'Captor and hostage, personal tensions, a taste of fear. Always goes down well with the viewers.'

'Theel came over as a real hard pro, didn't he? Then the cops gunned him down – but he took ten of them with him. What a way to go! You handled that with real class, Dynes.'

'Just doing my job as well as I can, Mr Gribbs. Now there's no need to be nervous. You just be natural. Think of it as easy money for an hour of your time. We can do it out here or in your ship, wherever you like.'

Gribbs realised he was sounding too eager. This wasn't how a hard man should behave. 'Well, maybe we will, maybe we won't,' he said lazily. 'I'm busy, as you can see, so you gotta make it worth while, because we're going to come away from this job well loaded. I reckon an interview with someone who's part of something that big should pay above scale.'

'Sorry, I'm only authorised to offer the standard bonus at this time. Remember, Mr Gribbs, you haven't found the treasure yet. If it all goes wrong at least you'll come away with something to show for it. Think of it as insurance.'

Gribbs turned it over and found the argument appealing. After a moment he nodded. 'OK, you're on.'

Dynes turned to the girl, who was still gaping at him. 'And are the terms satisfactory for you, Ms Brown?'

'You're actually offering me money for an interview while

he's holding me like this?' She jerked on the strap binding her wrists.

'Why not? I simply report things as they are. Surely, under the circumstances, you can see it makes sense to cooperate?' Apparently she couldn't find suitable words to reply, and Dynes continued: 'And let me assure you that if you are unfortunate enough not to survive this highly newsworthy event, the INA will be pleased to send your fee to your next of kin or nominated charity.'

For some reason she was still looking at him in disbelief, and Gribbs began to wonder if she ever watched the news channels.

'You're crazy!' she managed to choke out at length.

'Not at all. It is my legal right and duty under interstellar convention to observe and report without prejudice, fear, or favour for the purposes of information and entertainment.'

'But can't you see what he's doing is wrong?'

'Not my position to judge, Ms Brown. If the local authorities wish to take action in this matter, that would be their privilege and I would report their actions just as fully. As they appear not to choose to intervene, why should I?'

'But your turning criminals into... into media personalities!'

Dynes shrugged. 'A very biased point of view, if I might say so. One world's criminal is another's celebrity, and it's not for me to say if their choice is right or wrong. I just give the public what they want. It's up to them whether they approve or not, but after twenty years I think I know their tastes well enough, don't you?'

'Hey, who's in charge here, anyway?' Gribbs demanded impatiently, feeling there was too much talk going on, and giving a warning jerk to the rope fastened to Peri's wrist strap. 'She'll say her piece when the time comes if that's what you want,' he assured Dynes.

'That's fine with me, Mr, Gribbs,' Dynes said, the DAVE

drones flitting about to find fresh angles as Peri tried to pull away. 'I shall assume Ms Brown waives her right to compensation by default, and will be treated henceforth as a hostile news subject. Now, perhaps you'd like the interview to be inside your ship?'

'Yeah, maybe that would be best.'

He remembered he'd promised Qwaid he'd get the girl to the ship as soon as possible and keep her under wraps there while he waited for calls. For some reason Qwaid didn't like Dynes, and wouldn't want Gribbs associating with him like this. Still, as long as it didn't interfere with business, Gribbs couldn't see the harm, and afterwards it wouldn't matter. Besides, just suppose things didn't go to plan. Then he'd have made a smart move.

Dynes followed them into the *Falcon* with the DAVEs trailing after him.

After they had removed their packs and settled in the ship's crewroom, Dynes carefully positioned them and the two DAVEs for the interview. Gribb's admiration for Dynes rose as he saw how carefully he arranged things, having the girl, to her evident displeasure, kneel beside his chair to 'help the composition'.

'You want she should be mussed up a bit to?' he asked, trying to be helpful, remembering the look of Theel's captives.

'I think Ms Brown looks suitably distressed for the moment, except perhaps...' He reached forward and undid another button of the girl's shirt, ignoring her indignant yelp of protest, to reveal a little more cleavage. Gribbs preened himself nervously, trying to brush his straggly thinning hair straight.

'File Code: The Ultimate Treasure. Interview with George Erasmus Gribbs and Perpugilliam Brown,' Dynes said to one of the DAVEs, then turned back to them. 'Mr

Gribbs, let's start with a bit of background. Would you tell us, in your own words, why you turned to a life of crime?'

Inwardly Gribbs breathed a sigh of relief. He knew the sort of answer to give to a question like that.

'Well, I had no choice, did I?' he said regretfully. 'Back on Trainor Colony if you didn't take it you got nothing...'

None of it had been his fault; he was as much a victim as those he had stolen from. It was all down to the vids, the government, his parents, unlucky breaks, but never him. It wasn't fair that others had things he did not, and how else was he going to get them? He'd been good with his hands and had a way with circuitry, but who wanted to be an ordinary repairman all his life? OK, so he hadn't been starving, but there was more to life than food and shelter, wasn't there? Hadn't he as much right to so-called 'luxuries' as anybody else? All the commercials said so. Dynes seemed to understand perfectly and said nothing except to prompt and nod sympathetically.

'And what do you plan to do with your portion of Rovan's treasure if you recover it?' Dynes asked.

Oddly, he hadn't thought about that, except in vague terms. But he'd feel a fool if he had nothing to say. So he dredged up every fantasy he could remember and gold-plated them. It was hard work. Dynes continued to nod attentively, but Gribbs was worried that he was becoming boring. Out of the corner of his eye he saw that the girl's head was dropping as though she was dozing. He was putting his hostage to sleep on camera!

Perhaps Dynes noticed as well, because he suddenly turned to her. 'Ms Brown, how did it feel out on the plain when you thought you were going to die?'

The reply was tired and angry: 'What? Well I was scared spitless of course.'

'Of course,' said Dynes easily. 'And how does it feel to be Mr Gribbs's hostage for your friend's cooperation?'

'How do you think? Where do they find people like him

anyway: Henchman-U-Hire?' she snapped back sarcastically. 'He sounds like a total loser...' She faltered as though suddenly realising the likely consequences of her rash words and looked up fearfully. Gribbs lifted a hand ready to strike her and she cowered away, pulling on her tether. Then he looked at the camera and hesitated.

'Don't worry, Mr Gribbs,' Dynes said reassuringly. 'I can easily edit this part out, along with anything else you're not happy with. Just continue to be yourself. Forget I'm here.'

Gribbs looked down at the girl and felt a surge of pleasure at the power he had over her. Be yourself. Alpha would never have let them get as involved as this. Only the end result had mattered to him, to be achieved by the most direct and efficient means. But now there was no Alpha, and he was learning to make things go his way at last.

'Dynes,' he said slowly, 'do you want to see how George Gribbs keeps stupid girls who talk out of turn in line? Maybe it'd be worth something extra, eh?'

The girl's eyes widened in alarm. Dynes considered the proposition thoughtfully. 'There are certain information outlets that would pay a premium for such special items. But only as long as it is perfectly clear that you are not being influenced by my presence or any thought of remuneration.'

'Sure, right. No, you're not influencing me. I'm in charge, right? And I told her she'd better behave or else –'

Gribbs's wrist communicator bleeped. He made frantic gestures imploring silence from Dynes, then touched a contact. 'Yeah, Qwaid?' he said blandly.

'Just checking you got back to the ship OK.'

'Sure, no trouble.'

'Well you stay put until I let you know what we need.'

'I'll be here. Don't you worry about old Gribbsy.'

'Now put the Doc's girl on so he knows she's OK.'

'Here she is.' He held the communicator out to Peri. The Doctor's voice came through from the other end.

'Are you all right, Peri?' he asked anxiously.

'I'm fine so far, Doctor,' she said with an odd brightness, then added quickly, 'though Mr Gribbs was just going to punish me for speaking my mind and Dexel Dynes was going to film him doing it –'

Gribbs winced and snatched the communicator but it was too late. There were confused sounds from the other end, then Qwaid came on again. 'Gribbs! What are you playing at? Is Dynes there?'

'Yeah, but I didn't see there was any harm in it. The locals don't care –'

'Never trust reporters! They cut deals with the cops too. Anything you say about what we did in Astroville might help Jaharnus bargain for extradition, so get rid of him! And mind that girl doesn't come to any hurt. Right now the Doc's being a real star performer, so don't make me choose between you, understand?'

'Yeah, OK Qwaid. Sorry…'

'You will be, you idiot!' The line went dead.

Gribbs looked up in embarrassment to see Dynes and his drones focused intently upon him.

'Hey, were you recording all that?'

'Of course, Mr Gribbs, it's my job. Well, I think that'll do for now.' Dynes rose and made for the airlock, the DAVEs following like faithful dogs.

'Dynes, come back!' Gribbs pulled his gun as he ran after him. 'Stop or else –'

There was a retina-searing double flash of light from the drones that lit up the corridor. When his vision had cleared Dynes was gone. With a groan Gribbs stumped back to the crewroom to find that the girl was looking at him with fresh confidence and determination.

'Right,' she said, 'I want a comfortable room, some food and a shower. But for starters you can take this strap off.'

He raised his hand again, but this time she did not flinch

away. 'You heard your boss,' she said meaningfully. 'You've got to take good care of me or else he's going to dump you.'

Fuming but impotent, he hauled her to her feet, led her along to an empty cabin, removed her wrist strap, pushed her inside, and locked the door.

This wasn't how he'd planned things at all. And what was worse, Qwaid was beginning to sound as bad as Alpha.

Out in the woods not far from the landing fields, an indistinct form glided through the growing shadows. Limbs that were neither arms nor tentacles reached out and touched the barks of trees, as though it was curious about their texture. There was a hesitancy about its movements, almost as though it was searching for something.

Then it sensed movement and reacted instinctively.

One of Dyne's patrolling DAVE units drifted past. And, though its sensitive camera eyes looked straight at it from no more than five metres away, they did not register anything unusual.

As soon as the drone was gone the form appeared once again and continued through the woods, moving with notably greater assurance now. It was rapidly relearning old skills.

CHAPTER 14
THE LOST ONES

The raft bobbed slowly against the rocky shelf at the base of the cliff. Qwaid had made sure its mooring line was tied securely about a nub of rock, just in case they had to use it again. Now he, Drorgon, and the Doctor were inspecting the base of what appeared to be a stone slab staircase built into the sheer cliff face.

'How convenient,' the Doctor remarked, tapping the lowest projecting finger of rock thoughtfully. 'And how unlikely.'

'What d'you mean?' Qwaid asked.

'That we should find a ready-made means of ascent within such a short distance of our landing place. Either we were led here in some way, which is suspicious in itself, or else there are a number of these stairs along the length of the cliff. Somebody is certainly keen that we use them.'

'You think it's a trap, then?'

'Qwaid, I think this entire treasure trail is some kind of trap or other, though you simply won't accept the fact. But as there seems no other way up, I suppose we'd better get started. There should just about be enough daylight left for us to make it to the top.'

'Right, you go first.'

'Certainly,' the Doctor said brightly. 'That's very kind of you.'

'Uhh, Qwaid,' said Drorgon suspiciously, a frown creasing he sloping brow. 'Why's he so keen to go first?'

'He's just trying a wind-up,' Qwaid said.

'Am I?' said the Doctor. 'Perhaps I simply think it's preferable to going last.'

'Hey,' said Drorgon again, 'who's going last then?'

'You are, clumphead,' Qwaid told him. 'Now move!'

They began the ascent. The identical steps drifted

monotonously past them out of the mist.

'Keep your ears sharp so we don't run into Thorrin's lot,' Qwaid told the Doctor.

'In all probability they've either already made it to the top or are using a different stairway.'

'Well don't take any chances. I don't want any trouble up here in all this mist.'

They took a brief rest to ease their aching muscles, then pressed on. The Doctor began to peer ahead more intently, but the stairs did not end, nor did the mist thin. A gradual deepening of the grey suggested evening was drawing in. Eventually he stopped and exclaimed tersely, 'We seem to have a slight problem here.'

Drorgon swung his portable cannon around nervously with a grunt of alarm. 'What?' Qwaid demanded.

'Very simply, we should have run out of both cliff and stairs some time ago. I've been counting steps...' He explained his calculation with respect to the height of the cliff.

'Qwaid, what we going to do?' Drorgon growled unhappily.

Qwaid checked his own watch and began to feel uncomfortable. 'But that's crazy. You must have got it wrong.'

'You're welcome to continue, but you'll be wasting your time.'

Inside himself Qwaid knew the Doctor was right. There was an odd feeling about the stairway, but he just couldn't put his finger on exactly what. He tried not to show his alarm. 'But how's it done?'

'I'm not sure. It may be a mental illusion, or something mechanical...' Pulling a torch from his pack the Doctor bent down and examined the base of the steps carefully, shining the light at a sharp angle to the rock face. 'Ah...' he said at length. 'Look.'

Qwaid looked. There was a very fine groove cut into the smooth rock wall, running parallel to the line of the steps so that it just touched the leading edge of each. There were also fine vertical grooves that divided the mounting of each step from the next.

'Now look below the steps,' the Doctor said.

Qwaid peered between the treads and could just make out another groove running under the line of steps. 'So what?'

The Doctor smiled at him. 'Have you ever tried walking up an escalator that's going down at exactly the same speed?'

They had been slumped exhausted and despairing on the stairs for perhaps some while before Brockwell stirred. He had lain back with his head close to the rock wall. Unconsciously he found himself staring at the step mounts. After a minute his excited cry had roused them all.

'The whole flight of steps moves while we stay still?' Jaharnus said, once Brockwell had explained his theory.

'Someone has played a cruel trick on Old Jack,' Falstaff said angrily. 'The stones I must have shed upon this infernal device going nowhere. A plague upon them!'

'And they must have reversed as we descended,' Brockwell continued. 'The vertical grooves must be where the individual steps hinge to make the return leg along a channel somewhere inside the cliff.'

'A sliding stairway five hundred metres high?' Arnella said incredulously. Brockwell's gaze shied away from hers.

'That seems to be the case,' he mumbled.

'The Doctor warned us this place had been refined over a long time,' said Jaharnus.

'Well at least we know how it was done,' said the Marquis with relief. 'Of course, it wouldn't have worked except for the smoothness of the rock face and the mist. We had no points of reference to judge our true motion.'

'That was probably how it was planned,' said Brockwell.

'No doubt,' the Marquis agreed. 'But now how do we reach the top so we may resume our quest?'

'That at least is no problem,' said Thorrin breaking his long silence, and with some of his normal self-assurance returning.

Qwaid kept his hand near his pistol. He and the Doctor were alone and the Doctor's presence was beginning to trouble him. He suspected he was even smarter than Alpha.

On the Doctor's advice, Drorgon had been sent, much to his evident unease, walking down towards the base of the stairway. The Doctor had scratched a line just above one step and across the groove in the rock, and now, torch in hand, he waited patiently.

'This had better work, Doc,' Qwaid warned him.

'If the stairs move as a unit and they are designed to prove an efficient two-way trap for a moving person, then it has to... ah, look!'

Slowly the halves of the scratch mark on either side of the groove were separating. It was uncanny, and it was only by pressing his hand to the rock across the groove that Qwaid could tell that the section the steps were mounted on was sliding smoothly upward in response to Drorgon's descent.

'You see,' said the Doctor brightly, 'only a gentle acceleration at first, then building up to a walking pace. Carefully designed so you feel no jerk. It probably slows down just as gradually.'

Above them the mist was thinning at last and in a moment the open sky, studded with the first stars of evening, appeared.

Myra had volunteered to keep Brockwell company as he trudged down the stairs to make them carry the rest of the party upward. She was also there to provide an additional counterbalance, in case it took a certain minimum weight to trigger the mechanism. For a while they descended in silence as her thoughts dwelled on Qwaid and his likely progress so far, and how the Doctor and Peri Brown were coping. Since she could do no more than she was already doing, such speculations rapidly became morbid. She glanced at Brockwell, and was reminded that there were lighter aspects to their situation.

'That was pretty smart, the way you worked this out,' she said. 'Ever thought of becoming a detective?'

Brockwell smiled. 'Thanks, but I don't think I'd be very good at it.'

'You might. Scientists, like detectives, have to notice small but significant details I imagine. I do it all the time. Can't stop noticing trivial things.' She smiled. 'For instance, how long have you been in love with Arnella Rosscarrino?'

Brockwell almost fell and Myra had to steady him. His face was a picture of crestfallen alarm. 'But how did you know? Please don't tell her.'

Myra smiled sympathetically. 'I promise I won't say a word, but she might work it out for herself eventually. The way you avoid looking her straight in the face, and tripping over your own tongue when you speak to her. Away from her you're quite different.'

'Do you think her uncle has noticed?'

'I think he's too wrapped up in this quest business. Rather like Thorrin.'

Brockwell's face fell further. 'Yes. He's becoming... well, obsessed, I suppose. You aren't seeing him at his best, you know. He can be kind and –' His phone beeped and he took it from his pocket. 'Yes, Professor?'

'We've reached the top, Will,' came the satisfied reply. We can only see a line of rocks for the moment. The stairs are turning into a slot in the cliff. There must have been a similar slot at the bottom, but one of the steps must have been filling it too closely for us to notice. Probably just as it was meant to. We're about to jam the stairs so you can follow us up.'

There was a jerk underfoot and Brockwell and Myra staggered.

'Has it stopped down there as well?' Thorrin asked.

'Yes, Professor. We're on our way back up now.'

* * *

149

Qwaid turned away from the stairway slot they had blocked with a sliver of rock and peered suspiciously about him. It would take Drorgon a while to make it to the summit and he wanted to get an idea of the lie of the land while he had the chance.

In the fast-failing light it was evident that the rim top of the sheer cliff was crowned by a continuous jagged ridge of rocks, cut through by streams and small rivers that formed the waterfalls they had seen from the far side of the valley. Beyond the narrow parapet was a drab stretch of ponds and shallow lakes, streams and mud flats, reminiscent of a river delta. This glistening expanse was dotted with small islands. Some were merely jumbles of rocks rising a few metres above the sluggish waters, while others must have been anything up to a kilometre across, their outlines made shaggy with miniature jungles of small trees. As the gloom descended he noticed distinct yellow twinkles of light coming from several of the larger isles.

'Fires?' he wondered aloud.

'Apparently so,' said the Doctor. 'Or possibly simple torches. They don't appear to be either bright or steady enough to be anything else.'

Qwaid got out his binoculars and scanned the nearer islands. Under magnification and enhancement he saw what looked like lighted windows in the sides of rough shacklike structures, set along the narrow shorelines. They twinkled occasionally as figures moved in front of them, but he could make out no further details. Who lived here? The buildings were nothing like the neat domes they had seen near the landing ground. Was it dangerous, or might there be a clue here as to where to go next? He turned the problem over in his mind as he continued his sweep across the flats. Suddenly he halted. To their right and perhaps a little over a kilometre away, he saw a party of six figures leave the line of rocks and begin to pick their way across the mud flats.

'We're right where I wanted us to be, Doc,' he said with a grin. 'Soon as Drorgon gets up here we edge along until we're behind them. They should leave a clear enough trail in this ground to follow. Let them find out what's going on up here.'

Myra led the way, a rope from her belt fastened her to Brockwell, and the others followed in their footsteps. She used her staff to probe the way ahead of her. The danger of quicksand had immediately suggested itself in these conditions, and common sense dictated that she would be the best able to cope. She kept to the scattered slabs of rock that rose above the mud and clumps of wiry grass. Those channels they had to ford proved to be no more than knee deep, with a cool evening breeze rippling their sluggish waters. Patterns of tracks and blowholes in the mud indicated the presence of small animals, and they kept their guns at the ready in case they should encounter anything larger and more dangerous.

Thorrin wanted to reach one of the lighted islands before it was fully dark. He was certain there would be somebody there ready to provide a clue to the next stage of the quest. Myra was not convinced of his reasoning, but there seemed no better course to pursue and she did not want to risk falling behind Qwaid's party if by any chance they were already ahead of them. It would also be a relief to reach some sort of shelter. She felt uncomfortably exposed out on the bleak flats.

Their course took them past one of the smaller islets, a clump of rocks topped by a few straggling trees barely a hundred metres across. As they circled its tiny beach Falstaff said suddenly, 'Hold fast! Surely I saw something move up there.'

Even as they peered into the gloom, a fist-sized rock flew out of the shadows between two large boulders, hurtled over their heads, and splashed into the mud.

'Go away!' a whining voice shouted out in interlingua. 'Leave me alone! This is my land!'

Even as they looked at each other in bewilderment, another rock was thrown, this time landing at their feet and causing them to jump quickly aside as it rebounded between them.

'We do not wish you any harm,' Rosscarrino called back. 'We are simply... seekers. Can you tell us if we're on the right path to Rovan's treasure?'

There came a terrible wailing cry from the heart of the islet, followed by a stream of abuse and a further shower of rocks and pebbles. Dodging the missiles, they set off across the pools and mud flats at a run until they were out of range.

'Who was that?' exclaimed Brockwell.

'It didn't sound like a native.' said Arnella.

'Whosoever it was, they were sorely touched in the head,' said Falstaff, mopping his brow.

'It may simply be meant to confuse us.' Thorrin said resolutely. 'We shall continue on.'

It was almost fully dark when they reached the nearest of the larger islands, and they covered the last part of the way by torchlight. The ground rose slightly and the mud gave way to a narrow beach, fringed by small twisted trees and giant ferns similar to those on the other side of the mist valley. A little way along the scalloped shore was the first of a small cluster of structures they had seen from the cliff edge.

As they made a cautious approach they saw that the buildings were roughly made of poles, lashed together with vines and panelled with woven mats of reed. Feeble flickers of firelight shone out of unglazed windows, somehow failing to cast any cheer on the dismal scene. They smelled woodsmoke and food cooking and the stench of rotting fruit. A few snatches of desultory conversation floated out into the still air.

They reached the door of the largest of the shacks, closed only by a hanging rush curtain. Thorrin straightened himself up, checked his gun was lose in its holster, brushed the curtain aside and stepped within. The others followed.

Five men and two women of three different species were

sprawled on pallets of leaves and rush mats around the walls. A fire burnt in a stone grate in the centre of the room, the smoke simply escaping through a hole in the roof. The rest of the interior was bare, except for a stack of bowl-sized nutshell halves in one corner and a pile of rags in the other. The occupants, who, Myra now saw through the thin haze of smoke, were dressed in patched and faded clothes in varying degrees of decrepitude, looked up listlessly as they entered. But they merely let their gaze pass over them before dropping back to stare into the depths of the fire once more. None spoke a word of welcome or acknowledgment to the newcomers.

'How now, my fine fellows,' said Falstaff after an awkward silence. 'Not a single hail to greet Old Jack?'

One of the men grunted. Another turned to face the wall and pulled a matt blanket over him. Myra felt a shiver of disquiet. This was somehow more frightening than the creatures in the valley.

'I'm Alexander Thorrin,' the professor announced loudly. 'My colleagues and I are following the path to Rovan's treasure. Can you tell us which way to go from here?'

One of the women grunted without looking up. 'Idiot,' she said. 'We know what you are.'

One of the men mumbled, 'Turn back now, if you know what's good for you.'

Myra knelt down beside the nearest and shook him.

'Can you hear me? My name is Myra Jaharnus. Who are you? How did you get here?'

The man seemed to make a supreme effort, mumbling something that might have been a name, then: '…same way you did, of course…' Then he rolled away from her with his back to the fire and appeared to go to sleep.

'Are they sick?' Arnella wondered anxiously.

'Only sick at heart,' Falstaff said, with sudden unexpected perception. 'Their spirits are crushed. They have given up.'

'You mean… they were seekers?' said Brockwell. 'That man on the islet as well?'

'How else could they have all come to be here?' Falstaff said simply.

They looked at each other in dismay. Even Thorrin and the Marquis seemed subdued. Silently they left the shack, its occupants paying as little attention to their going as they had their arrival. As they walked away a ragged woman emerged from the next hut along. She glanced at them briefly with the same dull eyes and lack of interest as the others, then shuffled off towards the nearest line of bushes, undoing her belt as she went.

'It's too dark to go any further tonight,' said Thorrin, after they had gone a little way along the shore. 'We'd better camp here. I don't think those people will give us any trouble.'

'They seem barely capable of caring for themselves,' the Marquis said. 'How can thinking beings be reduced to such a state? Or are they all cowards with no backbone? Shalvis said there had been many seekers after the treasure over the years. Perhaps this is where some end up.'

'You don't suppose there might be a physical cause?' said Brockwell. 'Something in the food or water here that induces a state of extreme lethargy?'

Thorrin frowned. 'Mmm. It's possible, I suppose. To be safe we won't touch anything here. Our rations will last us for some days yet, if need be.'

'But can't we do anything for them?' Arnella asked. 'Make some tests, or something?'

'We cannot spare the time,' said her uncle flatly. 'This is not a medical mercy mission.'

'Whatever they are suffering from they must have brought upon themselves,' Thorrin pointed out. 'If those other islands are inhabited like this one, there must be a few hundred people here at least. They cannot all have arrived at once, therefore the later arrivals must have seen what we have. If they did not take sensible precautions in time, that's their own fault.'

Myra thought his attitude was rather callous, but didn't feel like arguing the point. They made camp along the shore out of

154

sight of the shacks. As soon as they had eaten they crawled gratefully into the big tent and closed it against the air of gloom that hung so heavily over the island.

From a tiny cluster of rocks a little way out into the mud flats, Qwaid watched the large island through his night-sight binoculars until the bright spark of Thorrin's campfire was extinguished. Then he slithered back down to the hollow, where they had made their own camp.

'Right, they won't be going anywhere till morning. And when they do, we'll be right on their heels.'

'You don't suppose they've found the treasure?' Drorgon said dismally.

'No, 'cos we'd have heard them celebrating even out here if they had.' He jerked a thumb at their attendant DAVE drone. 'And Dynes would be interviewing us about how it feels to miss out. Now get some sleep. You too, Doc.'

'Actually I don't sleep very much.'

'Suit yourself.' Qwaid pulled his thermal blanket up. 'Just don't try to sneak off, or anything. If Gribbs don't here from me regularly, saying the right words, you know what's going to happen to your friend. It would be a shame to mess up such a pretty piece as her.'

For a moment the light of their fire glinted dangerously from the Doctor's eyes, and it occurred to Qwaid that here was a man who could be pushed only so far.

'Oh, you can be sure I won't forget that,' he said coldly.

Peri tossed and turned in her narrow bunk on board the *Falcon*, unable to sleep. Now that her fear of Gribbs had been checked, at least for the time being, she was beginning to feel angry with herself. Why had she been so keen to come along? And to have dragged the Doctor into trouble as well was dumb stupid, she told herself scathingly. Of course she'd always longed for excitement and adventure, but this was not quite what she had bargained for. Were suffering and danger inseparable adjuncts to any adventure, she wondered.

All right. She'd just have to master her feelings and try to keep a clear head, and be ready to act when the time came. She was no superhero and was not sure how much physical violence she could inflict on anyone, however deserving. But if the opportunity arose, she would force herself to hit Gribbs over the head with the nearest blunt object. Dynes too for that matter – preferably with one of his own cameras.

Out on the fringe of the Gelsandoran system the fabric of space rippled.

The grey cabinet that had been Alpha's strongbox emerged from the discontinuity of hyperspace. For some minutes it flew on freely, sensors scanning busily. Then thrusters flared to adjust its course and it headed towards the inner system.

CHAPTER 15
DESPAIR

The morning light was grey and washed out, with that second-hand quality to it that Myra always found uninspiring. The air was heavy and the sun, though rising in a virtually cloudless sky, was filtered by a thin haze that hung over the waterlands, giving it a muggy dankness. Though she'd slept through the night she still felt tired and her legs ached from yesterday's climb. It was a small consolation that the rest were apparently no better, yawning in each other's face and responding in grumpy monosyllables. Even Falstaff seemed to be unusually muted, neither complaining nor boasting, and they breakfasted in almost total silence. Finally Thorrin appeared to rise above the general malaise and spoke at some length.

'I think it might be useful to spend a few hours here before we start off again. These people may know something about the conditions that lie ahead of us. I know that they were unresponsive last night, but perhaps those we saw were not typical specimens. They may also have been put off by our numbers. So I propose the Marquis and I question them alone.'

They all nodded and murmured ascent at this. Myra was grateful. She didn't feel up to starting another day's trek at that moment. The rigours of the valley and the ascent up the cliff must have taken more out of her than she had thought. When the meal was concluded, Thorrin and Rosscarrino plodded away towards the settlement. Falstaff sprawled like a beached whale on the sand, while Brockwell slowly began to pack away the camping gear.

Arnella rubbed her eyes lazily. 'I wish I could wake up properly.'

'Me too,' agreed Myra. 'Perhaps a swim might help – or maybe you'd rather not.'

Arnella managed a wry smile. 'Just as long as I can see the bottom, and we don't share the water with anything dangerous...' She paused, frowning. 'Have I thanked you yet for saving me yesterday?'

'Yes... I think so.'

They sat looking at each other stupidly for a moment, then Myra remembered. 'Shall we then?'

'What?'

'Swim.'

'Yes, of course.' Arnella took a deep breath. 'Anything to wake up.'

They set off in the opposite direction to the settlement. An outcrop of rock formed a tiny headland, and climbing this they found a sheltered cove on the far side, with a clear sandy bottom. Myra tossed a few rocks in first to see if anything was lying concealed in the sand. Then they stripped off their clothes and plunged in.

The water was not as cold as Myra had hoped for, but it was better than nothing and helped revive her somewhat. She swam underwater for several minutes, poking around the rocks and startling a few small crablike animals into retreating into their burrows. She surfaced with a splash and returned to the shore propelled by sinuous flicks of her powerful tail.

Arnella was sitting half in the water, letting her legs trail idly. Myra drew herself up beside her and they sat in silence for a long time, staring out at the glistening mud flats. A few wading birds were slowly pecking their way across the grey pools. Clumps of taller grasses stirred slightly in the light breeze. At least there didn't seem to be any particularly intrusive insect life here, she thought vaguely, though there did seem to be a low buzzing hum coming from somewhere. It took her a few moments to realise that Dynes's drone was hovering a few metres away, its lenses focused full upon them.

She blinked indignantly and nudged Arnella. 'Did you see that earlier? Has it been here all the time?'

Arnella gave a little start and fumbled about for her clothes to cover herself. But they were in a pile a few paces away, which seemed an immense distance in the heavy air, so she wrapped her arms about herself modestly instead and said, 'Go away! That's not polite!' with as much indignation as she could muster. The drone remained unresponsive. Arnella turned to Myra. 'Can't you arrest it… or something?' she muttered.

Myra shook her head slowly. 'It hasn't been here the whole time, has it? I mean, we wouldn't have just undressed in front of it like that if it had.' She was troubled by the thought that the drone had followed them from the camp, but for some reason she hadn't taken in the implications. Or had she noticed but not cared? She couldn't remember. Come on, she was a trained detective, she shouldn't miss such things…

She saw Arnella look down at her arms – as though mildly puzzled as to why she was hugging them around her – let them slowly drop and sink down flat on the sand. The momentary distraction caused Myra to lose her train of thought. Damn! What had she been trying to work out? She sighed. The sand was soft enough. The sun wasn't too hot or too cold. She lay back. There was no hurry. Wait for Thorrin and the Marquis to get back from… wherever it was. In a minute she had quite forgotten about the faint hum of the drone.

In the *Stop Press*, Dynes watched the sleeping figures curiously for several minutes, not in the least troubled by his invasion of their privacy, only deeply puzzled by their behaviour. It wasn't like Jaharnus to let it go so easily, nor for that matter a Rosscarrino. He sent the drone back to the camp. Falstaff was still sleeping, while Brockwell had finally packed most of the gear into the backpacks, and was now starting on the tent. Frowning, Dynes moved the drone closer. Brockwell was fiddling clumsily with the tent-frame release mechanism. After some moments he slowly sat back, pulled up his knees and rested his chin on them, apparently baffled by his task. Dynes peered more intently at the screen, then checked the monitor showing Qwaid's camp. Just what was going on out there?

It was mid-morning when Qwaid slowly lowered himself down to the camp hollow, yawning and blinking.

'Well, they're still there. Maybe they've found something.'

There was no response. Drorgon seemed to have fallen asleep again, while the Doctor was sprawled on his back resting his head on his interlaced fingers, with his hat draped over his face. Qwaid looked at them in mild disgust. 'Hey, am I the only one who does any work around here?' He kicked Drorgon's slumbering form. 'Your turn on watch.' It took a second kick before Drorgon heaved himself to his feet, took the binoculars and made his way ponderously up the rocky slope. Qwaid sat down heavily. 'Might as well wait. Nothing else to do here. Deadest place I ever saw. Give us a chance to get our strength back after all that climbing...'

There was a long silence. Then the Doctor slowly raised himself on one elbow and pushed his hat back, revealing a face creased with a frown. 'There was something... I think.'

Qwaid's head jerked up. He must have been dozing off. 'Eh... what?'

'Something else you were going to do... no, something we both had to do.'

Qwaid blinked at him. 'Was there?'

'Yes, yes...' the Doctor screwed up his eyes in concentration. 'Peri... you were going to call up your ship and I was going to talk to Peri... like we agreed.'

Qwaid nodded and wagged a finger. 'That's sharp, Doc. Might have forgotten that otherwise. That's what an education does for you.'

Laboriously he called up the ship. Gribbs's voice came on the line a little anxiously. 'Are you OK, Qwaid? You're late. I was just going to call up myself.'

'Yeah, fine. Get the girl so's the Doc can hear she's all right...'

There was a minute's pause, during which Qwaid found himself sagging slowly back against a convenient rock, then Peri's voice came through.

'Hello, Doctor. I'm bored but OK. At least Mr Gribbs has been minding his manners.'

Qwaid extended the communicator towards the Doctor, who blinked at it owlishly for a moment before replying, 'Good, Peri. That's… um, fine.'

'Doctor? Are you OK? You sound bushed.'

'Perhaps a little tired. We… er, did some climbing yesterday.'

'Are you sure you didn't fall on your head?'

The Doctor managed a slight chuckle. 'No, no… nothing like that.'

'Well if I didn't know better I'd say you'd been on the sauce.'

'Pardon?'

'Drinking. Are you sure you're fine?'

Qwaid realised the conversation was dragging along. 'OK, you've had your say,' he interrupted irritably. 'Take her back to her room…' There was something else he'd meant Gribbs to do. What was it? Oh yes: 'Gribbsy, listen. We're on the edge of this… uh, flat mess of lakes and small islands. We want to know how far it runs 'n' suchlike. When you've put the girl away, take the ship up so you can see what's ahead. Got that?'

'Sure, I'll have a go… if the locals'll let us.' Gribbs sounded uncertain. 'Are you sure *you're* OK?'

'Fine, fine. Call when you're ready.'

His hand dropped away from the comm link and he settled back against a rock. Say what you liked about it being boring, but it was certainly peaceful here. The Doctor was already lying on his back again staring into nothing. Drifting down from the rock summit above them came Drorgon's snores.

Vague pangs of hunger woke Myra, but it took her some minutes to work out where she was. The sun suggested it was nearing midday. Arnella was sprawled on the sand by her side. She poked her arm listlessly. 'Come on, let's eat.' She still felt tired, but there was fish in the water and fruit on the trees, so they wouldn't have to go far to find something. No, they were keeping to their own rations, weren't they?

Arnella stirred and looked at her blearily. 'What… where?'

'Back at camp.' There was something else. Oh yes: 'Your uncle and Thorrin'll be back. Probably found out…' What had they been doing? Never mind.

They got to their feet and started trudging towards the line of rocks. Then Arnella halted. 'Something wrong,' she said doubtfully.

They looked at each other. They were still naked. Their clothes were where they had left them by the pool. They trudged back for them, though it seemed a very long way. Dressing was complicated work. Fastenings seemed suddenly immensely fiddly, and they almost fell over a couple of times while stepping into their shorts. It should have been funny, but instead it was just deeply and depressingly annoying and a hugely unnecessary effort. Easier not to bother at all, thought Myra. But she persevered doggedly. Eventually, more or less properly clothed, they set out for the camp again.

The rocky headland had grown since they last climbed it an eternity and four hours before. Was it longer to go round wading into the shallows or to cut through the lowest cleft? The decision made Myra's head ache. Then Arnella began climbing and she followed because it was easier that way.

Halfway up Myra missed her footing and slipped.

Normally she could have saved herself, but there was something wrong about the speed everything happened, both in a dreamy slow motion and yet at the same time too fast for her to react. She cracked her right shin hard against a projecting rock before she thudded into the yielding sand. Her skin was tougher than a human's, and so the physical damage was slight. But the pain was still considerable, and as she lay on the sand she gave loud voice to a choice series of curses.

Then she clamped her lips shut as she realised what had happened. Arnella was looking down at her with vague concern.

'Are you all right?' she mumbled, slurring her words.

Myra leapt to her feet, savouring the wonderful pain in her leg that had shocked the fog from her mind. 'What the hell have we been doing?' she demanded. Arnella gaped back at her with slack-jawed incomprehension. Myra shook her so hard her teeth clicked, her claws digging into Arnella's flesh until she whimpered. But the light of awareness had returned to her eyes. 'Don't let it get you again!' she commanded.

Arnella managed to focus on her. 'I... I couldn't think clearly... what was it?'

'I don't know, but we're not waiting around to find out. Let's find the others and get out of here!'

They scrambled back up the rocks and down the other side, jumping the last few metres and rolling in the sand. Myra felt her leg protest again, but that was good: it meant she was alive and not half dead. They sprinted back towards the camp. Falstaff was where they had left him, while Brockwell was sitting with his back to the tent, which was still erect, toying with its packing bag as though unsure what to do with it.

Myra and Arnella yelled, and pummelled and slapped the two men into some semblance of alertness. Even in their panic Myra noticed a flash of genuine concern on Arnella's face as she forced herself to slap Brockwell on the cheek. Brockwell's expression as he came to and realised who was striking him was also worth treasuring, but she had no time to dwell on it for the moment.

'Finish the packing while I get the others,' she commanded. 'Watch each other like gyrehawks! The moment anybody looks dopey hit them!' And she sprinted off down the beach towards the shanty village, focusing her mind totally on finding the Marquis and Thorrin, and letting the ache in her leg stimulate her anger with every step.

The two were easy to find. They were resting in the shade of a rough awning strung from the shack they had visited the previous night. Sitting beside them were a ragged grey-haired woman (how long had she been here?) and a couple of other men. Bowls and cups made out of the half-shells of tree nuts were littered about them. Please don't let them be drunk as well, Myra thought. There was no time for half-measures. She snatched up two full cups and dashed the contents into their faces, then began the slapping and pummelling.

'Hey... what you doing?' One of the others was looking at her in vague bemusement. 'We were jus' drinking...' It hurt to see someone so enfeebled, but she could hardly dare to divide her attentions any further. Ignoring him she continued to work on rousing Thorrin and the Marquis.

When they began to respond she hauled them to their feet and sent them stumbling back in confusion towards their own camp, followed by the dull listless gazes of half a dozen lost ones who slouched in the shelter of their shacks. They met Arnella, Brockwell, and Falstaff pounding along the sands in the opposite direction with all their belongings. Barely pausing to sling their packs properly, they splashed out across the mud flats and away from the island.

Gribbs flung open the door to Peri's cabin.

'Out!' he commanded sharply. There was a look of fearful uncertainty on his face. Before she could rise from her bunk he had grabbed her arm and hauled her upright.

'Hey!' she yelped in pain and surprise, as he dragged her along the main corridor to the control cabin. 'What's wrong?'

'I can't raise Qwaid! If you're precious Doctor has pulled something, then he's going to hear you suffer!'

Qwaid was roused by his comm link beeping with shrill urgency.

'Yar... wassat?'

'I've been calling and calling,' came Gribbs's voice, heavy with relief. 'What's the matter with you?'

The girl's voice cut in: 'Doctor, are you all right? Please answer –' She broke off with a loud yelp and there came the sound of a smack on flesh.

'Shut up, you!' he heard Gribbs shout. There was another smack and cry from the girl. 'Stay there and don't move, or else I'll make you wish you'd never been born!'

The commotion seemed to have roused the Doctor. He was staring blearily at the comm link, then around at their camp and Drorgon's still form slumped on the rock above. Then he leaned forward and slapped Qwaid twice – hard.

The stinging blows jolted Qwaid. He reeled backward, reaching for his holster. 'Why you –'

'That's right – stay angry!' The Doctor's fresh boyish face was flushed, his deep eyes intense, his voice urgent and commanding. 'If we stay angry we can fight it!'

'What in hell –'

'Think how we've been behaving since dawn! We've been falling into a trap! Either something in the air itself or a mental field, inducing a state similar to the aftereffects of intoxication. Loss of concentration, reduced response to external stimuli, introversion, and extreme lethargy. We were becoming lotus eaters!'

Qwaid fought to clear his head. It was true: he had been feeling a little strange. 'Who… what?'

'Never mind. Just stay angry! Pinch yourself, bite your tongue! If we don't get clear right now we may never escape.' He scrabbled around for a fist-sized rock, forced himself to his feet and threw it up at Drorgon. There was an angry yell of pain. The Doctor picked up another rock and threw it after the first. Drorgon slid down the slope along with a minor avalanche of pebbles, his fangs bared, growling in anger.

'It's all right, Dro,' Qwaid snapped. 'He had to wake you. Something's been getting to us, into our minds, like we was drugged. We gotta get out of here fast. Gribbsy!' he shouted into the link. 'Get the ship up. Use the scope to find us the quickest way through this place.'

'OK, got ya,' Gribbs replied.

'Peri?' the Doctor shouted out as they snatched up their packs, 'keep talking. Don't let us drift off again!'

Her voice came back tremulously. 'I understand… but what shall I say?'

'Anything! Any outside stimuli to remind us what we're meant to be doing!'

'OK… right. Well… er, Gribbs is punching a lot of buttons… and the controls are lighting up… OK, I'm strapping myself into the spare seat… oh, there go the rockets, or whatever they are. We're rising… uh… it feels like an express elevator. I can see the pyramid and the wood dropping away under us. We must be a mile up already. There's the plain… all hazy and shimmering. We should be able to see where you are soon…'

Qwaid, Drorgon, and the Doctor ran from between the rocks and out across the mud flats. In the far distance were the specks of figures crossing the flats away from the large island. Qwaid focused his binoculars as they ran.

'They're in a hurry. Wonder if they were caught like us.'

'Where are we going?' Brockwell asked as they splashed through the mud.

'Away from that place,' said Myra determinedly.

'But how do we know this is the right way?'

'We'll chance it. Do you want to stay here any longer trying to get directions out of those poor drossers?'

'Is that a darker line… on the horizon ahead?' Thorrin panted.

Brockwell narrowed his eyes. 'Yes… I think so, Professor. Higher ground, maybe?'

'That'll do as well as anywhere,' said Myra.

'It's no use, Qwaid,' Gribbs said. 'All I can see beyond the plain is haze, even through the scope filters.'

'Well overfly us then,' Qwaid ordered.

There was a pause, then Gribbs's voice came back unsteadily. 'I can't... make it happen. Like in the pyramid when we tried to pull the triggers. I'm trying to move the stick forward... but I can't.'

'The Gelsandorans are making sure we play the game by their rules,' the Doctor observed.

'Try harder!' Qwaid shouted into the comm link. In the distance Thorrin's party had disappeared behind an island, and if they lost their tracks he knew they couldn't afford the time picking them up again. What would happen if they were here for another night and started to get tired?

'Its no good,' Peri's voice cut in. 'I can see him trying, but he simply can't make his hands work properly.'

'All right,' Qwaid relented. 'We'll just have to do the best we can for ourselves. Put the ship down again.'

'But how do I get to you when you've found the treasure?' Gribbs asked.

'Then we'll have won. No need to play any more tricks on us.'

'OK, I hope so. I'll just –'

'Attention, attention!'

A loud voice had issued from the control-cabin speakers and echoed clearly over the comm link. As he heard the harsh crisp tones, Qwaid stumbled to a halt, the colour draining from his face.

The voice was unmistakably Alpha's.

In the *Falcon*'s control room Peri saw Gribbs struck rigid; an expression of utter horror distorted his features. The unknown grating voice continued.

'This is a time-coded recording. As I have not reset this system for a significant interval, I must assume some misfortune has befallen me and this ship is being operated without my approval. To ensure no one profits from my incapacitation or untimely demise, I have installed a cutout circuit in the *Falcon* which will render all systems inoperative until freed by a certain code known only to myself.'

And all the lights on the control board went out and a moment later the hum of the thrusters faded away.

The *Falcon*'s nose dropped and it began to fall freely. Peri's stomach tried to climb into her throat and she swallowed to prevent herself throwing up. Terrified, Gribbs stabbed desperately at buttons on the control board, but nothing worked.

The wooded landscape of Gelsandor spun below them, growing larger by the second as they dropped out of the sky.

CHAPTER 16
A FRIEND IN NEED

The shrill whine of air speeding over the hull began to penetrate the control cabin. Through the forward ports Peri saw the green forest canopy rushing up to meet them. She heard both Qwaid and the Doctor shouting over the comm link but could not make her mouth shape any words of reply.

Gribbs suddenly ceased to stab at the useless controls, reached up over his head with both hands, grasped the raised bar of the headrest, and pulled forward and down sharply. A transparent tinted canopy unfolded out of the seat frame, covering his head and shoulders. With a sharp crack of exploding bolts, a section of cabin roof above his chair blew outwards, letting in white light and a blast of shrieking air. A telescoping guide rail sprang up from the back of his chair and through the open panel in the roof. A rocket charge ignited with a bang and a roar, and Gribbs and his ejector seat were blasted upward through the hatch and into the blue sky beyond in a cloud of smoke.

Peri gaped at the empty space beside her, then at the treetops that were beginning to blur across the viewport. She reached up, grasped and pulled.

The bolts cracked, the guide rail thudded, the seat charge ignited. For a moment she felt as though her spine was going to collapse under the acceleration. Then there was light around her and a shocking smack of racing air striking the front of her body and tearing at her clothes. The rocket charge cut and she tumbled freely for a second in silence. Then there came a vibration and a snapping of fabric, a jerk and a bounce and a gradual swaying motion.

She opened her eyes. Above her a parachute canopy blossomed reassuringly wide and full. Also above but far to one side she saw the mushroom of Gribbs's chute. Around her was the purple horizon of Gelsandor, while below was the receding tail of the *Falcon*. She watched in dazed fascination as it plunged towards the undulating sea of green. At the last moment she thought she saw it level off. Then it was enveloped in a cloud of vapour as though rockets were blazing furiously. When this had cleared the ship had vanished among the trees. She strained her ears, expecting the sound of an impact to reach her, but none came.

Qwaid and the Doctor were both shouting into the comm link. Even as he was threatening Gribbs with all manner of atrocities if he didn't answer, Qwaid saw the look of concern on the Doctor's face and knew the girl had indeed been the perfect lever to ensure his cooperation. And for a moment he felt a sudden flash of jealous resentment of the bond that clearly existed between them, because he knew, deep down, that nobody would ever care that much for Crelly Qwaid. And now he might have lost both her and the ship. Finally Gribbs's strained voice came back to them.

'I'm here, Qwaid. I had to eject. There was nothing I could do –'

'Peri? What about Peri?' the Doctor demanded.

'What? Oh, she got out as well. I can see her coming down in the woods.'

The Doctor's relief was palpable.

'What about the ship?' Qwaid asked urgently.

'I think the emergency retros cut in at the last second. It may have set down all right. But everything else was dead, Qwaid. You heard Alpha's voice –'

'I heard, now shut up!' Qwaid thought for a moment, then said, 'Listen, this is what you're going to do. When you get down, find the girl first and make sure you don't lose her again. That's real important. Then check out the ship if you can. If there's nothing doing, see if you can get into Thorrin's ship. Meanwhile, we'll keep on. You call us regular to see we're not going to sleep again, understand?'

'Gotya, Qwaid... Uh, the trees are coming up fast now. I'd better get ready to –'

There was a crash of branches.

Peri's ejector seat had ended its descent dangling just a few feet from the ground, and she was able to unstrap herself and drop the rest of the way with ease. Then reaction had set in, and, in the privacy of the still green woods, she had lain in a huddle and shivered for some minutes. When she recovered her self-control she sat up, wiped her eyes, and tried to think constructively, considering her options.

She didn't have the TARDIS key, so she couldn't shelter there, even if she could find it. The only other occupied ship was Dynes's, and she couldn't imagine his being of any help. She might be able to find the *Falcon* more easily since it was probably closer. But at all costs she had to keep clear of Gribbs. How long could she hide out in the woods? She no longer had her camping pack, but while the weather stayed fine she would be able to manage for a few days. Perhaps that would be enough. If she could find their town, would the natives give her shelter or simply ignore her? If they did, perhaps she could steal some food and –

'Have you any comments on your remarkable escape, Ms Brown?' said Dynes's voice in her ear, making her start violently.

A camera drone marked DAVE #4 was hovering beside her.

'Oh, why don't you just go jump in a lake!' she said in exasperation.

* * *

'We did manage to glean a few scraps of information from the islanders before we succumbed to the, ah, influence,' Thorrin explained as they plodded along.

It was good to have somebody talking: it kept them focused on what they were doing. The monotonous landscape made it all too easy to drift into that deadly torpor again.

'Yes, one was still quite a young man,' the Marquis continued, 'a university student who had come here with a party of friends. They'd bought the information off some cheepjack trader for fifty credits! They didn't really believe it was genuine, but they thought it would be "fun" to hunt for lost treasure over their summer vacation. He'd borrowed his father's yacht. Now he thinks he's the only one left. Unbelievable… and rather tragic.'

Myra noticed the expressions on the faces of Thorrin and Rosscarrino. Their pride had been shaken in more ways than one. Prior to encountering the island they had convinced themselves that they were really the first proper seekers of Rovan's treasure. Now they must be wondering how many more had come to Gelsandor over the years. Was the Doctor right after all? Were they going to be cheated of… What was she thinking? No! The treasure wasn't important, only catching Qwaid and his accomplices mattered.

'Did you find anything useful?' Myra made herself ask. 'Like the quickest way out of this place?'

'One of them did mention a forest that lay somewhere ahead,' Thorrin admitted.

'Well?'

'He called it the Forest of Fear.'

'That sounds cheerful.'

'Apparently it's where your worst nightmares are realised.'

He didn't, Myra noticed, dismiss the idea out of hand. A few days earlier it would have a been a different story, she suspected.

'Old Jack has memories best left undisturbed,' Falstaff cut in anxiously. 'Perhaps there is a longer but less perilous way to be found.'

'But we cannot afford the time,' said the Marquis. 'Have you no courage, man?'

'The better part of valour is discretion,' Falstaff countered, 'in the which better part I have saved my life thus far.'

'Nonsense,' said Thorrin. 'Whatever may lie ahead we're forewarned now. We've had a taste of the locals' mental tricks and know they can be overcome by concentration and strength of will.'

'Quite right,' said the Marquis. 'There'll be no turning back!'

Myra thought she saw a look of dismay flicker across the face of Arnella Rosscarrino.

The woods Peri wandered through, trailed remorselessly by DAVE #4, were overgrown and virtually trackless, unlike the neatly manicured glades she had seen near the Gelsandoran town. Her final descent through the upper branches had turned her around, and she was not sure in which direction anything lay. Still she trudged on in hope. If she chanced on the *Falcon* at least she might recover her pack. Then she could go after the Doctor and the others, though the thought of facing the trail alone terrified her even though she now knew some of its secrets. And she'd still be a couple of days behind the rest.

'What you need right now, Peri Brown,' she told herself aloud, 'is a friend and guide you can rely on, preferably with some faster means of transport than your own two sore feet.' She looked about her. 'Unfortunately it looks like the woods are fresh out of knights on white chargers right now. Even Rin Tin Tin would be better than nothing,' she added wistfully, recalling a Hollywood canine hero of the pre-war era.

'Looking for someone, are we?' said an all too familiar voice. Gribbs stepped out from behind a tree a broad grin on his mean face.

Peri turned and ran, DAVE #4 swooping after her.

'You stop right there or I'll shoot!' Gribbs shouted.

'You wouldn't dare!' she called back, twisting between the trees. A distant curse and running feet told her that she was correct. It was her only advantage. Gribbs's legs were longer than hers, and he had as much motivation to catch her as she did to stay free. She ran as fast as she could, desperately looking for some place to hide, but all the while Gribbs was slowly cutting down her lead. He was ten yards behind her, then five. His hand was reaching out for her shoulder.

'Gotya!'

His tug on her shirt pulled her off balance and she stumbled and fell heavily. In a second Gribbs's weight was on her back. With a heave he twisted her over and straddled across her middle, pinning her arms to her sides with his knees. Gasping to recover her breath, she looked up fearfully into his hard glittering eyes.

'Now I'm gonna make sure you don't get away from me again,' he promised, pulling out a cord and strap from his pocket.

There was a rumbling growl from the bushes a few yards away.

Peri had heard lions making similar noises in Africa, except this sound was far deeper, suggesting a creature of even greater bulk. Gribbs froze, and for a moment their eyes met in shared alarm. She saw his hand slowly slide down to the butt of his holstered pistol.

There came a crash and swish of branches and a thud of heavy feet. Gribbs yelled as he half rose, drawing his gun. Peri had a blurred impression of a large body passing right over her and knocking Gribbs off his feet. There was a boney thud as he hit the ground and a double thump of the creature's feet setting down after him. Then there was silence, except for breath being drawn into huge lungs.

Peri lay where she was, too frightened to look round after Gribbs, knowing she hadn't got the strength to run far and suspecting it would be useless to try in any case. Perhaps the creature would be satisfied with Gribbs, she thought selfishly. It would only be what he deserved after all. But there was no sound of her former jailer being torn limb from limb. Instead the great footfalls got louder. Then the creature loomed over her.

She'd never seen anything like it in her life.

A white, barley-sugar-twisted horn that would have graced any unicorn rose from its forehead. Its snout was as long a horse's head, but it was no herbivore as the long canines protruding from its upper jaw suggested. Its eyes were large, deep and intelligent. They looked out at her from what at first she took to be a contoured, metallic blue mask, except that she could see no straps or other means of attachment. Its neck was also armoured with overlapping metal bands and was equine in length, but more heavily muscled and covered with thick reddish fur.

The great head dipped towards her, the large nostrils flared. She closed her eyes in alarm. There was a snuffling and a sensation as though a vacuum cleaner hose were being run over her body. It was sniffing her! Cautiously she opened her eyes again, just as a long wet pink tongue emerged from the fearsome jaws and licked her neck and cheek in a friendly fashion.

She squirmed away, breaking into a hysterical peal of relieved laughter. 'Stop it – that tickles!'

The beast lifted its head and regarded her with patient interest. Slowly she got to her feet. With half an eye she noticed that Gribbs lay crumpled against the base of a tree some yards away. She thought she could see him breathing, but evidently he was not going to be playing any active part in proceedings for some time to come.

The beast was even more impressive seen in its entirety. If it had been a horse she would have said it stood maybe twenty-six hands high at the shoulder. Of course its broad three-clawed paws on furry white-stocking-marked legs were not at all horselike in articulation, nor was its long heavy tail, which ended in a cluster of wicked spikes. The rest of its body was covered in more of the red hair and armoured plates, but she could still see no sign of any fastenings. It was almost as though they grew out of its body like some partial exoskeleton. Perhaps that sort of thing was quite common on Gelsandor. Yet natural evolution alone could hardly have explained what could only be a saddle that grew out of the beast's back, complete with integral side flaps and pocketed stirrups.

'Well, you're quite something aren't you, Red? Who do you belong to then?'

The beast tossed its head but made no other response. Now she began to think furiously. It had to be a domestic animal that had got loose, but somehow she couldn't see Shalvis and those other robed monktypes owning something so magnificent. Perhaps it belonged to some group of locals they had not yet encountered, who might be less involved with the quest. And if it could be hidden, it might be encouraged to take her back to them. They would be bound to be grateful and might give her shelter. At least it would get her well away from Gribbs.

As she pondered, DAVE #4 circled in to get a closer shot of her new acquaintance.

'Aw, haven't you seen enough yet?' she said irritably.

With remarkable speed for something of its bulk, 'Red' twisted sideways and lashed out with one huge paw. There was a crunch of plastic and a dying crackle of sparks, and DAVE #4 lay crumpled on the ground.

'I think we're going to be friends,' Peri said with an approving smile.

She wished she had a sugar lump to offer it, but settled for cautiously patting the animal's massive flanks and talking in friendly tones. Its dense coat was soft and warm. She looked up at the saddle. How to mount an animal this size? There was no one to give her a leg-up, nor a convenient mounting block.

Soundlessly the stirrup flap in front of her extended like a long flat tongue until it hung at a convenient height for her to step into. There was even a bar lying across the flap at about shoulder level which she could use to steady herself.

'You're full of tricks, aren't you, Red?' She took a deep breath and stepped into the stirrup.

The flap contracted smoothly, lifting her upward. There was a hoop mounted on the pommel and she grasped it quickly as the bar disappeared under the saddle, threw her leg across, and she was seated. The right stirrup pocket contracted until she could slip her foot into it. A contoured plate that had been lying flat behind the saddle now rose to provide a backrest. It was almost like sitting in a high chair. She cautiously patted the furry back again.

'That's a good boy.' Only then did she realise Red's harness included no reins. 'Now, how I am I supposed to –'

But the great beast was already moving forward through the trees at a steady padding trot.

It was evening when Thorrin's party finally left the wetlands. They felt the ever-threatening lassitude lift from them, only to be replaced by a new sensation of expectant anxiety. Myra had half hoped there would be some neutral ground they could rest on, but the transition occurred over the course of a few paces. Clearly it was not intended they should have any respite.

Ahead was the edge of the forest. The trees were blackened, twisted and leafless – wooden skeletons with innumerable long, bare, twiggy fingers. Trailing from them were streamers of dry, grey moss. A little way inside the forest dark winged creatures flitted over the treetops, just too far away for those on the ground to make out their exact natures.

'Arden was never thus,' Falstaff observed nervously. 'But by my troth, is it not a theatrical setting? The Bard would have approved such gloom for his Scottish play, but Falstaff is no strolling mummer. I would find another path…'

'Oh no,' said Myra firmly. 'We're relying on you to keep our spirits up with more of those heroic stories of yours.'

But she could hardly blame him. The place reeked of a formless dread. It had to be contrived, yet knowing so made it no less real.

'Do we have to start now?' said Arnella. 'At least let's wait here overnight.'

It was a sensible idea. It would take an effort to press on in full daylight, but Myra thought even Thorrin and the Marquis would hesitate to push ahead with the evening drawing in. She wondered about Qwaid's party. Unless they got some extraordinary help from the Doctor, she didn't believe they'd have the guts to do it. Perhaps she should just wait along the edge of the forest for them, then there'd be no need to –

She came to herself with a start. She'd been trying to find an excuse not to go on. The forest was already affecting her.

'What we need is a good fire to cheer us up,' Rosscarrino said with slightly forced heartiness.

'An excellent suggestion,' Thorrin agreed. 'A really big fire.' He strode forward to the nearest of the trees and pulled at the moss. It crackled at his touch. He kicked at a dead branch lying on the ground, then licked his finger and held it up in the air. 'Plenty of firewood. We shall start it here.'

'But Professor,' Brockwell said anxiously. 'you might set light to the tree.'

'Exactly!' said Thorrin, with a calculating gleam in his eyes. 'And with any luck a sizeable portion of the forest with it, if it's all as dry as this. There is a slight breeze in the right direction which should help.'

'But you can't,' exclaimed Arnella.

'Why not? This is no time for half measures, and it's evidently good for nothing else. As Sir John pointed out, it is clearly a contrivance of the natives. And since they have proven themselves quite ruthless when it comes to setting their traps and hazards so far, they can expect nothing less in return. Let us see how frightening they can make a field of ashes. If they think they can intimidate Alex Thorrin so easily, they can think again!'

Gribbs stirred and slowly sat up, resting his back against the tree. The wood was filling with gloom around him as the shadows of evening lengthened.

He was aware of a terrible pounding in his head, and a dull ache along his back where he had hit the tree. Feeling sick, he looked around for the red beast that had knocked him down, but, thankfully, there was no sign of it. Unfortunately, neither was there any sign of the girl.

What would Qwaid say when he found out he'd lost her again?

Then inspiration, brought on by his own splitting headache, struck. As soon as his mind had cleared a little, he called up Qwaid.

'I found the girl,' he said brightly, 'only she took a knock on the head when she landed and she's still out cold.'

'Are you sure she's all right?' cut in the Doctor's anxious tones.

'Sure,' said Gribbs easily. 'I've seen these things before. She'll come to in her own time.'

'OK,' said Qwaid, coming back on the line, 'but as soon as she does, you check the *Falcon*, right?'

'I'll do that, Qwaid. Just you leave it to me. How are you doing? Been staying awake?'

'What do you think? At least we're nearly clear of this muck.

There's a line of trees ahead. Maybe another wood…'

Drorgon's voice spoke out in the background. 'Qwaid. See that? Looks like a fire…'

'Yeah, it is. We'll take a closer look. Call you again.'

Gribbs broke the connection with a sigh of relief. He'd bought himself some time. Now all he had to do was really find the girl – and keep an eye open for that creature as well. He struggled to his feet and drew his pistol. It wouldn't catch him by surprise again. The sudden awful possibility occurred to him that the creature might have eaten her. How would he explain that to Qwaid?

Peri was having the ride of her life. Red was bounding through the trees on a curious but effective loping run, forcing her to hold on tightly to the pommel hoop and duck overhead branches. Gradually the forest opened up and in the failing light she now saw they were moving along a familiar, well-marked pathway. Were they headed for the pyramid after all?

They passed a couple of the robed locals. Peri expected some sort of reaction, but they merely stepped politely aside to let them by, then continued on their way.

Through the trees to one side she saw a large metallic dumbbell form resting on widespread strutted legs. A spacecraft. She was back in the landing grounds. And then in the glade before her was the TARDIS.

Red padded to a stop beside the ersatz police box and waited expectantly.

'Now how did you know where to bring me?' Peri asked him. 'Did you scent my trail from the other day, somehow? Well it was a nice try but I haven't got a key, so…'

Then she saw that the TARDIS's door was ajar.

Thorrin stood back and admired his handiwork. Tree after tree was catching as the fire began to eat its way into the dead forest.

Wood popped and dry grass and moss crackled and hissed, sending clouds of sparks into the air. The others shaded their faces from the heat, but Thorrin seemed positively to bask in its intensity. The first of the trees toppled and shattered, showering a cloud of sparks and blazing fragments across the ground. Myra saw Brockwell take Thorrin's arm protectively.

'You'd better step back a little, Professor. It's not safe standing so close.' Another tree collapsed, setting small tongues of flame flickering across the matted tangles of dry grass that fringed the forest edge.

'We had best retire to the mud fields,' said Falstaff, mopping his brow. 'We must resist their soul-sapping doldrums while this conflagration burns itself out.'

With Brockwell half dragging Thorrin, they turned their backs on the blazing trees.

The tiny fires that had been smouldering about them seemed to suddenly burn brighter. Before they could take half a dozen steps they had flowed and merged into two arms of flame that crackled out from the forest through the grass and met with a roar, encircling them in a wall of fire.

CHAPTER 17
NIGHTMARES

Peri ran though the TARDIS shouting out the Doctor's name. But the twisting corridors only echoed to the sounds of her own words. She'd hoped that somehow he had managed to return to the craft, but evidently it was empty and, oddly, though she felt reassured to be within its dimensionally folded walls again, it seemed somehow less welcoming than it had been. But then what had the door been doing open? She was sure she'd seen the Doctor close and lock it when they'd set off.

Well at least she could shut herself away in here from Gribbs. But for how long? Having set out on a treasure hunt the thought of cowering away inside the TARDIS didn't feel right. Besides, what about the Doctor? Those crooks would hardly just let him go when they learnt she'd escaped. She had to try to do what she could for him. And perhaps now she had a better chance, if she could count on her new friend to help. For some reason Red seemed to have taken a liking to her and showed no inclination to return to wherever he came from. Now might be a good time to reinforce that bond.

She dialled up a heaped assortment of synthetic meat bars from the food machine, found a large bowl and filled it with water, and took it outside. Red was still sitting in a half crouch, patiently waiting where she had left him. She made a great fuss of him while she opened a few bars and let him sniff at them. He consumed each one, then the rest as fast as she could feed them to him, wrappers and all. Afterwards he drank deeply from the water bowl and then lay down protectively in front of the TARDIS's door, like some monstrous guard dog.

She wished him goodnight and closed the door, feeling

really safe once more. Tomorrow at first light she would set off after the Doctor and the others. And there seemed a good possibility that she would be riding at least part of the way.

Arnella was screaming, arms flung about her uncle, as the wall of fire grew higher and closer. Brockwell was stamping on small fires that were springing up about them, while Falstaff slashed wildly at them with his sword. Thorrin was swinging about, glaring at the blaze as though attempting to hold it at bay by the sheer force of his will. It should have burnt out in seconds, Myra thought. No grass can burn that long or that fiercely, so it has to be another trick. But she could smell the clothes scorching on her back. Was it real fire artificially enhanced or simply an illusion? Could you die from the illusion of fire if it seemed real enough?

Suddenly Thorrin shouted above the roar of the flames, 'This way – it's our only hope!'

For a moment Myra thought he had gone mad. He was pointing into the forest. But then she realised the outer wall of trees had burnt down, revealing cool darkness beyond, overhung by a pall of black smoke.

They stumbled forward, picking their way rapidly across the still smouldering embers, choking in the fumes, the heat scorching their feet. The DAVE drone tried to follow them, but a flaming branch smashed it to the ground. It's an ill wind… as terrestrials say, Myra thought. Then they were beyond the blaze, staggering between the twisted tree trunks and breathing in cool air.

Then the fire came after them.

It leapt from tree to tree, each almost exploding into flame, forcing them to run deeper into the forest to keep ahead. As the trees burnt they contorted still further, writhing into even more fantastic shapes. And as each burnt it seemed to scream. A thin terrible wailing cry, a continuous ululation of agony. Arnella clamped her hands over her ears as she ran to shut out the terrible noise.

'It's heated sap and water vapour escaping through splits in the woods!' Thorrin shouted, sounding less certain than his expression would suggest.

But as the fire sheathed each tree they began to see faces picked out by the flames and the peeling bark. Myra could make out distinct eyes and noses, with mouths gaping in time with the cries. They were too precise to be chance formations. Thorrin stared in horror and disbelief, but the terrible faces would not go away.

'You killed them, you killed them!' Arnella shouted wildly.

Flaming branches uncoiled and lashed out, as though the tree beings were trying to take their revenge on their destroyers before they died. Falstaff cut at one branch with his sword and then, seeing a dark gap between two trees, he darted off, moving with surprising speed for his bulk. In a few seconds he was gone.

Before Myra could decide whether to follow him or not, a howling wind tore through the forest, whipping up dead leaves, ash, and glowing embers into a choking turbid fog. She heard the others calling out, but though she groped about her she could find nobody. She stumbled on blindly, eyes and nostrils clamped shut against the unbreathable atmosphere. How long could humans survive it? she wondered desperately.

Then the skies opened as the black cloud above the forest dissolved into a torrential downpour, washing the smoke and ash from the air and drenching the blazing trees with hissing roars. In moments everything vanished in a haze of steamy vapours. The cool rain felt like balm to Myra's scales, even though it had not improved visibility. The ground was fast turning to mud and she could neither see nor hear anything of the others. Exhausted, she slipped and slithered into the lee of an earth bank and sat down to wait for it to pass.

Qwaid urged them on into the shelter of the nearest clump of trees on the edge of the forest as the torrent descended. The fire they had been approaching was swallowed up by the downpour, and in seconds the only sign that it had existed was the pervasive odour of damp ashes.

As they huddled out of the rain and wind he tried to raise Gribbs on the comm link, but all he got was static.

'Must be the change in the weather,' he said aloud, more for his own benefit than the others'. Silently he wondered if Gribbs had simply turned off his receiver. Perhaps he'd fouled up again and didn't want to admit it. What if he'd got the ship working and decided to give up on them? No, he wouldn't do that – would he? What other surprises had Alpha left for them? Maybe the ship was booby-trapped and Gribbs had tried to take off and it had blown up. He could still see that last image of Alpha's face on the monitor...

'I don't like it here,' Drorgon rumbled, swinging his great head about anxiously and fingering the stock of his cannon. 'It feels... bad.'

'You don't have to like it, just be quiet and do what you're told!' Qwaid shouted back. 'We say what's bad around here. Others worry about us, got it?' He was surrounded by fools, but he mustn't lose their respect. And yet it was getting harder to think of new things to say. Then he realised the Doctor was looking from one to the other of them with solemn intensity. 'What?' he demanded, his voice cracking under the strain.

'It's begun,' the Doctor said. 'Another form of mental attack. The opposite of what we experienced out on the mud flats, I think. You must both force yourself to remain calm, whatever stimulus you feel. Do you understand?'

There was something very compelling and soothing about his voice. Qwaid swallowed, forcing himself to concentrate.

'You hear him, Dro? You keep cool, yeah?'

'But I feel it, Qwaid. It's all round us.'

'No it ain't!' Qwaid said, very much afraid that Drorgon was right but desperate not to show the depth of his own fear.

Even as he spoke he saw a tiny flicker of motion out of the corner of his eye that disappeared when he turned to look properly. Then there was another. Somehow he knew they were shadows of half-formed things that should never see the light of day. He drew out a torch and flicked it about after them, but they always evaded the beam. He began to flinch and jerk at the slightest movement. A heavy raindrop worked itself through the branches and landed on his cheek, where he dashed it away with a whimper of terror. Drorgon fired his cannon at something unseen out in the darkness, then shone his own torch only to discover he had blasted their tenacious DAVE drone to fragments. For a moment that cheered him enough to force a chuckle. But the dread returned, growing deeper by the minute.

The Doctor was sitting with his fists clenched and eyes shut apparently fighting his own demons. 'However real they seem they aren't there,' he said quietly, as though repeating a mantra. 'I am master of my own mind.' Then more loudly: 'I deny you, do you hear me?'

The storm lessened and the rain swept away, leaving a clear sky tinted by the last cold blue glow of the vanished sun. The Doctor forced his eyes open, looking suddenly haggard. 'I suggest we get back on to the mud flats. I think we can manage the lassitude better than this, at least until morning.'

'Yeah... right,' agreed Qwaid, his breath coming in ragged gasps.

They all three made to stand up. But they couldn't. Something was wrapped around their ankles holding them fast. With a sobbing cry Qwaid shone his torch down at their feet.

Pale glistening roots as thick as ropes were curling about their legs.

* * *

Back in the *Stop Press*, Dexel Dynes cursed loudly.

That was the third DAVE drone he had lost inside a couple of hours. His expenses for this story were going to be steep.

Rapidly he reprogrammed the second of his patrolling DAVEs and sent it on its way. But it would take over an hour to reach the scene of the action, and meanwhile he was as good as deaf and blind. The blank screens on his monitor array stared back at him like dead eyes. The scene of the year might be taking place somewhere out there this second and he might miss it!

That possibility was the only thing in the galaxy that really frightened him.

When the steam and rain lifted Myra found herself all alone, sitting on the edge of an ephemeral flood stream that gurgled away between the trees. The only other sound was the incessant dripping from the naked branches.

She looked around her curiously. 'Hey, where is everybody?'

There was no reply. Taking out her torch, she got up and began to make a circle through the trees, keeping the stream at the centre and calling out their names. There was still no reply. Where could the others have got to? Nobody would have gone far in these conditions. Fifty metres at most.

She scratched her hip irritably, then realised she was feeling hot and itchy in several places. Some ash from the fire must have got into her clothing and between some scales. She tugged out a flap of her jerkin and shook it about, but the itching only became stronger. She twisted around and shone her torch on her side. The smooth supple hide across her hips was disfigured by a swollen patch of flesh, dotted with loose scales. With trembling fingers she touched the patch. A few scales dropped to the ground and a flap of skin peeled back to reveal a spongy grey mass of fibres beneath. A fetid odour reached her nostrils.

Myra gave a tiny gasp of horror. The torch fell from her

nerveless fingers and she sank to her knees. She had terminal sporiform necrosis – the most hideous disease a Tritonite could contract.

Even now she could feel the fungus growing across her body, burning and itching as her skin flaked away. She tore at her clothes, staggered forward and fell into the tiny stream. The fungus was invading her face, eating away her eyes. She tried to scream but her tongue was useless. As her sight faded the last thing she saw were the scales of her body floating away down the brook like dead petals.

The mud sucked and gurgled around Willis Brockwell. He'd been following Arnella's voice when he had blundered into some kind of bog in a hollow between the trees, and had rapidly sunk in up to his waist. Looking about desperately, he saw above his head a tangle of vines that trailed from an overhanging tree branch. If only he could reach them he could pull himself free! But every time he stretched up a hand, his fingertips brushing the vine, it seemed to twitch out of his reach. He sank a little lower – and the vines dropped slightly as well, remaining cruelly that merest fraction beyond his reach.

Then he heard a light laugh.

Arnella was sitting on a tree root by the side of the bog. She had something in her hand – trailing vines that ran up into the branches over his head. And he knew it was she who had deliberately lured him here to his death, and who was even now tormenting him.

'Ms Rosscarrino... Arnella! Help me, please!'

But she only looked down at him with aristocratic disdain and laughed again as, slowly but inexorably, he sank deeper into the mire.

Thorrin halted, panting, flashing his torch about him. Where had the others got to? Why did they have to wander off like that, leaving him to make all the decisions? No discipline or foresight, that was the problem.

He found himself in a sort of natural amphitheatre floored by a carpet of dead leaves and encircled by trees. There was no other exit, so impatiently he turned to retrace his footsteps.

But the path he entered along was now blocked by a hunched and twisted tree with branches trailing to the ground. He flashed his torch around the hollow, but its high banks were completely ringed with the trees, forming a living fence about him. Even as he stared at them their branches began to sway as though stirred by a breeze.

But there was no breeze.

'Alex Thorrin,' whispered a voice out of the dry rattle of thousands of twigs.

'Who are you? Show yourself.'

'We are all around you. Can you not see us? You are accused of callous murder.'

'What? That's absurd. This is no court… and I'm no murderer!'

'But you are. Earlier this night you acted out of arrogant self-assurance. Instead of waiting to find another way you thoughtlessly attempted to dispose of an obstacle in your path. Your fire killed our people.'

'Your people? Trees? No, I don't believe you exist. It was an illusion created by natives. This is all an illusion now.' He clutched at his head. 'Get out of my mind! Talking tree men belong in some childish fantasy.'

'Do you know that for a fact? Can you prove it absolutely, or is this a further example of your arrogance? You, who think of yourself as educated, know only the minutest fraction of the myriad forms life takes throughout the universe.'

'Yes, but I want to learn more.'

'Then you admit your ignorance? You admit you might have been wrong?'

Thorrin looked about him wretchedly. 'I… don't know. I

didn't mean any harm, but I couldn't afford any delay. It's vital I reach Rovan's treasure as soon as possible.'

'Why are you so impatient?'

'There's so much to do and learn, so little time.' He looked around himself again. 'Please, won't you let me out of here?'

'More impatience. But it is too late for you, Alex Thorrin. Now you must pay the price for your crime.'

The dead leaves swirled around him, brushing against him with their papery forms. They were autumn and winter, sucking the life out of him.

'You cannot deny the seasons…'

He saw the skin of his hands greying and cracking as they drew the years out of his body.

Too late, too late, they whispered.

Then he was nothing but a swirl of dust dissolving into the wind.

Nobody knew where Arnella was.

The Marquis ran through the forest from one person to the next, but there were only looks of incomprehension on their masked faces. And it was becoming steadily harder for him to make himself heard, what with the people getting taller all the time.

Or was it he that was getting smaller?

He looked down at himself and saw he was dressed in rags. No wonder they didn't take any notice of him any more. He couldn't be very important looking like this. But he kept on tugging at trouser legs and skirts asking for Arnella, because nothing would work without her. The masked people laughed and started to throw coins at him, which stung as they struck, but evaporated when they hit the ground before he could pick them up.

And he shouted and begged until finally one of the giants condescended to look down at him from his eminence.

'What a poor little man you are. What's your name?'

And he couldn't remember any more. He was nobody. He was nothing.

A great foot was raised above him and descended, grinding him under its heel.

Arnella was hopelessly entangled in the middle of the thorn bush. The more she struggled, the deeper the thorns bit. Only by staying absolutely still did she make the pain go away, and then the bush supported her in surprising comfort. She called out for help but nobody answered, which made her angry rather than frightened.

After a while she began to feel thirsty, but she could not reach the flask in her pack. Then she saw a bunch of plump grapes hanging from a wild vine that grew through the thorn bush. Why hadn't she noticed it before? The bunch was just by her head and she had only to turn to bite one off. It was delicious and she ate some more, but the bunch did not diminish. The grape juice was like wine, and she began to feel light-headed.

Then came the flapping of many wings.

Dark shapes flitted out of the darkness and settled on the bush. She could not make out their exact forms, only their red eyes alive with hunger. She twisted away from them but the bush held her fast. The creatures closed on her, probing with their tiny sharp fangs, their needle proboscises and leechlike mouths. They fastened to her exposed neck and wrists, or stabbed delicately through her clothing with exquisite pain. They gorged off her lifeblood, but did not suck her quite dry.

After what seemed like hours they departed in another flurry of wings, leaving her weak and trembling, her clothes stained richly with her blood. And she knew they would be back the next night and the next. She had to eat the grapes to sustain herself and to feed the parasites, and as long as she did so she would not die. The thorn bush would protect her from all other dangers save these. It was her shield and her prison.

And that was her fate and she would never escape.

She began to scream.

'You ran away from them again,' the voice taunted Falstaff from out of the darkness. 'Just like you always do when there's any real danger.'

'But I am trying,' he protested, puffing and putting his back against a tree.

'Are you? Or is this all another sham? You were searching for your honour, remember?'

'Honour, what is honour? A word. What is that word? Honour. What is honour? Air. Can honour set a leg, or take away the grief of –'

'Enough. I've heard it all before. When are you going to find some lines of your own?'

'Where have you heard this before? You have the advantage of me, sir. Who are you?'

'Can't you guess? When are you going to stop hiding?'

'Hiding? Hiding from what?'

'How about this?'

A sword stabbed out of the darkness. Falstaff parried more by luck than judgment. The blade appeared again out of nothing and he hacked wildly at it while trying to edge around the tree. But the blade wouldn't let him.

'Running away again? What happens when you can't run away? Will you stand and fight at last? Have you the courage?'

The blade was weaving about him, but now he thought he could see a vague shadowy form beyond it. But however he cut and thrust he could not seem to touch it. And he was tiring. He was going to die.

'Frightened of delivering the winning blow? Frightened of committing yourself perhaps?'

Falstaff made one last desperate thrust. Somehow it got behind his opponent's guard and he felt his blade sink home. The other blade instantly dropped to the ground, leaving him with his own transfixed. And for the first time he saw who he had been fighting.

His own contorted body was skewered on the end of his blade, its features frozen in a mask of horror.

But why was there no blood? Why did his doppelgänger not collapse but instead hang on his blade as light as a feather?

With a trembling hand he reached out and touched the face of his image – and it crumpled like paper. The whole body was a mere shell.

'Ah,' said the voice, 'an empty man. More deceptions. You have found yourself it seems.'

'That's not me!'

'Isn't it? Have you looked closely recently?'

Falstaff clutched at his own chest, feeling his fingers sink into nothing. He tore his coat open, but there was only empty blackness within. And hanging there a grubby label bearing his real name.

As fast as Qwaid, Drorgon, and the Doctor tore and cut at the roots with their knives and bare hands, more sprang up to take their place. The severed ends lashed and writhed about like white worms; even Drorgon's strength could not break the thicker roots. Slowly their feet and lower legs were becoming further tangled in the clawing roots, which began to tighten, cutting off their circulation.

Qwaid used his pistol, set on a narrow beam, on the roots about his feet. Wet earth exploded in a scorching cloud of steam. Scalded, Qwaid yelled out and dropped the gun, which fell beyond his reach.

In desperation Drorgon turned his cannon downward.

'Don't do that – you'll blow your legs off!' the Doctor shouted.

'We're dead anyway!' Drorgon snarled.

'Then try it against the trees behind us first. Maybe they're controlling them!'

Drorgon twisted around and blazed away at the gnarled trees that clumped at their backs. A trunk exploded in a shower of splinters. Several of the roots at their feet lashed about wildly, then fell limp.

'Again,' said the Doctor.

Bolt after bolt smashed into the spinney of trees. Severed branches fell to the ground, slowly contorting before they were still. More roots fell away, and one by one they managed to tear their feet free, only to fall helplessly on to their faces.

Lower legs numbed from the crushing force of the roots, they could only crawl away across the tussock grasses until they felt the melancholia of the mud flats descend upon them. When they shone a torch back to see if the root things were pursuing them, they saw they no longer writhed, but merely stood torn and burnt in the midst of churned earth. Beyond them shattered tree stumps smoked slightly, looking quite innocuous. Slowly, as they rubbed life back into their legs, it became harder to believe they had ever been anything else.

'Was it something real,' Qwaid demanded, 'or was it a mind trick?'

'A bit of both, perhaps,' the Doctor said, 'but I wouldn't like to say exactly what or how.'

Faintly, from the depths of the forest, came the sound of a scream, either of pain, or fear they could not tell. The Doctor started forward automatically but Qwaid restrained him.

'If they're having a taste of what we've just been through, that's their problem. You work for me, remember?'

In the reflected torchlight, the Doctor's face tightened into a mask of contempt. 'One day you'll learn there's more to life than your own selfish ambitions, Qwaid. But will it be too late?'

'I'll risk it,' Qwaid retorted. But his eyes shied away from the Doctor's angry gaze.

They remained where they were, alert but uneasy, until the sky greyed with the first light of morning.

CHAPTER 18
SHOOTING STAR

The first flush of dawn was just beginning to tint the sky when Peri opened the TARDIS door and carried out Red's breakfast. The great beast rose and stretched, then nuzzled against her in a friendly fashion. As she watched it eat she wondered if her plan was feasible. Could she really expect this animal she had known for only a few hours to take her where she wanted to go? Yet she sensed somehow that she could rely on him. At least his owner hadn't turned up in the night, and none of the locals, who seemed to have everything around here pretty much taped, had raised any objections. She had to assume it was at least permissible to make the attempt.

Peri had replaced her supplies and pack from the TARDIS's stores, and now saw there were convenient eyelets on the back of Red's saddle to fasten it securely. She didn't like the idea of leaving the TARDIS unlocked, so when she was sure she had taken everything she needed, she pressed down the door control plunger on the console and dashed out before the inner double doors could swing ponderously shut.

As on the previous evening, the stirrup flap lowered to help her mount, and soon she was seated in the saddle again. She patted the great body under her. 'Now I want you to go through the wood where all the signposts are. I can remember part of the way –'

But Red was already trotting off across the glade in the direction she wanted. How did he do it? Had the Gelsandorans bred a type of animal that could respond to mental commands? It was no more fantastic than many other things she had already experienced. Peri tried to relax in the high-backed saddle and not worry about it. Don't look a gift horse in the mouth she told herself. Especially when it has teeth as sharp as this one.

* * *

Gribbs watched them set off from the cover of the trees.

He'd wasted several hours the previous night in a fruitless search before he realised where the girl might have gone. It had then taken him a while to get his own bearings and strike the parkland around the Gelsandoran town, before finding his way to the landing fields. He'd kept well clear of Dynes's ship, hoping not to pick up another camera drone. The lock of Thorrin's craft had defeated him. He'd need his full toolkit to crack it. That left the Doctor's ship. He'd found the right glade but had boggled at the odd box shape sitting in it. It had to be a shuttle pod; the main craft must still be in orbit. He would have investigated further but for the massive and all too familiar form that lay beside it. He'd fingered the butt of his pistol, but had decided not to risk taking his revenge just now. Besides, he wasn't sure his gun would be powerful enough to deal with something that size, and merely wounding it and making it angry hadn't seemed like a very sensible idea. And so he had waited for dawn.

Should he follow them, or find the *Falcon* and see if he could override the cut-offs Alpha had installed? How long could he pretend to Qwaid and the Doctor that the girl was still unconscious?

Then a flash of light caught his eye. A brilliant but slow meteor was cutting lazily through the still dark eastern sky. Even as he watched it with natural appreciation, he saw its nucleus grow brighter and its tail foreshorten.

Hey, this was a big one.

The tail vanished altogether and the nucleus appeared to become stationary in the sky, but growing steadily brighter.

Suddenly it seemed to be heading straight for him!

Gribbs threw himself to the ground. The meteor flashed dazzlingly overhead and vanished behind the trees. Any sound of impact was lost in the earsplitting sonic boom of its arrival, which hammered the earth under him, before climbing back up into the sky and gradually receding to a distant rumble.

Cautiously, when he was sure he was not going to be showered by impact debris, Gribbs picked himself up and looked about him, trying to work out where it had hit. Over the treetops he could just make out a thin thread of grey smoke rising to catch the first light of day.

He checked its bearing on his object compass still set on the *Falcon*'s signal. As far as he could estimate, the meteor had come down not far from the ship. It would be just his luck if it had been damaged by a freak chance like this.

Anxiously he set off through the woods.

Myra saw the meteor from the dead forest as it cut its sparkling arc across half the dawn sky.

She was lying on her back staring up through the stark branches of a tree. Very slowly the events of the previous night fell into place, and with a sudden rush of horrified recollection she sat bolt upright. She was half clothed, filthy with mud and shivering with cold, but she was alive!

Fearfully she examined herself for any sign of disease lesions, but her skin was smooth and sound once more. Had it ever been otherwise? A nightmare – it had all been a nightmare! No, she corrected herself, something worse than that. It had to have been the Gelsandorans doing, playing on her greatest fear. Now, with her head clear, she remembered that sporiform necrosis took months to prove fatal, yet last night she had believed without question that it was spreading and killing her in minutes. Suddenly she understood how the lost seekers had come to be on the mud flats, trapped between the nightmares of the forest and the monsters of the valley.

Her pack was still lying where she had cast it aside. With it and a pool of clean water she hastily made herself respectable once more. Then she set off to find the others.

Drorgon examined the muddy footmarks in the blackened ground.

'They all scatter here.' he pointed. 'Run in all directions. Which one we follow, Qwaid?'

Qwaid looked about at the charred swathe the fire had cut through the forest, then glanced at the Doctor. He had his hands in his pockets and was staring about keenly.

'Well, Doc? Any suggestions?'

'I'm afraid my boy scout spooring skills are somewhat rusty. But it does occur to me that if a group of people have become separated in these conditions, they will try to find each other again by signalling in some way, so if we simply stay quiet and listen –'

A distant hail floated through the trees to them.

'– then we might learn where they are.'

Voices, which had so mysteriously failed to carry the night before, now enabled them, gradually, to reassemble. Nobody asked what they had each suffered, nor volunteered any details of their own, but Myra could read in their faces that it had been as bad for them as herself. Arnella fell sobbing unashamedly into her uncle's arms, while Brockwell looked at her with a very curious expression. Thorrin's face was haggard, and Myra thought his hair was actually greyer. They could feel the menace of the forest still pressing close about them, but it was bearable by daylight and in company.

Eventually only Falstaff was unaccounted for.

'We cannot afford to waste time in a search,' Thorrin said after they had called his name for some minutes. 'Either he'll follow our trail, or else return to his ship. He knows the hazards now, so he should be safe enough.'

The Marquis nodded in agreement. 'Yes, we must press on.'

Myra rounded upon them both angrily, 'How can you be so callous! Suppose he's trapped somewhere. I wouldn't leave a kazarn slime rat here for another night like that! We find him, however long it takes, Professor. Have a little patience for once!'

Unaccountably, Thorrin flinched, but said nothing.

Gribbs came upon the meteor crater before he reached the *Falcon*. It had landed within half a kilometre of the ship. The impact had flattened a couple of trees and started a small grass fire, which was already dying down, but otherwise had done surprisingly little damage. The crater was only five metres across and very shallow. More like the blast pit of a rocket, Gribbs thought idly. Then he looked again. In the centre of the crater was a heap of blackened remains that he had first taken to be a burnt bush or shards of rock. But now he looked more closely he saw regular sharp edges to them, and here and there a glint of metal. Puzzled, he circled the still hot crater. There were strange regular marks running from its centre out across the charred earth and grass. At the point they left the crater he identified them. They were the tracks of a set of caterpillar treads.

Suddenly he began to wonder if it was really such an extraordinary chance that something had landed just where it had.

Pistol drawn, he followed the trail. When the tracks reached fresh grass the impressions remained clear. Through the trees ahead of him he saw a familiar form. It was the *Falcon*, resting on her landing legs amid a few torn branches and another swathe of blackened earth, but otherwise looking perfectly sound after her plunge from the sky. And the tracks led straight for her.

Gribbs made a cautious circuit of the ship, but there was no sign of movement. The track prints led up to the main hatch, he noticed, but did not return. The hatch itself was closed.

What should he do next? Qwaid should know somebody else, presumably more treasure seekers, had arrived here and were apparently using some sort of reconnaissance vehicle to spy out the land. But he wouldn't be pleased to learn it had somehow got aboard the *Falcon*, especially if he found out he'd been lying about the girl and so wasn't there to prevent it. On the other hand, how long could he afford to wait and do nothing?

Then the decision was made for him as the main hatch swung open.

'Don't skulk amongst the trees, Gribbs. Come inside, I want to talk to you,' Alpha's voice boomed from the darkness within.

For a moment Gribbs thought he was going to faint, and the world blurred around him while a sick knot began to tie itself in his stomach. Then he recovered, swallowing down hard.

'Do not keep me waiting, Gribbs.'

There was a slightly odd quality to the voice, but It definitely did not come from the cabin speaker. It was not a recording. It was Alpha.

'M-Mr Alpha, sir...' he called out tremulously. 'It was Qwaid's idea. Me and Drorgon had nothing to do with it, honest.'

'To do with what, Gribbs? You'd better come in and tell me all about it. In fact I want you to tell me everything that's been happening for the past few days, Gribbs. Every detail. Do you think you can do that?'

'Y-yes Mr Alpha... uh, you aren't angry with me?'

'That rather depends on what you've been doing, doesn't it? But I will be angry if we continue this conversation in such a manner any longer, Gribbs. Come inside at once.'

Swaying like a man mounting the steps to the guillotine, Gribbs climbed the ramp and peered inside. The hatch closed smoothly behind him, not quite muffling his involuntary cry of fear and amazement.

In the white pyramid, Shalvis lifted her head as she let her mental projection fade.

'Alpha has arrived as expected,' she announced to the assembled Seers.

'And our powers will not affect him?' one asked.

'No. In any case our trust is inviolate. We may not interfere directly. Evil though he is, Alpha has rights. He must be defeated within the laws of the quest. We can only hope that all else we foresaw also comes to pass.'

Falstaff was huddled in the hollow at the base of a tree. He stared at them blankly at first as Myra gently encouraged him to uncurl, and mutely accepted a drink from her flask and a ration bar. For some reason he kept pawing uneasily at the front of his jacket. Slowly, full awareness returned to his eyes.

'My,' he said shakily, 'but Old Jack's soul was put through the mangle last night and no mistake. Perhaps this was a step too far. I suggest a strategic retreat. I should never have ignored my own dictum: discretion is the better part of –'

'We've heard it,' Thorrin said sharply. 'But nonetheless we are going on. You can follow us or not as you wish.'

'Exactly,' said the Marquis, regarding Falstaff with a trace of contempt. 'Some of us have an obligation to fulfil –'

Arnella, who had been very quiet, suddenly said, 'Uncle, please don't talk about obligations!' And she turned her back on him and stomped away.

Through the screen of trees they watched the other party gradually assemble itself and set off. Qwaid let them get safely ahead, noted the course they were following, then he, Drorgon, and the Doctor moved on to a parallel path.

'Isn't it about time you called Gribbs?' the Doctor reminded him. 'I want to be sure Peri has recovered safely.'

Qwaid tapped the call button. It took Gribbs a minute to answer, and when he came on the line there was a slightly forced tone in his response.

'Hi, Qwaid. Everything's fine here,' he said quickly.

'It had better be. What about the ship?'

'Oh, it's fine too. Came down on the emergency retros. I managed to get in and override the cut-outs Mr Alpha had installed. It's all ready any time you need it. Soon as you find the treasure we'll be over to pick it up. Just give the word –'

'OK, OK. Now what about the girl? The Doc's worried about her.'

'Oh, she's fine…'

'Well put her on.'

'Er, right. Yes. I'll, er, just get her…'

There was a pause, then Peri's voice came over the line. 'Hi, Doctor. I'm fine, how are you?'

'Are you sure? You must have had quite a knock.'

'Just a bit of a headache. Mr Gribbs has been a perfect gentleman looking after me, but I think he's only going to stay that way as long as you keep helping Qwaid. So please find the treasure as soon as you can so I can get out of here.'

Red had found his way through the woods with little help from Peri. The misleading signposts were still blank, and she could only recall for certain a few of the turnings, but Red had bounded along with hardly a pause. She wondered if he had a better idea of where they were going than she did. Was he scenting their previous trail? Of course: this was his own back yard, so to speak, and a specially bred carriage animal, the product of exotic genetic engineering perhaps, might be created with the ability to find his way about with little or no guidance.

The wood thinned and then before them was the unreal expanse of the tiled plain. Peri scowled at the prospect of crossing it for the third time, but it had to be done.

'Now you've got to step carefully here,' she said firmly to Red, hoping her words or thoughts were getting through. 'We've got to find the right sequence of colours, otherwise the ground drops out from under your feet, and that's no fun, believe me.'

But even as she spoke she felt the pocketing around the stirrups contract up and around her feet and calves, holding them fast. 'Hey, what are you doing –' Simultaneously the saddle back and the pommel hoop hinged and slid forward respectively, forcing her into a posture not unlike that of a racing jockey. Red gathered his legs under him as though to spring.

'Now just a minute –'

He bounded forward and Peri had to save all her breath for hanging on. Red was following the rainbow sequence perfectly, but he was touching only every other tile.

Gribbs turned off the comm link and nervously faced the other occupant of the *Falcon*'s control cabin, trying not to make direct eye contact as he did so. They were nothing like Alpha's eyes had been, for a very good reason, but he still did not want to look at them.

'That should put their minds at rest, don't you think, Gribbs?'

'Uh, sure, Mr Alpha. That was, er, some performance on your part.'

'Simply a voice synthesiser unit, Gribbs. I accessed the ship's log recordings of your recent conversations with Qwaid and duplicated the girl's voice and superficial mannerisms. Now all we have to do is allow Qwaid and his assistants to locate Rovan's treasure and give us its location. From the recordings it seems that this "Doctor" person is not unintelligent. He should compensate for Qwaid's grosser deficiencies.'

'Oh, right, Mr Alpha. He will that. And when he's done that we just… pick it up?'

'More or less, Gribbs. I want to give Qwaid a surprise, you see. You do think he'll be surprised to see me, don't you?'

Oh, he'll be surprised, that's for sure, Gribbs thought miserably.

The far edge of the dead forest was marked by a continuous line of fencing. Through this they could see an open expanse of rocky ground.

The fence itself was formed of black tubular posts, perhaps three metres high and spaced some ten metres apart, linked by black rails slotted alternately into them. There was not enough space between the rails to pass between them, but Myra judged that it should be simple enough to climb over, the horizontal rails making in effect broad ladder-like steps. She wondered vaguely what material they were made of. It had to be extremely rigid to support itself without any apparent sagging over such long spans. She reached out to test it, then jerked her hand back with a yell.

'What's wrong?' Brockwell asked with concern. 'Is it electrified?'

'No, but don't anyone touch it. Look carefully at the edges of the rails.'

Cautiously they did so.

The rails were similar to thin I-beams in cross section, and about twenty-five centimetres broad. But the horizontal edges of their upper and lower flanges were literally razor sharp. In addition, another razor-like ridge rose perpendicularly from between them, pointing vertically up and down. Any attempt to grasp or step on the rail for the purposes of climbing would result in serious lacerations.

'Hmm, an ingenious contrivance,' said Thorrin, examining the railing.

'A cruel trap,' said Myra. 'Suppose you reached it at night, with some imaginary horror at you heels? Would you notice the blades in time? How well can you apply bandages with your fingers cut to ribbons?

'Cruel perhaps, but necessary,' the Marquis said quietly.

'I beg you pardon?' said Brockwell.

'Never mind,' said the Marquis.

'Whatever its morality, it prevents us from leaving this evil place,' said Falstaff. 'And I for one do not propose to spend another night here.' And he reversed his staff and drove its metal ferrule hard against the side of one of the vertical blades. Despite its thinness, it did not break or chip, and the rail itself merely shivered slightly under the force of the blow.

'Some sort of toughened synthetic,' Thorrin pronounced. 'We must either wrap enough spare items of clothing and bedrolls over it to protect ourselves while we climb, or else see if our pistols can be set to burn through a section.'

'Can we dig under it?' Brockwell wondered. He bent down and experimentally began scooping at the earth below the lowest rail. Suddenly he jerked his hand away. There was another rail buried just below the surface, linking the bases of the fence posts.

'Oh well, it was a good idea,' said Arnella sympathetically. Brockwell risked a small quick smile of thanks.

The Marquis was looking up at the trees, some of which overhung the fence. 'Perhaps it would be possible to swing over on our climbing lines.'

'We could try sliding one of the rails aside,' said Myra, who had been examining the nearest fence post. 'They don't seem to be secured in any way, and the slots they sit in run right through. I think I can push the end of a rail from the other side…' She thrust the end of her staff into the slot, and the rail, surprisingly light for its size, slid free and dropped to the ground. It was as easy as that.

At least Falstaff had the decency to laugh heartily. Thorrin looked put out.

With a rail removed it left a gap of almost eighty centimetres, through which they stepped carefully one by one. There was a sense of palpable relief to have the fence between them and the forest.

'I think we should replace this section,' said the Marquis, once they were all safely through. 'Should those criminals come this way it may slow them down.'

'I shouldn't think it will make much difference,' said Thorrin, with a touch of his former self-assurance. 'They must be far behind us by now.'

'Don't underestimate Qwaid,' Myra said sharply. 'He might not have Alpha's brains, but he's determined. And if he's forced the Doctor to help him he might not be short of brains either.'

'I bow to your superior knowledge of the mental processes of the underworld,' said Thorrin heavily. 'By all means replace it. But then can we please proceed?'

They gingerly edged the rail back in place by lifting it with their staffs. Then they set off across the open rocky plain, leaving the dark line of the dead forest, and all its nightmares, behind them.

As they plodded across the rocky wasteland, Willis Brockwell dropped back until he was walking beside Myra. 'I'm sorry about the professor,' he said quietly.

'What do you mean?'

'The way he spoke to you back there. It wasn't like him. I know, I've worked with him for years. I mean he can be short tempered and a bit overbearing at times, but he usually apologises for it afterwards. It's this quest business. He's become... well, fixated on finding this cursed treasure. I never thought money would have that sort of effect on him. He's made enough of it already after all.'

'Well, you never can tell what touches people that way. Like the Marquis, for instance.'

'Yes. What did he mean by "cruel... but necessary"?'

'I don't know. I don't think either of them are telling the whole truth about what they're doing here.' She looked at Arnella, trudging along beside her uncle with her head down. 'She may know half of it, and perhaps that's what's troubling her – which I suppose doesn't make you any too happy either.'

Brockwell nodded regretfully. 'I wish she'd talk to me... but she's got her pride.'

'Haven't we all? And then of course I know even less about

"Sir John Falstaff" over there, and that bothers me intensely as well.'

'Still, I suppose that makes us the only two relatively uncomplicated people here right now, Inspector.'

She looked at him coolly. 'We'll have to see, won't we? Fear, greed, and the prospect of coming into a fortune like Rovan's treasure sometimes do strange things – even to the most uncomplicated of people.'

They topped a slight rise in the ground, and they heard Thorrin exclaim, 'What on earth is this?'

CHAPTER 19
BLOODLINE

Red made a final bound and landed on the grassy fringe that bordered the far side of the tiled plain. The saddle back straightened and the pocket stirrups released Peri. She slid stiffly to the ground, massaging her aching back and thighs.

'That was some ride,' she admitted. 'Can't you give a girl some warning when you're going to pull a stunt like that?'

Red contrived a look of puppylike sorrow.

'Oh, all right. I didn't mean it like that,' she said, petting him and feeding him another meat bar from her pack. 'We must have crossed five times faster than on foot, which is quite a bonus. Now let's have a look through here...'

With Red padding along behind her, she made her way through the miniature jungle of fern trees until they came to the edge of the valley. Even the high sun had failed to disperse the mist blanket, and it remained unbroken except for the few crowns of the tallest trees close to the terraced steps. A series of deep honking cries floated up to her, followed by a throaty roar, which made her shiver.

'The boys and girls are still at their fun and games I guess,' she said, trying to sound offhand. 'From what I heard over Gribbs's radio, there're some berries that repel the things down there, only I don't know if it'll work for you as well. It's OK for me to take the risk, but it's unfair to put you on the spot.'

Red tossed his head and gave a defiant snort.

'All right, so you can lick anybody twice your size. But then there's that lake to cross, which means I'd have to build a raft, which might take some time. And the trick stairs. Will you be able to get up them?' She pursed her lips and looked along the misty valley thoughtfully. 'Well, there's nothing to say we can't try another way, as long as we meet up with the Doctor

211

somewhere on the far side. They didn't have time to explore, but I can cover a whole lot more ground on you. Let's try some lateral thinking and check out the side of the valley first.'

She remounted and Red turned his head to the right, setting off in a long loping stride along the valley rim.

Dynes ate a pack meal without taking his eyes off the monitor screens, following it down with a couple of stimtabs. No time for sleep, now that his instincts told him things were starting to build towards a climax.

He'd sent replacement DAVE units at top speed to the last recorded positions of their predecessors in the hope of re-establishing contact with his subjects. Even now they were searching the dead forest. He had lost Peri completely, and could only hope he might find her by chance. Via a DAVE he'd investigated the pseudo-meteor crater and had followed the tracks to the *Falcon*. He had no idea what they signified, or if Gribbs was back inside the ship, but he was running short of drones and couldn't afford to leave one there on the off chance.

Now he could only wait and see.

The rocky plain was cut through the middle by a deep river gorge, on the far side of which they could see cool and inviting green trees and stretches of open grassland. The gorge itself, however, was more forbidding, and quite unlike anything Myra had ever seen before.

'They certainly do go in for some impressive feats of engineering,' Brockwell observed, raising his voice over the roar of the waters.

'If they hope to overawe us, they are wasting their time,' said Thorrin firmly. 'It's simply another challenge.'

The river ran white and foaming some twenty metres below the level of the plain. This was partly due to the fall along its course, and partly to the turbulence generated by its banks, which resembled nothing less than two sets of interlocking saw teeth. The teeth were made of stretches eleven or twelve metres long, Myra estimated, which then turned a precise right angle, zigzagging in and out alternately, so that the sheer-cut sides on the opposite banks exactly paralleled each other. At no point did they come any closer than the same eleven or twelve metres. The remarkable construction stretched away into the distance on either side of them, without a bridge in sight. The river banks for fifty metres back were quite smooth, with not a single place where a grapnel might take hold.

'We either set off along the bank until its nature changes, or work out a method of crossing where we are,' said the Marquis.

'Even if I went into the water and had a line to keep me from being carried away, I couldn't climb up the other side,' said Myra.

'We've got some climbing gear with us,' said Brockwell. 'You might be able to manage with that.'

'Enough for twenty metres of sheer smooth rock?' she kicked the planed stone bank. 'And I'll bet this is hard stuff. They won't make it easy for us.'

'Old Jack is no spider,' said Falstaff. 'He does not swing across perilous chasms on threads of gossamer secured by pins.'

Thorrin, who had been scowling at the scene before him in silence for some minutes, slowly began pacing along one of the angles of the bank. Then he took out a stylus and notepad, sketched something rapidly, and gave a satisfied smile. 'I have solved the problem,' he announced. 'We shall need some sections of that post rail from the edge of the forest.'

'Excuse me, Professor,' said Brockwell. 'They might be strong enough, but I'd say they'll be almost a metre too short to reach across.'

'Of course, we can bind two lengths together,' said the Marquis. 'But... won't those razor edges cut the cord?'

'No, there is no need to waste time tying anything together,' said Thorrin. 'It's simply a matter of elementary geometry. A childish puzzle. Just bring the rails and you will see.'

The Doctor was examining the fence with interest, while Qwaid angrily applied first aid to Drorgon's hands.

'Now do you see why I brought him along?' he said. 'Next time don't try smashing anything down until I tell you.'

'Sorry, Qwaid,' Drorgon rumbled. He looked up through the fence across the plain. 'We got company.'

They remained motionless as Brockwell and Jaharnus appeared over a slight rise. They approached the fence a little way to one side of them, carefully removed four of the long rail sections, then set off back across the plain, dragging their acquisitions carefully behind them by their flat ends.

'Now I wonder what they need those for,' said the Doctor.

They made their way along to the gap in the fence and stepped through. As they did so there was a hum and swish in the air and a DAVE unit flew past them and vanished over the skyline, while a second came to a halt a few metres away, lenses gleaming.

'I thought we'd seen the last of them,' Qwaid groaned.

'You want me to blast it again, Qwaid?' said Drorgon eagerly, hefting his cannon.

'Cruckbrain! We don't want to let them ahead know we're here. Just ignore it and keep moving.'

They progressed slowly, so as not to run into Thorrin's party. Eventually they crested the low rise and saw the strangely symmetrical gorge cutting across the plain. On its far side Thorrin's party could be seen heading towards a line of trees and green fields. Qwaid waited until they had disappeared, then they made their way down to the edge of the river.

'Ah, so that's what they wanted those lengths of fencing for,' said the Doctor.

Two sections of railing had been laid side by side across the V-shaped space between two of the gorge's teeth, as far out as they would span. The two others had been laid side by side from the centres of the first two out across the river to the tip of the projecting bank opposite, forming an inverted T.

'An instant footbridge. Those of a specially nervous disposition can even shuffle across on hands and knees,' the Doctor said. He looked at the ends of the fence rails where they rested on the edges of the bank, then at Qwaid. 'You might notice that they serve their purpose with barely a handsbreadth to spare, which can hardly be coincidental.'

'All right, so we're playing the locals' games to give them material for their mind studies or whatever,' Qwaid said. 'So what? As long as I get what I came here for, they're welcome to whatever they can learn from my mind.'

'And I'm sure they'll find it a most interesting study,' the Doctor said sincerely. 'But all this effort and planning would go to waste if too many people succeed in reaching the treasure. Either it has been removed piecemeal years ago, or else there's a catch to the whole business.'

'No, it's here,' Qwaid said passionately. 'I can practically taste it! Your job is to get me to it, that's all. If they try any null moves after that, then it'll be the time to start worrying.'

They cautiously crossed the improvised bridge and walked on.

Straggling brush and stunted trees gave way to more substantial growths. Soon they came to a simple rustic fence surrounding a field filled with rows of low leafy plants with spreading leaves and purple heads. In a more distant field small figures could be seen harvesting what might have been wheat. They came to a lane rutted by cartwheels and shaded by tall trees hung with small spiky blue pods. As there was no one else in sight they started down it.

'Are these more seekers, or locals?' Qwaid wondered.

'I've no idea,' the Doctor admitted. 'But it does seem remarkably peaceful and well established.' The hedge on the other side of the lane was overhung by the trees of an orchard, heavy with tempting multicoloured fruit. As they passed, Drorgon reached up and picked a few, sniffing them appreciatively.

'Forget that and keep your eyes open,' said Qwaid.

Drorgon scowled and put the fruits in his pack.

High roofs showed over the hedgerows, and they were soon passing between wooden buildings whose large double doors and cavernous interiors revealed themselves to be barns. Beyond them came the the first of a row of small houses, with glazed windows, shingled roofs and rough stone walls. Qwaid hesitated, then led them into the nearest barn. It was dusty and warm, a third full of the local equivalent of hay, with an upper loft reached by a rough ladder. They climbed this and found a platform with a loading door and pulley block. Qwaid peered through the cracks between the loose-fitting door and its frame.

He could see over the roofs of the nearest houses to some sort of village square. Outside one of the larger buildings were several chairs and tables, seated at which were a handful of people. Facing them was Thorrin's party. After a few minutes of apparently amicable conversation, Thorrin led the others into the building, their DAVE unit following.

Qwaid settled back on a pile of straw. 'Couldn't be better. Now we wait and see how they get on. Pass us one of those apple things, Dro.'

The building was the public meeting house and sole hostelry of Braal, the largest settlement in the Country of the Enlightened – as the villagers seated outside had proudly explained.

'Why, 'tis a cousin of the old Boar's Head,' said Falstaff.

It was the sort of room Myra had seen only in historical reconstructions. Clusters of timeworn trestle tables and chairs ringed a room ceilinged by smoke-blackened beams. Though the day was warm, a large fire blazed in the brick-backed hearth. Above a stained counter rows of tankards hung on hooks over several differently sized casks resting on their sides on blocks. From a room beyond came the aroma of cooking. No doubt it was crude fare prepared in unhygienic conditions, but after a few days eating only ration bars it smelled very enticing.

A fat Torkein man was tending the bar. He gave their DAVE a curious glance then waddled over to them; his lower pair of arms were still busy wiping a cup with a towel, but he made a friendly gesture of welcome with his upper limbs.

'How can I be of service, ladies and gentlebeings?'

'One of the men outside said you served food and drink,' said Thorrin. 'But I don't suppose you accept stellars or credit charges?'

The innkeeper grimaced. 'You, being strangers, won't know any better, but here we don't have anything to do with money in any form. We, or our forebears, were all seekers once, but we've found a better way now. Fair exchange of labour or goods. If you've anything to trade against a meal I'll consider it.'

After some haggling, they bartered two eversharp camping knives for a full meal and all they could drink. The innkeeper passed the orders through and directed a rosy-cheeked human woman to load a tray with tankards. As she delivered them to the table, Falstaff said something quietly to her that made her blush and giggle.

'The men outside also mentioned that Rovan's treasure is not far from here,' Thorrin said, trying not to sound too eager.

'That's true,' replied the innkeeper noncommittally.

'And that later on, people who knew about the last part of the quest trail would stop by here?'

The innkeeper shook his head almost sadly. 'Ah, so you're still set on your goal, despite what you've suffered.'

'Certainly,' said the Marquis.

'Well that remains to be seen,' said the innkeeper. 'I warn you now, it's not a safe road for any who try to venture beyond our borders. You'll turn back now if you know what's good for you.'

'Thank you for your advice,' said Thorrin firmly. 'But we'd still like to talk to anybody who knows about the trail. They will be in later?'

'Oh, yes, they stop by. You wait a while and everybody stops by here, even if only once.'

There was a path cut into the steep valley wall, hidden from the middle of the valley by the haze. Peri, examining it through her binoculars, thought it looked a bit like the tracks the Incas had made across the Andes. It was just as precipitous in places, but it seemed continuous and certainly crossed over the end of the lower mist valley. She looked at it doubtfully.

'Is it likely,' she said aloud to Red, 'that after five thousand years at this treasure quest game, the Gelsandorans would leave such a simple way open to get around their pet monsters down there, not to mention all the traps beyond it?'

Red gave a snort, which she chose to interpret as agreement.

'Exactly. So it can't be as simple as it looks. Unless it's some really mean double bluff. Perhaps they reckon nobody will try it exactly because it looks too easy. I don't know. But it sure would save a lot of time.' She sighed. 'I guess we've got to give it a go.'

The path began a little above the level of the tiled plain, reached by a narrow track that switchbacked up a jumble of rocks. Then the ground fell away to one side and Peri found herself looking down on to the perpetual mist bank that shrouded the valley. Perhaps it was best that she couldn't see all the way to the ground, she told herself, leaning slightly towards the rock wall on her right. The track was just wide enough to take Red's bulk, and she just hoped they wouldn't meet any other traffic.

They were halfway across the end of the mist valley, and Peri was beginning to think she had been worrying over nothing, when she heard a distant rumble. She looked up at the sky, but it wasn't thunder.

Red bounded forward as the avalanche crashed down upon them.

The food was plain but plentiful and filling. Falstaff consumed three huge portions and continued to flirt with the serving woman. Arnella found the spectacle of the fat man making a fool of himself in public mildly embarrassing. After the meal Jaharnus sat a little apart from the others and appeared to be brooding over her drink, while Thorrin and her uncle engaged in conversation each person who entered the inn, attempting to learn more about the final stage of the quest. During the process they in turn were probed about their own adventures, which were treated with a curiously grave fascination by the locals.

This left Arnella and Brockwell alone at their table sipping rather coarse but warming wine. There was an awkward silence, which Arnella eventually broke.

'So, it looks as though we might be getting near the end of our journey,' she said, then thought angrily: Why did I say something so mindlessly obvious?

'It seems like it,' Brockwell agreed quickly. There was another silence, then he seemed to make an effort to meet her eyes. 'Excuse me for asking…'

'Yes?'

'But you don't seem, well, very happy about the prospect.'

'What do you mean?'

'Well, I would have thought the idea of coming into vast wealth would have made you a little more cheerful. I mean, I understand you and your uncle have some money problems, and this would seem to be the ideal solution.'

'It's all more complicated than you realise,' she admitted, then added defensively, 'For that matter you don't seem so overjoyed yourself.'

'No, well there are… personal reasons for that.'

'Well I have my personal reasons too,' she said haughtily.

For a moment there was silence, then they suddenly laughed into each other's face. It had been a long time since Arnella could remember laughing aloud.

'That was a very silly exchange,' Arnella admitted. 'You'd understand if you knew…' She glanced around her, but nobody was paying them any attention. She looked back into Brockwell's lean, serious face. Despite his dislike for her kind, she thought he would understand. 'Uncle wants it to remain a secret as long as possible, but now we're so close it doesn't matter. You'll know soon enough if we succeed, and if we fail… well then nothing matters any more.'

'Succeed at what?'

She took a deep breath. 'The treasure's important, of course, but not just for our own fortunes. You may not know it, but there are still factions on a few of the worlds Rovan once ruled, even after all these ages, who'd like to have his Empire reborn. Now that the Terrestrial Empire is falling apart they see a chance. But they need funds – and someone to lead them. Someone whose lineage can be traced back to Rovan's line, or at least as close to his parents as possible. But so much information was lost during the fall that nobody living now can prove they're of the same line, let alone who would have right of succession.'

'After all these years, does it matter?'

'Oh yes, it does to some. And it might help bring stability to the region, but only as long as there's an undisputed ruler.' She took out her money-card folder and showed him a picture of the book. 'That's the Book of Lineage of the Empire. It contains the genetic records of all Rovan's ancestors. He took it with him when he disappeared and my uncle thinks it's still with the treasure. If we find it we may be able to match it with our own ancient family records of only slightly later date to prove a connection with Rovan's line.'

'You mean your uncle might be another emperor?'

'Oh no. The most direct line of descent is through my father.' She gave a half-smile. 'I'm potentially the next empress.'

He looked at her in amazement.

'Perhaps you find that offensive, being anti-royalist?' she added.

He blinked and recovered his tongue. 'Why do you think I'm particularly anti-royalist?'

'Well… the way you've always looked at me. Or rather didn't look at me… until now.'

'That!' He seemed genuinely astonished. 'That was because I'm… uh, shy. Not because of titles.'

'Oh,' Arnella said. 'I just wondered. I mean you seemed to have no trouble looking at that Brown girl.'

'Well why not? She seemed friendly and it was polite. But I don't think she's… I mean I think you are much more…'

'Yes?' Suddenly it seemed very important that she know what he really thought of her.

He flushed. 'Since I first saw you I thought you were the most…' He looked down at his drink and frowned. 'I think I may have had too much of this…' he said, then slumped forward striking his head on the table with a thump.

She reached out to him, trying to stand as she did so, and found her own legs would not support her. She sank backward, looking around dizzily for help. Falstaff was also collapsed over his table, a tankard of wine on its side forming a pool under his head. Jaharnus, her uncle, and Thorrin were slumped in their chairs, heads lolling on their shoulders. The locals they had been talking too were simply watching them in silence.

The last thing she remembered was the innkeeper looming over her.

'You should have turned back when you had the chance,' she heard him say as though from a great distance. Then everything was swallowed up by a velvet blackness.

CHAPTER 20
TRIAL

Arnella fought her way slowly back to consciousness. Dimly she became aware of lying on some hard surface and voices around her, then someone raising her head and forcing water between her lips. She coughed and spluttered and blinked gummy eyelids open. A blur lit by grey light resolved into Brockwell's concerned face.

'Hello,' she said faintly, her tongue feeling thick and useless in her mouth.

He smiled down at her. 'Hello. How do you feel?'

'I think... that wine was a little strong.'

'It was drugged.'

'Oh...' She was still drowsy and the implications of his statement took a few moments to sink in. 'The innkeeper?'

'Yes. And everybody else in the village as well, apparently.'

She made herself breath deeply, trying to clear the cobwebs from her mind. 'My uncle?'

'He's here, and the professor and Falstaff and Jaharnus. They're still feeling rather groggy, but I think they'll be all right. They drank a little more than we did.'

'But why did they do it? And where are we?'

'I don't know, but I'm sure they'll tell us soon enough. We're in a sort of prison, so it looks like they're prepared for this kind of thing. You can see if you sit up – not that there's much to it.'

With an arm from Brockwell she sat up, resting her back against a rough wall. Her head swam for a moment, then she began to take in her surroundings.

The cell was quite large, with stone-slab floor and block walls. A small, heavily barred window let in pale grey light.

'Is it morning or evening?'

'Morning by my watch. It must have been quite a powerful dose they gave us. They weren't taking any chances.'

The cell held half a dozen low, rough, wooden trestle beds, covered by thin, straw mattresses. Falstaff lay on his back on one snoring, while her uncle and Jaharnus were sprawled on their sides. Thorrin was half sitting up, head cradled in his hands. The forth wall of the room, opposite the windows, was formed out of a thick latticework of bars, let into which was an equally sturdy door. Beyond that was a dark, stone-flagged corridor and a second row of bars. Behind them stood a figure dressed in a pale frock coat and striped trousers who was staring across at her.

'Hello, I hope your feeling better now,' he said.

'Doctor? How did you get here?'

'Well at Qwaid's insistence, we've been following you rather closely for some time. We saw you arrive and settled down to wait in an empty barn to see what you'd do next. Unwisely, as it turned out.'

'Why? How did they catch you?'

'Drorgon had procured some tempting local tree fruits as we went along. We ate them while we waited. And that was the last thing I remembered until waking up here. A salutary lesson: crime does not pay.'

She stared at him aghast. 'They drugged the fruit on the trees to catch seekers?'

'Apparently so. They must have been watching us all the time as well, since they evidently found us quickly enough.'

'That's... frightening.'

'It does suggest a rather unwelcoming attitude to strangers, doesn't it?'

She now noted the two figures still slumbering on pallets in the cell with him. 'Where's your friend? Is she... all right?'

'Peri? She's fine, as far as I know. Gribbs took her back to Qwaid's ship to ensure my cooperation.'

'Do you think they can do anything to help us?' Brockwell

asked practically.

'Unfortunately the locals seem to have removed anything that remotely resembles a weapon, or that might be useful in aiding our escape. And that includes all our communicators. So even if they could help, they won't know exactly where we are. We were taken before Qwaid sent an update on our latest position. Gribbs must be getting quite worried about us by now.'

Gribbs turned back from the communicator. 'It's no use, Mr Alpha. He still doesn't answer.'

'So Qwaid is still functioning as efficiently as ever, I see. Give them another hour, then we shall have to take action ourselves. In the meantime, check the ship's systems and ready her for takeoff. I shall release the override locks.'

'But the natives won't let us fly over the quest zone. I tried, but I couldn't make my hands work the controls.'

'So I understand, Gribbs. But it is always a risk to place too much reliance on a single form of defence. I doubt whether these people have any conventional weapons, and I suspect that illusions and other mental subterfuges will not affect me now.'

'No, boss. I guess they won't.'

Their captors waited until they had all recovered before coming to fetch them. Their hands were shackled and a number of burly men armed with swords and short-handled pikes ushered them out into the morning light. Two DAVE drones were waiting outside for them, giving a surreal touch to the procession as they were marched through the narrow streets of Braal to the square. Some children playing in front of a house watched them pass with wide, curious eyes, until a woman dragged them inside hastily.

Their destination turned out to be the inn. Inside they found the bar had been removed to make way for a low wooden podium and nine chairs on which they were made to sit. The tables in the rest of the room had been replaced by several rows of benches. Seated on these were fifty or so villagers of all ages and races. Arnella searched for some sign of sympathy in their faces, but saw only stern concentration. The DAVEs glided into position at the back of the room, studiously ignored by the crowd.

The innkeeper had removed his apron and replaced it with a simple black sash across his chest. His friendly, open manner of the day before had also undergone a dramatic change.

'I shall conduct the proceedings against you, and interpret the will of the people of Braal when it comes time to pass sentence,' he announced.

'Wait a minute,' said the inspector. 'I'm Inspector Myra Jaharnus of the Astroville police force. 'I am currently pursuing those two men over there on suspicion of murder. The third man, known as the Doctor, is a potential witness to the crime. But he is not associated with those two in any other way, and to the best of my knowledge is only aiding them under duress.'

'Thanks, Inspector,' Qwaid snarled bitterly.

'May I point out to Your Honour that I'm merely a humble bodyguard, hired for my prowess with a sword?' said Falstaff ingratiatingly. 'And I really have little knowledge of what any of these people intended to do on your fair world. If I have inadvertently given offence, please accept my humblest apologies.'

'Is this true?' the innkeeper asked Jaharnus.

'No. He's just a congenital liar,' Jaharnus said flatly, and the others nodded automatically. Falstaff looked deeply offended.

'All this will be taken into account when passing judgment.' the innkeeper said.

'But it's my duty to bring him and those three over there back to Astroville,' Jaharnus protested.

'Your duty does not have precedence here, nor do we

recognise your laws. They are a product of a diseased society.'

There was a murmur of appreciation from the crowd.

'Innkeeper, judge, and philosopher,' Jaharnus retorted angrily. 'What do you do in your spare time?'

'Your attitude betrays the stratified envy-ridden society that has shaped you. Here we each perform those tasks we are best suited for without such distinctions.' He turned to address Thorrin's party. 'Before many witnesses, you have repeatedly expressed an intention of continuing with your misguided attempts to acquire Rovan's treasure. Is that not so?'

'But that's no crime,' Thorrin protested.

'Do you admit that is your intention?'

'Well, what if it is?'

The villagers in the public benches groaned as though in dismay.

The innkeeper turned to Qwaid, Drorgon, and the Doctor. 'You were observed following in a devious manner and spying upon the first party. Do you deny your intention was to steal from them what they would acquire, thus compounding their crime?'

'I want to see my lawyer,' Qwaid said. 'I don't admit nothing until I've got proper representation.'

'Here your silence or lack of cooperation is taken as an admission,' the innkeeper said simply. Qwaid started to protest, but was jabbed in the back by one of the guards with the butt of a pike until he was silent again. The innkeeper looked at them all gravely. 'You collectively stand accused of greed, acquisitiveness, selfishness, and avarice. How do you plead?'

'What nonsense,' said the Marquis. 'This is not a court of law. What gives you the right to judge us?'

'We are those who have been reborn into the way of truth and enlightenment,' said the innkeeper solemnly. 'We have renounced the greed and lust for wealth and power that first drove us or our ancestors here. Now we live simply without the misery that money and desire for petty valuables brings.

This has been our way for centuries. Even the Gelsandorans do not dispute our right. All those who wish to pass through our land and beyond the rainbow must first answer to us!' He gestured at the DAVE drones hovering at the back of the room. 'Let your watcher see justice done, and broadcast the truth far and wide so that this sad tide of misguided seekers will someday cease. Now, how do you plead?'

'Not guilty,' said Thorrin contemptuously.

He turned to Qwaid, who shrugged: 'Not guilty.'

The crowd shook their heads and muttered.

'Then we shall debate your case and you may speak in your defence.' He faced the Marquis. 'Should you acquire a portion of Rovan's treasure, what would you do with it?'

'Well, most would be sold.'

'And do any of your companions think that is wrong?'

They looked at each other, unsure of how to respond, or where the innkeeper's line of argument was leading.

'Look, I understand you think money's wrong, but we have to have it or some equivalent,' Brockwell said. 'Your small society might be able to get along with barter, but ours can't. It's too complex.'

'Has it tried?' the innkeeper challenged him. 'But it is the dissemination of an evil force we are most concerned with at present.' He turned back to the Marquis. 'How will these items be transformed into money – an auction, perhaps?'

'Probably, for most of it.'

'Where it will be fought over by collectors, each trying to outbid each other?'

'That's up to them.'

'And might these valuables be the object of continuing envy and desire? Perhaps even leading to theft?' He glanced at Qwaid. 'Or even murder to obtain them?'

'That's pure speculation!'

'But is it impossible?'

'Well... no.'

'Is it not in fact a certainty that this will happen sooner or later, at least to some of the items in such an obscenely magnificent hoard as Rovan's?'

'I suppose it may – but that's hardly our fault.'

'Ah, the abrogation of responsibility. Such a base excuse. Can you not see that it is your responsibility? You had the choice not to embark on this selfish quest, knowing the likely consequences for others, yet you still did so!'

There was an angry murmur from the crowd. The innkeeper seemed to rise to it, for he gestured dramatically with both pairs of arms.

'Do you need this money because you are starving, any of you? Or because you were incapable of exchanging honest toil for the necessities of life? No!'

The crowd applauded.

When the noise had abated, the innkeeper looked at the Doctor. 'Is it true you accompany these two criminals under duress?'

'Yes, because I fear for the safety of my friend, who is currently being held hostage by their accomplice.'

'So you put your friend's safety, a single life, above the far greater evil that would result from inflicting Rovan's treasure on the galaxy.'

'Well of course, but I –'

'You have said enough. I judge there is no mitigation.' He turned to the inspector. 'And you, who claim to represent law and order: tell us what punishment these criminals would receive if we let you take them back to your home for punishment?'

'That is for the courts to decide.'

'But is it likely to be death?'

'No. We do not sentence people to death on Astroville. It would not bring the deceased back to life –'

'What is their likely fate?'

'A term in prison, then psychiatric examination and –'

'Will this ensure there is no possibility of their offending again?'

'Well, no treatment is a hundred per cent certain, but –'

'So you admit you are willing to risk them continuing their criminal activities. What is to prevent them returning to Gelsandor and attempting to perpetrate their crimes afresh?'

'Listen, I just represent my system of law to the best of my ability!'

'As do I!' the innkeeper replied simply. 'I also find no mitigation in your case.' He turned to the crowd. 'You have heard the evidence. What shall the verdict be?'

There was a stirring of many whispers and heads turned this way and that as each consulted their neighbour. Then one man in the front row stood up.

'Death!' he said.

Another stood. 'Death!' And another and another and the chant grew louder.

'Death!'

Arnella felt cold and curiously detached, as though she was not really hearing the words and they could not possibly apply to her. As though at the end of a long tunnel, she saw the innkeeper turn to them.

'Such is the verdict of the Enlightened of Braal. Let it be carried out within the hour!'

Dynes had watched the drugging and capture of both groups the previous day, uncertain as to the entertainment value of this unexpected interruption to the quest. The problem was that drugged people in cells provided little sustainable interest.

A few of the locals had enlivened things slightly by throwing stones at the DAVEs in an attempt to bring them down, but he had pulled them clear in time – he could not afford to lose any more cameras. Once they realised he was not going to interfere, however, they had more or less ignored the DAVEs as long as they stayed clear of the prisoners, stubbornly refusing any of his relayed requests for interviews. He had debated how long to leave the DAVEs on station, but his instinct told him to be patient.

And now it was paying off.

He had the chance to record a genuine primitive execution. And Peri and Gribbs were still lose somewhere, he reminded himself. Their reactions should be interesting when he found them again, and they might yet win through to the treasure, providing a satisfactory conclusion to the whole feature.

It was at moments such as this, when he was about to witness death, that Dynes felt most intensely alive. This apparent paradox and any associated psychological ramifications did not bother him unduly. He simply regarded it as the natural reaction of a professional craftsman seeing his skill and dedication repaid.

For what was the ultimate payoff in life except death? It was the one thing that bound all his disparate viewers together. It was their unifying fear and yet also their darkest fascination – especially if it was unnatural. They might turn away sickened afterwards, but they would watch it that once and remember who brought those images to them for the rest of their lives.

That was the supreme accolade as far as Dynes was concerned. Apart from the awards and bonuses this sort of report brought him, of course.

Carefully he began to plan camera angles.

It took six men to drag Drorgon out of the inn, three to manage Jaharnus, and a surprising two for Brockwell. The others did not put up much of a struggle, partly due to shock. The Doctor went unresisting, although his deepset eyes flashed about him as though he was searching for any possible means of escape.

But it seemed they were not be given the opportunity. With

the jury from the inn swelled by the crowd that had been waiting outside, they were led out to a field on the edge of the village, the DAVEs gliding along in their wake. There a line of posts had been driven into the ground, while around their bases were heaps of kindling.

At the sight of them Drorgon roared and began struggling afresh, while Qwaid began to curse their captors. Thorrin went white and Arnella gave a little whimper. They couldn't really mean to do it. They couldn't!

'I'm so sorry, my dear,' her uncle said to her brokenly.

'You call this justice!' Jaharnus shouted.

'Not very sporting,' said the Doctor to the guards dragging him along, his voice amazingly level. 'Traditionally you're meant to put us back in our cells to contemplate our fate just long enough for us to work out some ingenious plan of escape.'

'Do not chide Old Jack for his cowardly words earlier,' said Falstaff, as though in apology to them all. 'I have more flesh than another man, therefore more frailty.'

Arnella's wild eyes met Brockwell's.

'I just want to say,' he shouted desperately, 'that I lo–'

The sun was blotted out by the angular form of the *Falcon* as it tore over Braal and the execution field less than fifty metres over their heads.

Tiles were lifted from roofs and chimney stacks toppled. Then the blastwave of displaced air and the sluggish sound trailing in its wake hit them with mind-numbing force. The crowd scattered in confusion, and many who could never have seen a spacecraft or heard a thruster exhaust before dived for the ground and buried their heads in their hands. A whirlwind of whipped-up dust and debris billowed across the field, reducing visibility to a few metres.

As Arnella lay sprawled on the ground, still dazed by the suddenness of it all, she saw the Doctor act.

He crashed shoulder first into the one man he had never let

out of his sight, knocking him to the ground: the jailer with the master key to their manacles on his belt. Brockwell and Jaharnus, momentarily free of their stupefied guards, caught on immediately and joined him, jumping on to the man, kneeing and kicking and fumbling with their bound hands for the keys.

Arnella saw a guard running towards the struggling group, kicked out her feet as he passed, and saw him crash satisfyingly to the ground. Before he could recover she shuffled forward and kicked him in the head repeatedly until he lay still; she was surprised to find she had within her such hatred and determination to live.

Then the Doctor's hands were free and he was twisting round with incredible speed to release the others. Two more villagers appeared out of the pall of dust that was falling all around them, but by then Jaharnus was free. She snatched up a sword and swung it viciously, driving them back. Then Brockwell had a hand under Arnella's arm and he was pulling her upright and unlocking her shackles.

To one side Drorgon and Qwaid were struggling with three of their guards, who had resisted the general panic. Brockwell kicked viciously, opening a path through the mêlée to Drorgon's shackled wrists, and freed them. Heaving himself upright, Drorgon picked up one hapless man and smashed him down on the other two with bone-shattering force. Then he snatched up two discarded pikes and, swinging them like flails, charged at another ragged knot of guards while Brockwell freed Qwaid.

Falstaff, perhaps by accident more than design, had rolled backward on to a local and was effectively keeping him pinned to the ground. Brockwell unshackled Falstaff, and then her uncle and Thorrin, who were still lying dazed by the sudden turn of events.

The villagers fell back under their captives' unexpected resistance, and for the moment they had the centre of the field to themselves, apart from the dead and wounded. Arnella saw Qwaid rise from the prostrate figure of the innkeeper with a bloody dagger in his hands, and she found her disgust at his action surprisingly muted.

Then the *Falcon* came in for a second pass, sending most of the remaining onlookers around the edge of the field running or crawling back to the shelter of the village. The ship made a tight turn and returned with landing legs extended and underjets blasting. It touched down in a fresh cloud of dirt and smoke, its side-hatch ramp dropping open. Qwaid and Drorgon led the frantic dash towards it and were first up the ramp, which immediately hinged upward again before the others could set foot upon it. Then a fresh blast from the underjets sent them cowering backward.

'No!' shouted the Doctor in dismay. 'Peri!'

Unheeding, the ship soared up into the sky, leaving the Doctor to stare helplessly after its receding form.

'Peri,' he said again faintly.

Jaharnus tugged at his arm. 'Sorry, but we've not time to spare. We've got to get out of here.'

'Aye,' said Falstaff, puffing up beside them. 'Let us tarry not but vacate the field of battle triumphant.'

Captured weapons in their hands, they ran for the trees at the far edge of the field. Rising beyond them were the valley walls, closer together than before and indicating that the valley was narrowing. Then they were among the trees and crashing through the brushwood, the DAVE units following after them.

Slowly, still gasping for breath, Qwaid hauled himself off the deck of the *Falcon*, where the pressure of their rapid ascent had briefly pinned him.

He heard a growl of shock and alarm from Drorgon and looked up.

A glittering machine in the shape of a large humanoid torso

supported by a blocky tracked base was staring down at them. Its eyes were glowing red photosensors set in an expressionless silver face.

'So here you are at last, Qwaid,' it said impatiently, in the unmistakable tones Alpha had once used. 'I trust you have obtained some useful information from this latest escapade?'

After what seemed like hours of desperate flight through woods and spinneys, ducking down along hedgerows to avoid detection from outlying farmhouses, Thorrin finally called a halt. They were in a narrow tree-lined gully and they threw themselves down on its earthy banks exhausted, gasping for breath.

It was not until she had recovered a little that Arnella realised the Doctor, Jaharnus, and Falstaff had vanished and only one DAVE remained.

'Where are the others?' she asked.

'I think we lost them in the thicker woods,' said Thorrin. 'Forget them. They're on their own, just as we are. Besides, why should we share it?'

Arnella blinked at him stupidly. 'What?'

'Don't you realise from the way the villagers behaved? We must be very close to it by now. We must stay alert for any clues.'

Arnella saw Brockwell was as shocked as she was. 'After all we've been through you're still thinking of the treasure?' he asked in disbelief.

'Thorrin is quite correct,' said her uncle. 'We can't turn back now. If any of this has any justification it will be through our success. Find the treasure and we will have proved ourselves worthy. Come on!'

With a heavier heart than she could ever remember, Arnella stumbled after her uncle as Brockwell followed after Thorrin, each drawn by bonds of loyalty that were stretched now to their limits.

* * *

235

The *Falcon* was set down in some woods several kilometres from Braal.

The Alpha robot talked more volubly than the original, which was fortunate because Qwaid felt too shaken to string together any meaningful remarks at that moment. Behind its glittering bulk, Qwaid saw Gribbs making fearful apologetic gestures.

'This mechanism,' said Alpha, gesturing at itself, 'was something I acquired many years ago, together with an experimental device that purported to transfer a copy of one's mentality into a cybernetic brain. Having no natural offspring of my own it seemed an interesting opportunity to ensure the continuance of my line, in a manner of speaking. After all, I had nothing to lose by the attempt. So I regularly copied my brain patterns into the memory banks of this device to ensure it was up to date with my affairs, while still keeping it dormant. A timing circuit was set to power up its systems automatically after a certain interval if left unattended.

'And it seems to have worked perfectly. The transition from flesh and blood to cybernetic organism has been remarkably easy. My pleasures were always of the more intellectual variety, and these new senses seem perfectly adequate for their continuance. In fact I feel there may be distinct advantages to the transition. I seem to be immune to the mental forces the natives employed to prevent you overflying this area, for instance. A fact to which you owe your lives.

'Naturally, when I first became conscious in this new body I was somewhat put out to discover I had been ejected into free space, but I had anticipated such contingencies. The strongbox was in fact a disguised emergency capsule, enabling me to complete my journey and track the *Falcon* to its landing site. And there I found Gribbs, who has been updating me on your activities since we parted company.'

Qwaid had finally gathered his wits enough to speak up.

There was really only one question he had to ask.

'So… you're not, er, angry at what we did, boss?'

'Your thinking is muddled, again, Qwaid. Why should I be angry?' It pointed to itself. 'I, this unique consciousness, would not be alive now except for your actions. What happened to my former self was done to another person whose mind pattern I happen to share. You need have no fear of revenge on that account, for you have done this version of me no harm.'

Qwaid brightened slightly. Alpha's next words deflated him again.

'However I do not tolerate incompetence any more readily than my former incarnation did. You will now tell me everything that happened since you last made contact. And, as I said earlier, you had better have some useful information to impart.'

The DAVE unit looked on impassively as Myra, the Doctor, and Falstaff crouched panting in the shelter of a thicket. They were scratched, dirty, thirsty, and hungry, having managed only to snatch a drink from a stream and eat a few wild berries during several hours of desperate activity.

In the distance they could hear the cries of the search parties calling to each other. They had been evading them all afternoon, but now the valley was rapidly narrowing. Would they run out of room before they ran out of pursuers?

'Don't these people ever give up?' Myra wondered in exasperation.

'Fanatics and monomaniacs,' said the Doctor simply, 'do not give up that easily. We offended their fragile self-justification and sole reason for being. Apart from killing and wounding several of their number, of course.'

'That was self-defence!'

'They won't see it that way.'

'They must have turned out the entire countryside to look for us. I hope the others got clear.'

'If we can stay out of their hands until it's dark, then we've got a chance,' the Doctor said.

But even as he spoke they heard a distant baying. It was faint at first, but as they strained their ears it grew steadily closer.

'Hounds!' Falstaff exclaimed.

'Yes, they must be using dogs to track us... and I'm very much afraid they've got our scent!'

'So there is only the somewhat elliptical mention of "beyond the rainbow", by the innkeeper/judge that remains unexplained from this whole affair,' Alpha concluded, after Qwaid had dredged his memory of everything that had happened, and Drorgon had contributed his minimal observations.

The robot's torso swivelled smoothly, and its tracks whirred as it rolled up the lounge, then reversed direction. Alpha was pacing up and down, Qwaid realised.

'"Beyond the rainbow" is a slender thread to go on, but I suppose we must simply make the best of it.' Alpha rolled close to Qwaid so that he had to look up into its expressionless metallic mask of a face and the glowing eyes. 'But are you absolutely sure that's all? You've left nothing out?'

'Nothing, boss. On my life.'

'How apposite,' said Alpha.

Qwaid only saw the long slender silver blade that sprang out of the robot's right arm for a split second. Then the arm had blurred as it swung in a punching movement up and into his ribcage, and a spear of hot/cold fire burst within his chest.

'Yes, there are considerable advantages to this new body,' Alpha said absently, letting him slide to the deck.

'Not revenge, Qwaid, but sensible pre-emption. Apart from being a careless thinker, you've demonstrated that you're really not very trustworthy. This is my second life, and I'd be a fool to risk it to the likes of you again...'

But Crelly Qwaid heard no more.

CHAPTER 21
BEYOND THE RAINBOW

Eventually even Thorrin's ruthless determination to press on had to give way to common-sense reality.

From being a well-equipped expedition with the latest outdoor gear, they had in a few hours been reduced to a party of lost and hungry people, stumbling through unknown countryside in the near darkness. Cart tracks and farm land were far behind them, and if they continued any farther they would inevitably have an accident. They had to find shelter and trust to luck that they would not be discovered before morning.

They came across a clump of trees where the wind had heaped up dry leaves about the hollows between widespread roots, and there they halted. Exhausted, they could only rest fallen branches against the largest of the trees to give additional cover, heap the leaves around them, and lie still.

In the darkness, Arnella felt Brockwell take her hand in his. She did not pull away, but instead let her head rest on his shoulder.

In minutes, despite their resolve to take turns keeping watch, they were all asleep.

The lights of their pursuers bobbed and weaved through the trees behind them. Myra thought the excited howls and yelps of the hounds seemed closer at their heels by the minute.

But there would be no surrender. Even Falstaff seemed determined to go on to the bitter end. How did he keep his great bulk in motion for so long? she wondered. He wasn't fast, but he never stopped. He must have legs like tree trunks.

Myra still had the sword she had acquired that morning, and had already decided she would rather die fighting than risk capture and a terrible death at the stakes in the field. The blood of her less civilised ancestors not long out of the pools of her homeworld still coursed through her veins. Nobody would say she had not died well or done her duty to the last. Her only real regret was that it looked as though Qwaid had escaped the justice he so richly deserved.

She hoped they'd let Peri Brown go unharmed. The Doctor had not mentioned her again, but she knew he was more worried about her safety than his own. Myra was coming to quite like him. How would things have turned out if she had decided to trust him and not stow away aboard his improbable spaceship? she wondered ruefully.

Her confused thoughts were jarred by the sight of torches ahead and to their right. This was it.

'Find something to get our backs to!' she said.

The baying of the dogs got louder, and a fierce cry went up from the hunters as they closed in.

'Once more unto the breach dear friends...' Falstaff panted.

'That's not one of your lines,' gasped the Doctor

'I plagiarise,' Falstaff admitted with unexpected frankness, 'amongst other faults...'

Then from out of the darkness beyond the lights came a throaty roar of such volume that it drowned out the barking of the hounds. The eager shouts of the hunters became confused cries of alarm. The tremendous roar sounded again even louder, reverberating through the woods, and some solid body crashed through the brush with a thud of heavy feet. Snarls of hounds became yelps of pain, mingling with shrieks and yells of fear from their masters. Flaming torches fell to the ground or were carried away into the darkness. In minutes the hunting party had retreated in confusion.

'That's twice today,' said Myra faintly. 'I don't know how many more of these eleventh-hour reprieves my nerves will stand.'

Heavy footsteps padded towards them.

'Always assuming this is a reprieve,' said the Doctor.

An electric torch beam stabbed out of the darkness to illuminate them.

'Am I glad I found you at last!' said a relieved voice.

It was Peri Brown.

'I have had the most frightening ride of my life,' Peri stated with feeling some while later, as they sat around a fire under a tree gratefully consuming ration bars from her supply. 'Avalanches, bridges collapsing under me, a sort of thick ivy stuff that wraps itself around your legs if you stand still for a minute, mysterious sheets of black ice. At one point I felt so depressed I almost gave up, but Red just kept on going. Then when we came down off the cliff path there was this fast river to cross, but he swims really great – he has webs between his claws, you know. And then… well, if it hadn't been for him I'd have never made it. He seemed to know where to find you, but don't ask me how.'

They all turned again to the great bulk that was crouched beside them like some faithful dog. It growled at the DAVE unit, which was keeping a discreet distance. Myra found herself smiling at Red ingratiatingly. Anything that big she wanted on her side.

Peri was looking unhappily at the Doctor. 'I'm real sorry I talked you into all this, Doctor. I let this treasure hunt thing get to me.'

'Don't worry,' he said lightly. 'I would probably have become involved, one way or another. I usually do in these situations. I'm simply glad you aren't still on board the *Falcon*. Gribbs did a good job fooling all of us.'

'Well, the next place we go, choose somewhere quiet and deserted,' Peri said. 'I could do with the rest.'

'I'll bear it in mind,' the Doctor promised. 'And now I think we should try to get some sleep. After all, it's been a busy day.'

* * *

Arnella woke to the dawn light and Thorrin's cry of delight. Stiffly they pushed away their crude blankets of leaves and staggered across to where he was standing on a small knoll.

Before them, through a rift in the trees, was the tapering end of the valley, illuminated by the low golden rays of the morning sun. The line of cliffs was broken at one point by a broad waterfall, which must have been the ultimate source of the sawtooth gorge river, the wetlands, and the mist-valley lake.

And in the haze of spray at its base hung a rainbow.

'Beyond the rainbow!' Thorrin said, his voice hoarse with emotion. 'That is what the innkeeper meant. Rovan's treasure is behind there. It must be!'

He was haggard and unshaven, his face scratched and his hair awry. Arnella thought she saw an unhealthy grey pallor suffusing his skin. But there was a fire in his eyes that was sustaining him beyond the normal limits of endurance.

'Yes,' said her uncle. 'That's it. We're so close now. Come on!' And the two started forward.

'No,' said Brockwell firmly.

The two older men stopped, astonished by the tone of his voice. Brockwell continued in the same manner.

'Think what you're doing! At this moment we cannot afford to think of anything but our survival. Marquis: I know what you hope to find, but you daren't risk Arnella's life in the process.'

'You don't understand, young man,' said the Marquis. 'I cannot risk failure now. A line of succession is more important than any one life. You cannot ignore duty and responsibility. I'm going on alone if need be.'

'Professor,' Brockwell begged. 'You always prized logic so highly. Can't you see this is an illogical risk? Nothing can be that important.'

'No, Will,' said Thorrin, almost sadly, 'it's you who aren't thinking logically. Do you think I have been chasing after trinkets and baubles all this time? It's so simple. Just ask yourself: what would have made somebody like Rovan leave his empire as he did? And why did he need to take such a treasure with him? There's only one rational explanation, and I assure you it is worth risking everything for. Now, I'm going on. Whether you come or not is up to you.'

And he and Rosscarrino continued down the hillside towards the rainbow. Arnella looked up at Brockwell, tears in her eyes.

'We can't let them go alone,' she said simply.

'I know,' Brockwell sighed.

The *Falcon* lifted from the woods, leaving Qwaid's body lying where it had been dumped from the hatch.

Gribbs and Drorgon sat very quietly as Alpha took the ship up into the morning sun. They were tired and frightened. Alpha did not seem to need sleep any more, and had spent the night considering the information to hand and reaching no useful conclusion. The silver face was impossible to read. Just how angry and frustrated was he?

But then, as he levelled the ship off, he looked through the side port and suddenly said, 'Of course. How absurdly simple!'

The distant drone of the *Falcon*'s motors echoed out of the sky as they were breaking camp. The Doctor peered upward through the overhanging branches.

'Now I wonder where he's going. Not back towards the Gelsandoran town.'

'He's coming lower,' said Myra. 'Maybe he's going to land...'

They looked at each other for a moment, then Myra hastily pulled off her boots. Peri saw her toes were long and claw-tipped. She used them to good effect as she rapidly shinned up the tall tree at their backs until she had a clear view.

'I can see them. They're heading towards the valley wall... there's a waterfall... Doctor, I can see a rainbow! Remember

what the innkeeper said? The *Falcon*'s heading straight
for the fall... Hell, it's gone through! Did you hear that?
It went straight through the waterfall!'

'Dexel Dynes, it is time for you to come with me.'

Dynes jerked his head away from the monitors with
an uncharacteristic gasp of surprise.

Shalvis was standing in the cabin beside him.

'What? How did you get in here?'

'It does not matter,' said Shalvis placidly.'As your devices
have informed you, the quest has entered its final stage. I
thought you would prefer to witness it in person. An
"exclusive, on-the-spot report", as you would say.'

Dynes suddenly beamed.'Just let me get my hat.'

Gribbs looked nervously about him at the spacious
cavern, which was lit by the twinkling diffuse light
refracted through the wall of water that concealed its
mouth. Drorgon, standing beside him, was clearly just as
apprehensive.

Alpha, by contrast, rolled briskly past them and down
the ramp. 'Come on, Gribbs, Drorgon,' he ordered, his
voice rising above the muted thunder of the falls. 'Don't
you want to be rich?'

Several tubes and canisters had been clipped to the
mid-section of Alpha's tractor body, and in one hand he
held a heavy-duty rifle blaster. Recessed lights in his
casing snapped on, illuminating the mouths of a several
smaller tunnels that led off the larger cavern. After
examining them carefully for a minute, he chose the
most central and started down it, with Gribbs and
Drorgon following reluctantly after him.

There was a narrow path that ran around the lake at the
base of the falls and behind the curtain of water.

Drenched by the perpetual mist the thundering torrent threw up from the lake, Thorrin, the Marquis, Brockwell, and Arnella picked their way cautiously over the slippery rocks and stepped gratefully into the cavern. The first thing they saw was the *Falcon*.

'I thought it was heading this way,' Arnella said.

Her uncle's shoulders sagged a little. 'Perhaps we're too late.'

'No,' said Thorrin. 'If the treasure was meant to be found that easily it would simply be lying here in the open. Look, there are some tunnel mouths at the back. There's still a chance for us to catch up.'

The ship seemed quite empty, and after carefully skirting round her they faced the row of smaller caves. The ground before them was hard and gave no clue to which one the others had chosen. Brockwell looked down a couple of them.

'These could lead anywhere. And we haven't any torches.'

'Then we shall explore each one by touch on our hands and knees if necessary,' said Thorrin. And without another word he led them into the left-hand tunnel.

The Doctor pointed to footprints in a patch of mud on the path beside the falls.

'Thorrin's party. They must be worse off than we are now. Why didn't they have the sense to give up?'

'Well, we're here as well,' Peri pointed out.

'Perhaps our reasons are nobler now,' said Falstaff softly, as though speaking to himself.

'So you're not after Rovan's treasure for yourself any more?' Peri replied half mockingly.

Falstaff turned to her, wearing a more serious expression than any she had yet seen. 'Mistress Brown, there is more to life than beads and baubles.' He looked again at the path that led behind the waters. 'Honour pricks me on. Yea but... no. I'll do it this time.' And he led the way, leaving the others to exchange curious glances.

Red's claws scrabbled over the slippery rocks, but he reached the cavern behind the fall and there growled at the *Falcon*.

'It's all right, boy,' Peri assured him. 'I don't think there's anyone at home.'

The Doctor was looking about the cavern and the tunnels leading off it with a disappointed expression on his mild face. 'Hardly very original, is it?' he observed.

'What do you mean?' asked Jaharnus.

'Cryptic clues, waterfalls, caverns, dark tunnels. The traditional resting place of hidden treasure. But have the Gelsandorans included the usual trimmings?'

'Doctor, please don't talk in riddles,' Peri begged.

'I mean will there be some final tricks or traps to catch us when our guard is down.' He suddenly rounded upon them, his usual flippancy melting away and his eyes flashing in deadly earnest. 'Remember: this has all been, in part at least, an elaborate experiment run by well-mannered people who don't care whether we live or die! Take care where you put your feet and don't trust anything you see.'

And he stepped into the right-hand tunnel.

Thorrin's party no longer had torches, but patches of a mossy plant gave off a pale luminescence that, once their eyes had adjusted, was just sufficient to find their way. It was not, however, bright enough to distinguish the trigger stone in the floor that depressed with a click under Brockwell's foot. Circular panels set at waist height dropped away along both sides of the tunnel. Arnella screamed and Brockwell threw himself flat.

Nothing happened.

After a minute he very cautiously rose to his knees and peered into one of the holes exposed by the panels.

'It's empty,' he said in surprise.

They examined the other recesses. There were no

crossbows set on hair triggers, or pneumatic blowpipes loaded with poisoned darts, or even modern energy weapons. They were all empty.

Alpha's enhanced vision system detected the tripwire before he triggered it. Moving well back he ordered Drorgon to toss a rock at the wire.

A roof panel several metres farther along the corridor fell open with a crash, forming a steep ramp. Down this rolled a spherical rock that almost filled the corridor and bounced towards them at surprising speed. Before they could retreat further it crashed into Alpha's metallic body.

And rebounded without a sound and rolled to a stop.

Alpha reached out a glittering arm and prodded the boulder. His fingers sank into a soft, yielding substance.

'A painted ball of sponge!' he exclaimed coldly.

Though the Doctor and Falstaff were leading at that point, the trap caught Peri and Jaharnus. They heard the click of a pressure plate and the whole length of corridor under them abruptly dropped, the end farthest behind them falling the most until it was a forty-five-degree ramp, sending them tumbling backward. Peri had a momentary horrified image of a wall of spikes waiting at the bottom of the incline, but before they could slow their fall they had hit.

Something crumpled. She waited for the pain but none came.

She saw the others peering down at them from above, Red whining sympathetically. 'Are you all right?' the Doctor called out anxiously. Jaharnus twisted round and picked up a shard of one of the spikes. It was thin card, rolled into a narrow cone.

'It's a bad joke!' Peri said angrily.

'Would you rather they'd been real?' said Jaharnus.

* * *

With a sudden hiss, clouds of white vapour billowed out of concealed vents, flooding the corridor in front and behind them.

'Run!' shouted Brockwell.

They dashed forward, trying not to breathe, but there was too far to go. Thorrin was forced to take in a shuddering lungful of air. Then another.

'Wait… I don't think it's dangerous.'

The others stopped in bewilderment. Curiously Thorrin examined one of the nozzles still fitfully expelling the vapour.

'I think this is just… dry ice,' he said, then looked about him angrily. 'Why are they toying with us?'

The tunnel sides fell away on either side of Alpha's party and large half-seen forms seemed to lunge out at them. Gribbs and Drorgon blasted several in their alarm before they realised sheepishly that they were simply skeletons of long-dead monstrous beasts.

'What is going on here?' Alpha demanded, but Gribbs and Drorgon could not give an answer.

The Doctor halted them before a suspiciously neat checkerboard-tiled section of passageway with a large dark void above. Only by shining a torch upward could they make out the hundred or so weighted spears suspended like lethal stalactites above the board. They found rocks and tossed them on to the tiles before attempting to cross. But strangely not one tile released a single spear.

Brockwell drew back his foot just before stepping on the fine grid of wires that crisscrossed the floor ahead. Cautiously, he removed his belt and used the buckle to short the grid out. There was an impressive crackling and sparks showered brilliantly from the sides of the passage. He frowned and very lightly flicked a fingertip across two of the wires. The sparks erupted again, but he had felt not the slightest of shocks.

They crossed the grid to the accompaniment of further spectacular but quite harmless pyrotechnics.

Alpha turned a corner and stopped abruptly.

'What is it, boss?' Gribbs asked anxiously.

'Something different, Gribbs.'

The section of corridor before them was long, plain, and high. Its upper half was filled by a huge block of stone, suspended by some hidden means so that it just cleared the side walls by a couple of centimetres. There was no way past it. Alpha examined it closely, confirming that it was real stone. With all his strength, Drorgon could just set it swaying slightly, indicating that it was hanging freely, and must have massed a few hundred tonnes. If it was released while somebody was in the corridor below it would crush them flat.

'It's so obviously a trap,' Alpha said, 'but is it as harmless as the others?'

'Like I said before, somebody is playing some really sick jokes around here!' Peri fumed, pulling the sticky threads of a giant cobweb from her. A spider six feet across was still twirling slowly on its thread before her. It was, as they had ascertained only after its dramatic appearance, made of rubber. Red sniffed at it curiously.

'I don't think anything has been placed here simply for the fun of it,' the Doctor corrected her gently. 'I think there is a far deeper purpose.'

'But what?' Jaharnus said, looking anxiously up and down the corridor, grasping her sword more tightly.

'A final warning, perhaps: that they can kill us any time they wish if we continue? Or is it meant to symbolise something: traps that no longer function guarding a treasure that is no longer there?'

'You've thought that all along, haven't you, Doctor?' said Peri quietly.

'Let's say I believe it is a strong possibility.'

'So you're saying I should be prepared to be disappointed?'

'I thought you'd renounced treasure hunting?'

Peri grinned. 'Well, I thought, as we're here anyway and if we sort of stumbled over it, we might as well take a look…'

They rounded the next corner.

'Ah… now this is something a little different,' the Doctor said.

There was a massive stone block suspended above the corridor.

The Marquis prepared to step under the slab that overhung their section of corridor. Arnella was trying to stop him.

'Please, Uncle. This one might be real.'

'I have not come this far to give up now.'

'It could be suicide!' Brockwell said. 'Professor, talk some sense into him.'

Thorrin looked anything but stable himself. 'I don't know, any more,' he said faintly. 'Perhaps it is real, perhaps another fake. Is it to test our resolve, or ingenuity? But I don't see any other way to test it than we already have. It is worth every risk but this… a paradox.'

Brockwell was looking at him in dismay. The Marquis pulled free of Arnella.

'I refuse to cower here paralysed by uncertainly,' he said, and stepped boldly forward.

Fearfully, Drorgon had stamped on the floor under the block, thrown rocks, and done everything else Alpha had commanded in order to spring any hidden mechanism. The block still hung there menacingly.

'Such an obvious hazard, whereas the others were hidden,' Alpha mused. 'Is that the actual intent? To trap us into knowingly passing under it? There is nothing else for it. Gentlemen, I need a volunteer…'

* * *

'Either it will fall and you will die, or else it will not and you will live. It certainly makes you think,' said the Doctor, staring at the slab. 'Is that its purpose? To decide what value you really put on your life? Do you gamble everything on a fifty-fifty chance – the toss of a coin?'

'Doctor,' said Peri, 'there's no end to second-guessing this thing and wondering if its a bluff or not. I don't think I can stand waiting here much longer. We have to find out the truth!'

'The truth? Is that fundamentally what its all about?'

And then they heard Falstaff say softly, 'Cowards die many times before their deaths: the valiant never taste of death but once…'

And he ran through the passage under the block.

They looked at each other in surprise, then dashed after him, Red bounding along excitedly in the rear, followed by the DAVE unit.

The block did not fall.

Falstaff was lying sprawled on his face on the far side.

They rolled him over and the Doctor examined him anxiously, then grinned. 'He's all right. Heart beating like a trip hammer. Fainted from shock, I think.' He slapped Falstaff's face lightly. 'Come on, Sir John. You've made it. Wakey, wakey…'

His eyes flickered open, and he stared at them for a long moment. 'Preston Loxley the Third,' he said faintly.

'Pardon?'

'Preston Loxley the Third. It's my real name.'

'Ah,' the Doctor said slowly. 'Well we had surmised it wasn't really Falstaff.'

'Why the deception?' Jaharnus asked suspiciously.

Loxley/Falstaff heaved himself up until he rested against the wall. 'It's nothing sinister, Inspector; just sad, perhaps. But you may not understand my reasons.' Peri thought his speech sounded strangely bland now, shorn of its antique frills and allusions. He sighed. 'You've always known who you are and what your purpose is in life. I haven't. My family was wealthy but completely undistinguished – and so was I. Other people had personalities that shone out – I had money, a glib tongue with nothing worth saying, and a slight weight problem. I wanted to be genuinely interesting: a real character. Someone people would remember, instead of wondering afterwards: who was that fat man anyway? Then I came across Falstaff in some ancient texts. It was a revelation! Here was somebody who was fat, a cheat, and a liar, and yet he was popular. People forgave him his faults. And so I, well, borrowed him.

'That was years ago. I've grown into the part since, you might say. But life sometimes rather cruelly imitates art, you know. Falstaff was a coward at the core... and I slowly discovered that so was I.'

'So you came on the quest to prove yourself?' said the Doctor.

'Yes. But it's hard to abandon a character just like that. It's so much easier to keep up the barrier, and to go on making up excuses and talking your way out of trouble.'

'There's nothing wrong with talking your way out of things,' said Peri sympathetically.

'If it's only your own life at stake, perhaps not,' said Loxley. 'But eventually you run out of words, and must either stand your ground... or abandon others in need. As I attempted to back at the inn or did in the forest.' He looked at Jaharnus. 'Sorry, Inspector.'

Jaharnus smiled. 'I think you've made up for it now. I'm not sure if I would have taken the risk.'

'But you have always had something worth preserving. It was only through taking the risk that I discovered if I had also.'

'And have you?' the Doctor asked.

Loxley rose to his feet. Peri thought he stood a little straighter than before. 'Yes, I believe I have,' he said slowly. 'Shall we continue? I'm still afraid, but I'll try never to let you down again.'

A tunnel curved away before them. A brighter light was reflected along it from some hidden source.

'I think this might be it,' the Doctor said.

The end of the tunnel opened into a large brightly lit chamber. After the dark of the tunnels Peri squinted in the glare until her eyes adjusted. It was panelled with white marble. Several tunnel mouths identical to the one they had emerged from opened on to it, together with four heavy metal doors set in the facing wall. Thorrin, the Marquis, Arnella, and Brockwell were grouped a little to one side, looking dishevelled and bewildered. Standing before them in front of the four doors were Shalvis and Dexel Dynes, flanked by two DAVE units.

Even as Peri took this in, another party emerged from a tunnel to their left. Gribbs and Drorgon she recognised at once, but she flinched in surprise at the sight of the tracked silver robot thing that accompanied them. Where had they found that?

Nothing, however, seemed to disturb Shalvis's equanimity.

'Your quest is over,' she said gravely. 'Welcome to the antechamber of Rovan's treasure vault.'

CHAPTER 22
CHOICES

'Now you are all gathered as was foretold,' Shalvis continued, 'the final stage may begin.'

The silver robot raised the wicked-looking gun it was carrying. 'I think not,' it said in a harsh, precise voice. 'You must be the one called the Speaker. You will follow my orders.'

'Alpha?' said Jaharnus, incredulously, gaping at the thing.

'Inspector Jaharnus,' it replied, with incongruous cordiality. 'As alert as ever. As you see, reports of my demise were premature – in a manner of speaking. Qwaid, however, is definitely no longer with us: a victim of his own shortcomings.'

Red growled at Alpha, and the machine swung his gun round to cover him.

'You will keep that beast under control or I will kill it,' he said coldly, as Peri patted Red placatingly. 'I assure you my weapons are amply powerful enough.' His glowing eyes passed over the rest of them. 'You will all note that we are the only armed party present, and I for one am not constrained by any mental inhibitions against using weapons.'

'He speaks the truth,' said Shalvis calmly. 'We have no power over an artificial mind such as his.'

'So I trust you will be reasonable,' Alpha continued. 'If you will open the way to the treasure and do nothing to prevent my associates loading it on to our ship, there need be no unpleasantness.'

'That is not possible,' said Shalvis.

Alpha raised his gun and pointed it directly at her heart.

'You may kill me and all these present,' Shalvis said calmly, 'but it will not gain you the treasure. You see only the surface of this chamber, but its true functions are far more complex than you can possibly comprehend, and beyond the reach of any force you can employ. A certain procedure must be followed. Only once it is complete may the ways be opened according to Rovan's wishes. Then you may make your own choice as to which treasure you wish to take from Gelsandor. Choose well and you can leave enriched without any need for violence.'

Peri thought she detected the first edge of doubt in the Alpha robot's voice. 'What do you mean: "which treasure"?'

'Because the legacy of Rovan is more complex than you imagine. It is a measure of your ignorance that you were not aware of that obvious fact. Ask your companions or anyone in this room, if you disbelieve me. Though your mind is closed to us theirs are not, and they can recognise the truth when a Gelsandoran speaks it.'

Gribbs was nodding quickly. 'It's right, boss. They tell you if they're going to lie. This is the straight stuff.'

'Does the treasure include any more illusions?' the Doctor asked Shalvis almost casually. 'I suspect you're very good at them.'

'The only illusions will be those you create for yourselves.'

This seemed to decide Alpha. 'That is something I shall not be troubled by. Very well, do what you have to. But no tricks.'

'There will be none. Only self-deception by those who cannot recognise the simple truth when it is presented to them – as Rovan wished it to be.'

She walked over to the first door on the left, which had, Peri now noticed, a slight green tinge to the metal it was composed of.

'This way leads back to the woods where you landed. If you do not wish to proceed further I advise you to choose this path. Remember, there is no shame in being satisfied with what you have already achieved. That is something to treasure in itself.'

She moved to the next door, which was tinted a pale yellow.

'This door will only take you into the lesser treasure room and nowhere else. Within it there is a collection of ephemeral material wealth, but nothing more of true and lasting value. I advise you not to enter this room unless that is all you wish for the rest of your life.'

The next door was tinted blue.

'This will bring you to what you most desire, if you do not possess it already. Only take this path if your need is of the utmost urgency, and you are certain beyond doubt it can be satisfied in no other way. I promise you will find what you seek, but once you are committed there is no return.'

She moved to the final door, tinted in red.

'Through here is the ultimate treasure. It is beyond meaningful description, limit, or measure, to make of what you will. But nevertheless, I expect many of you will be disappointed at what you find if you choose this way.

'Those, then, are the paths of Rovan. Now you must choose one, and only one, to follow. There are no second chances, and you must live with the consequences of your choice for the rest of your life. Take as much time as you wish and decide well.'

An intense silence descended in the chamber, broken only by the slight hum of the DAVEs as they flitted about catching close-ups of their intense faces. Dynes was silent, but his lips moved slightly as he subvocalised his observations to be recorded by his throat microphone.

Despite Alpha's menacing presence, Peri felt herself drawn by the thought of what might be behind the doors. She looked from one to the other. Just suppose she chose the big one. She saw the same look of calculation on the faces of Jaharnus and Falstaff/Loxley.

Then she caught the Doctor's eye and he gently shook his head.

* * *

Gribbs looked from one door to the next in an agony of indecision.

He knew he'd been given the exact truth by Shalvis, but he didn't know what to make of it. Lies were easier to handle.

'I don't like this,' Drorgon said unhappily.

'Which one do we chose, boss?' Gribbs asked plaintively.

'Let the others make up their minds first,' said Alpha.

He sounded calm and collected, but Gribbs noticed a slight whirring from his locomotor tracks as they jerked forward and backward by tiny fractions.

Thorrin and the Marquis edged forward even as Brockwell and Arnella pleaded with them. Thorrin licked his lips, eyes darting between the blue and red doors.

'Which of them, if any, represents most closely the path Rovan took?' he asked Shalvis.

'I cannot tell you that,' she replied. 'He did not want his choice to influence others.'

'But you promise these choices have been presented to us exactly as Rovan wished?' the Marquis asked.

'Exactly so,' said Shalvis. 'We have kept our trust according to his instructions.'

'The blue door... it has to be,' muttered Thorrin.

'Yes, he had to have provided for the future,' said the Marquis, half to himself.

'Uncle, please no!' Arnella begged. With a shudder she forced herself to add, 'I... don't want to go through with it any more!'

He turned terrible eyes towards her. Not so much angry but shocked and uncomprehending.

'Arnella... you cannot abandon your birthright... your duty! Not after we've survived all these tests to prove we are worthy. Yes, that's what they have been for, you see: to choose a worthy successor when the time came! You are of Rovan's blood and somewhere in there is the proof. You will be the first empress of the Cartovallian line for almost forty-five centuries! Think what that will mean!'

'I am thinking!' said Arnella wretchedly. 'I'm not sure it will bring so much good. If the old empire was so wonderful, why did it fall so easily? Why is the Terrestrial Empire falling now? Things change. This may not be a step forward but a step back. Listen: in the forest I had a nightmare. I wasn't sure what it meant then, but now I know. I was imprisoned within a bush of thorns, being sucked dry by these flying parasites, but being fed by a vine that was part of the bush. My blood and their wastes fertilised the ground and so the vine which fed me. Day after day. It was a living death. That is what this will mean and I won't do it!'

'If your father could hear you now!'

'Oh, Uncle… this search for the book killed him and has changed you terribly. It must end. If the people want an empress that badly they'll find one, but not simply because she happens to share a handful of genes with Rovan's line.'

She felt Brockwell put a hand on her shoulder and squeeze gently. The Marquis's eyes flashed at him.

'It's you! You've poisoned her against me, against her duty!'

'No, sir. I love your niece, but I've said nothing to her about this. There hasn't been the opportunity. It's her choice… and I think it's the right one.'

Arnella looked up at Brockwell and smiled, though her eyes were wet with tears.

'Then… it is left to me,' the Marquis said brokenly. 'I will keep the succession alive alone. Goodbye, Arnella.'

He walked stiffly towards the blue door. Arnella reached out for him, but Brockwell held her back. 'No. It's his right.'

The door fell open at his touch and he passed through. They had a glimpse of a corridor beyond, then the door swung silently shut again.

Thorrin looked at the door, then at Shalvis.

'Can any number use the same door?'

'Any number. One person's choice does not alter the next person's chance of success in any way. So it has been for thousands of years.'

Thorrin licked his lips again, as though weighing every word. 'But only the worthiest ever reach this far?'

'I cannot make any assessment of their individual worth.'

'Surely not many... only the select few. That has to be what he intended...'

Brockwell was looking at Thorrin in concern. 'Professor, just what is it you think is in there?'

'I told you to think, Will! Why else would somebody like Rovan, who had everything he could possibly desire, come here? For one thing only: the reason I'm here. The ultimate treasure is immortality!'

Suddenly there was silence. Everybody in the chamber looked at him. Thorrin gazed back at them with blazing eyes.

'What else could it be? Can nobody else see it but me? Why else did he bring all that treasure? It was the price he paid to them!' He stabbed a finger at Shalvis. 'The treasure's probably all gone now, but that doesn't matter. But which door? The one she said herself was the ultimate or the other?' He glared at Shalvis who looked back impassively. 'That harpy knows, but she won't tell! One last test, but is it another bluff? That was what those traps were telling us. Rovan would want company over the millennia, but only the best, the most worthy. All this was set up to provide them for him, do you see?'

'Professor... Alex,' Brockwell said gently, 'Just because something is possible or even logical, it doesn't necessarily make it true. She warned us about self-deception... and I think you're deluding yourself.'

Thorrin seemed not to have heard him. 'The possibilities! What I could learn if I could spend ten years, or fifty years studying a single subject. My most productive time is already behind me, but if I had it back again a thousand times over, think what I could accomplish? Come on, Will: help me choose. We shall go in together. Bring your lady. Eternity will be lonely, but it will be worth it!'

'No,' said Brockwell. 'Not this time, Professor. I think you're wrong, and I think it might be dangerous.' He glanced across at the impassive Shalvis. 'There's more going on here than we know. You take the chance if you want, but I have too much to lose now.' He took hold of Arnella's hand.

Thorrin spared him one pitying glance, then he returned to his agonised deliberations. 'Am I certain there is no other way? Yes. Is my need urgent? Yes. Therefore I will find it...' Suddenly, appearing to find his inspiration, he rushed forward through the blue door and vanished.

'Can we wait for them, just in case?' Brockwell asked.

'Certainly,' said Shalvis. 'But you may have to wait a long time.'

Alpha broke the silence. It seemed to Peri that he had reached a decision as well.

'Gribbs, Drorgon. Go through the yellow door. Stay in communicator contact.'

'Boss. Are you sure?' Gribbs asked nervously.

'I have the measure of it now, Gribbs.' He flashed red eyes at Shalvis.

'I really wouldn't send them in there,' the Doctor said quickly. 'If you think about Shalvis's description carefully you'll understand. What she said was the literal truth, not a bluff!'

Gribbs and Drorgon hesitated.

Alpha swung his gun around to point at the Doctor, causing Red to growl again.

'I have heard something of your intellectual acuity, Doctor. But do not try sow the seeds of confusion now. This is a trap for the greedy and obsessed. But my wants are modest. I will be satisfied with the so-called "lesser treasure". Now go.'

Gribbs and Drorgon cautiously pushed open the yellow door and walked through. It swung closed behind them.

* * *

Beyond the door the passage, lit by glow panels, stretched straight and unbroken for ten metres to another door, similar to the first. It pushed open just as easily.

'Well, Gribbs?' came Alpha's voice over the comm link.

'There's another door, boss… and another. They're very thick, boss, and they keep closing behind us.'

'Just keep going!'

'Yes, boss… more passage… another door… uhh.'

'What is it, Gribbs? Talk to me!'

The room was dazzling, and it took Gribbs a moment to adjust. Then what he saw briefly robbed him of the power of speech.

Exquisite jewellery and precious stones were carelessly heaped about like sand dunes. Small pearls and loose gems crunched underfoot. In between them were bars of gold, platiniridium, silver, blue electrium, all stacked into improbable pillars and columns taller than his head. Resting on stands were complex fluted forms of rainbow-hued crystal and paintings of ancient scenes, richly glowing as though they had been finished just yesterday.

'Gribbs… Gribbs!'

'It, it's p-packed floor to ceiling,' he stammered. 'There must be tonnes and tonnes of it!' Drorgon give out a wild howl of delight as the full realisation dawned upon him. 'There's jewels, an' those old paintings you like, and, and… You were right, boss! Rovan's treasure! We've found it and it's all ours!'

CHAPTER 23
DESTINY

The Marquis pushed open the final door.

The chamber beyond was dimly lit, but filled with myriad subtle sparkles from the piles of jewels that were heaped about the corners. But he hardly gave them a second glance. There was only one thing he wanted to find. His heart beat faster as he saw at the far end of the room a golden lectern bearing Rovan's crest. He approached it with faltering steps.

On it rested the Book of Lineage of House Cartovall.

Reverently he wiped the dust of ages from its gem-studded cover and turned the broad creaking pages with trembling hands, searching for the right section. Yes, here they were: the genetic files. He pulled out his pocket holo-scanner, ready loaded with his ancestors' DNA pattern, and ran it across the pages of dense lines of tiny genetic code symbols.

There: a sequence illuminated with a flickering interference pattern. A match. It was the final proof!

Carefully he closed the book and lifted it from the lectern, comforted by its weight. And now he noticed a door in the far wall. Hugging the book to him, he cautiously made his way through the door and down a short passage.

This opened on to the bottom of a wide vertical shaft with a circle of daylight at its upper end. Resting on the shaft floor was a spacecraft of antique design, grimed with dust but apparently sound. On its side he could just make out the Cartovallian crest. Rovan had left transport for his successor. If it would carry him back it would be further proof of his claim to the throne, even though that honour should have gone to –

'Uncle! Wait.'

It was Arnella's voice. She emerged from the tunnel behind

him, and ran to his side, her face wet with tears.

'I'm sorry, Uncle,' she said. 'I was foolish to let that man influence me. But I know my duty now. Will you forgive me?'

His heart filled with joy. 'Of course I will, my dear.'

They entered the ship and took their seats. The controls were oddly arranged and slightly clumsy, but he rapidly mastered them. The thrusters were noisy but serviceable, and they carried them up the shaft and away from Gelsandor.

Soon they were out among the stars and on their way home.

Already the Marquis could picture Arnella's coronation. The Cartovallian line would be restored, bringing peace and stability to the new empire. It would happen just as he'd always dreamed...

Thorrin stood in an empty chamber. Just as he had suspected, there was no sign of any treasure. But there was something in the darkness.

Picked out by a single spotlight was a stand bearing a perforated tray, in which were slotted plastic phials of a deep-blue fluid. About half the slots were empty. As he stepped towards it there was a flickering in the air, and the projected image of a man materialised in front of him.

It was unmistakably Rovan himself, but dressed, Thorrin noted, in a more recent style than that of his own era. The recording smiled.

'Welcome to eternity, my friend. By reaching this chamber you have proved yourself worthy to share in something wonderful beyond imagining, and to accompany me on a journey into infinity. The phials you see before you contain the true secret of Gelsandor. A perfected pantropic genetic booster: the elixir of life. As you must know, no properly structured organism need ever die from mere age, as long as the body cells can be adjusted to repair and replicate themselves indefinitely. That is what the formulation in these phials will do.

'Drink one measure, it is all you will ever need. Leave the rest for those who may follow after you. Then I will give you instructions that will guide you to me in person. Together we shall learn the secrets of the universe. We shall see suns being born and dying. If we have the desire we shall last until the end of time!'

Thorrin picked up one of the phials, broke it open and swallowed the contents. It burnt inside him, and for a moment he felt dizzy. Then a wonderful warmth began to infuse his bones. He looked at his hands, and thought he could already see the fine wrinkles across their backs begin to fade.

He had made it. And the only limit to what he might accomplish now was his imagination...

Gribbs was feeling weak from laughing and shouting. He saw Drorgon slump back on to a drift of precious stones and followed suit, panting heavily. It was rather like being drunk. That was it: they were drunk with riches. The sound of Alpha's voice from his comm link gradually receded until it was no louder than the buzz of a fly.

Gribbs took one last shuddering breath, then he heard nothing more ever again.

In the antechamber, Alpha continued to shout into his communicator.

But there was no reply.

'I told you not to send them,' said the Doctor despairingly, his voice more brittle than Peri had ever heard before. 'She said there was nothing of true and lasting value.' He turned to Shalvis. 'What is the major constituent of the atmosphere in the lesser treasure chamber?'

'An inert gas, Doctor, to help preserve the artworks.'

'Then there was no more oxygen than they took in with them?'

'That is correct.'

'What ghastly irony! They get their ephemeral wealth for the rest of their lives exactly as you promised – except that they are already dying!' he snapped back angrily.

'Yes.'

Peri trembled, feeling sick. 'I know they were scum… but how could you be so cold blooded?'

'We are simply keeping our trust,' Shalvis replied, apparently unperturbed. 'I advised them not to pass through that door. Remember, I warned you all when we first met of both the dangers and the rewards of the quest.'

The Doctor shook his head sadly. Arnella and Brockwell glanced anxiously at each other, then at the blue door through which the Marquis and Thorrin had gone.

'How fortunate,' Alpha grated, 'that in my new form, I do not require oxygen. An inert atmosphere will not trouble me at all. I shall examine this chamber.'

He clipped his rifle to his side and rolled towards the door, which opened smoothly once again at the slightest touch, and passed through. The door began to swing closed behind him even as Peri noticed how thick and heavy it was.

Then Alpha's metal hands appeared around its edge as he fought to pull it back open. It slowed but did not quite stop and Peri realised it must be power-driven. Alpha began to force his tracked lower body back through with a scraping of metal. They could hear the whirr of servo systems under load.

'We can trap him in there!' the Doctor shouted, throwing himself forward and pressing back against Alpha's gleaming torso. As though coming out of trance the rest joined him, except for Shalvis and Dynes. Red growled and whined at the back of the press of bodies.

But Alpha was too strong. Despite their efforts he was forcing his way back out. With a final shrill of metal he shot free, knocking them to the ground almost contemptuously with sweeps of his massive arms. Then he turned to Shalvis.

'I congratulate you: an elementary but effective trap. I only noticed there was no means of opening the door from the inside just in time.'

'They are designed to let people in, not out,' Shalvis admitted calmly. 'If you recall, I said it would only lead to the chamber. And both it and the doors are lined with collapsium, and would be quite impervious to your weapon.'

'But it has failed,' Alpha pointed out triumphantly. 'And now I know the location of the real treasure, I shall find some means of obtaining unobstructed access to it, however long it takes.' His glowing eyes flickered across the rest of them still sprawled on the floor. 'But you will not witness my success. As I had cause to explain to Qwaid shortly before his own demise, I do not indulge in revenge. This is merely sensible pre-emption to ensure you will trouble me no further…'

His rifle unlatched itself from the casing and sprang into his hand. They started to scrabble uselessly away from him. Red stood over Peri protectively, growling at Alpha.

'Remember I'm a neutral press observer, Mr Alpha,' Dynes called out quickly. 'I'd like to arrange an exclusive –'

Alpha's gun blazed twice, and two of the three remaining DAVE units exploded in midair. Red gave a ferocious snarl of warning. Alpha swung his gun round.

'No! Red, don't!' Peri screamed.

Red sprang as Alpha fired.

The energy bolt struck Red in the chest, passed straight through 'him and out of his back, blasting his saddle mount free. But his momentum carried him on and he struck Alpha, sending him skidding back on his tracks to crash against the wall. Alpha fired again, burning a long furrow into Red's flanks. But somehow Red remained on his feet, and tore the rifle out of Alpha's grasp with one swipe of his massive forepaw. With a whirr of tracks Alpha drove forward, his hands reaching out to clasp Red's neck. Red twisted his head and his huge jaws snapped shut about Alpha, teeth grating on metal. With a tremendous heave Red jerked the glittering body aloft, even as Alpha's fists beat upon his snout and jaw, smashing into his mask of armour plates with ringing blows. Red began to shake him as a terrier would shake a rat, his head snapping from side to side. But he was standing so that on each alternate swing Alpha's head and shoulders were dashed against the hard wall with ringing crashes. Silver arms flailed uselessly and shards of broken metal started to fly free. Suddenly, blue smoke hissed from Alpha's strained joints.

There was a sharp bang, a crackle of electricity, and a shower of sparks. Red sank to the ground. With a final effort, his neck twisted and his jaws jerked open. Alpha's mangled form was tossed aside, writhing and jerking, whirring and sparking fitfully. Incoherent groans and gurgles came from its voicebox. Gradually they subsided. The flailing arms froze, and the baleful glowing eyes in the half-flattened cranium dimmed and went out.

Warily they got to their feet. Jaharnus picked up Alpha's rifle and edged forward until she could kick his outstretched hand. It did not move.

'It's all right,' she said with a sigh. 'He's finished.'

'All find their just reward on Gelsandor, both good and evil,' Shalvis said.

Peri was not listening. She was staring down at Red's scarred body as it lay very still. She touched his furry side, but there was no trace of a heartbeat. Her eyes filled unashamedly with tears. 'Why did he have to be so brave?'

The Doctor patted her consolingly on the shoulder.

'He was certainly a remarkable animal,' he agreed.

'A noble beast,' Loxley proclaimed sincerely.

Arnella and Brockwell approached Shalvis. 'We have to

know,' Arnella asked brokenly. 'What has happened to my uncle and the professor? Are they... dead as well?'

'No,' said Shalvis calmly. 'Knowing you have chosen another way and cannot follow or aid them in any way, do you wish to learn their destiny?'

They exchanged searching glances, then nodded. Shalvis turned to the others.

'Have you decided yet? You must choose not to go through the blue door before I can reveal this.'

'My job's done,' said Jaharnus. 'Green for me.'

'And I', said Loxley. 'One bold deed is enough for the day. And I shall have enough genuine tales to tell now.'

Peri simply shook her head, still staring at Red.

'Certainly not,' the Doctor confirmed.

She looked questioningly at Dynes, who had rapidly recovered his composure and was directing the single remaining DAVE in recording the remains of Alpha and Red.

'Can I get a better shot from inside?' he asked simply

'Not substantially,' Shalvis replied.

'Then count me out.'

Shalvis crossed to the blank wall beside the four doors and touched its surface. The wall seemed to become transparent, like a giant screen. The image on it was softly lit, but they could clearly make out Rosscarrino and Thorrin reclining side by side in full body-contoured chairs. Their eyes were closed and they lay very still.

'Are they asleep?' Arnella asked tremulously.

'In a manner of speaking. When an impossible dream becomes an obsession, and life becomes intolerable while it remains unfulfilled, then only illusions can bring release. The Marquis would never have believed Rovan did not leave the Book of Lineage amongst his treasury, nor would the professor accept that we do not possess the secret of immortality. The truth would have destroyed them. They are at peace now, and will live out their lives believing they succeeded...'

The screen viewpoint slowly withdrew to reveal the rest of the chamber, and they saw it was huge and filled with row upon row of the contoured chairs. Each bore a still figure. There were creatures of many races in all manner of costumes, some ragged and torn, but none of them stirred. Every single one of that silent multitude slept the same eternal sleep as the Marquis and Thorrin. And as the viewpoint glided between their ranks, Peri realised that most of them were very, very old.

'Despite what you may think, Rovan was not entirely unmerciful, and neither are we,' Shalvis said.

The screen darkened and the image of the sleepers vanished.

Peri shivered. Arnella and Brockwell remained staring at the blank wall for a long time, then they slowly turned and walked hand in hand through the green door that led back to the surface. Loxley and Jaharnus followed at a respectful distance.

'Any final comments?' Dynes asked hopefully, as he and the single surviving DAVE headed after them, leaving Peri and the Doctor alone with Shalvis.

Peri glanced sadly once more at Red's still form. Then she frowned and edged closer. 'Doctor, why is there no blood?'

Before he could reply a swirling shimmering light enveloped Red's body, and it seemed to shrink inward. Then the light was gone and in its place stood a familiar form, with the ghosts of the wounds Red had suffered dissolving into its silver body shell as though they had never been.

'Kamelion?' Peri gasped in disbelief.

'I had interfaced with the TARDIS shortly before the Master took control of me,' Kamelion explained in his familiar deferential tones, having politely allowed them a few moments to recover. 'Also, I have a pseudo-metabolic extension into the fifth dimension, where I store or draw on mass to suit varied body forms. It was through this and the tenuous interface link that my mental pattern survived, trapped within the TARDIS's hyperdimensional fields. But I was confused and could not contact you nor regenerate a new physical form. It was not until we arrived here that I was released.'

'Ah,' said the Doctor knowingly, glancing at Shalvis.

'Yes, we were responsible,' Shalvis admitted. 'We foresaw Kamelion's coming and his part in the defeat of Alpha. Through an illusion we made you think you had locked your TARDIS when you left on the quest. This allowed us to bring an amorphous plasmoidal form we had created within reach of Kamelion's mind. With our help he was able to make the initial transition. This did not break the spirit of our trust with Rovan, nor was it totally selfish. Our actions were already part of a potential future, and in a manner of speaking Kamelion was on a quest of his own. Remember, it is our purpose to aid seekers of whatever kind to achieve their true destiny. And defeating Alpha was part of Kamelion's.'

Peri turned back to Kamelion. 'But why didn't you appear to me like this first off?'

'On Sarn I had caused you alarm and pain in this form. You would have been mistrustful to see it once again. Yet there you had also called me "friend" and cared for me, and I wished to repay that kindness. So when I traced your mind pattern in the woods, I analysed your desires and combined them in a form that would best serve and reassure you.'

Peri suddenly understood. 'Just before you appeared I was thinking of heroic dogs, knights in armour, and America. And I got something that combined all three, right down to the patriotic colour scheme!' She chuckled. 'It was a great disguise, Kamelion. I'll always remember "Red". But it's good to have you back as you are.'

'Thank you, but I regret I cannot rejoin you.'

'Why not?' the Doctor asked.

'This form is unstable, Doctor. Too many of my functions were lost with my original body, and they can never be regained. Gradually I would lose control of my patterns and become a liability once more. I have decided it is best if I leave you now with, if I may so call it, dignity.'

'No!' Peri exclaimed. 'Not again...'

But even as she spoke she realised Kamelion was fading. She began to see through him, as though he were turning into ice which was slowly vaporising before her eyes.

'Kamelion, you must hang on,' the Doctor said urgently. 'There may be a way to stabilise your new body.'

'Thank you, Doctor, but it is useless. You granted me a merciful release once, now allow me the same freedom to choose my ultimate destiny. It has pleased me to redeem myself. I hope I have fulfilled my functions adequately and given satisfaction.' He was growing fainter by the second.

'Yes you have,' Peri said desperately, 'but please don't go like this!'

'Do not concern yourself any further, Peri Brown, or you Doctor. I am finally at peace...'

She tried to touch him one last time, but there was only a shape of mist. 'Goodbye...' she said simply.

Then he was gone.

Peri swallowed hard and wiped her eyes. She looked up at the Doctor and saw a look of tender compassion. He put a reassuring arm around her shoulders.

'I know, it's not fair. But the universe is not fair, it just is. At least Kamelion had a chance to make good second time round, which is more than most beings get. Let's remember him at his best,' he suggested gently, 'acting with courage and purpose.'

She sighed. 'I'm just sorry I started this whole thing.'

'But if we, and especially Kamelion, hadn't been here, things might not have gone so well for everyone else.'

'I suppose so,' she agreed.

'And what's more,' he added, his voice lowering to a conspiratorial whisper, 'Remember, Dynes will never know what a scoop he's just missed: Heroic Beast Really Reincarnated Shapeshifter Android!'

Peri had to smile at that thought. Then she frowned and looked at Shalvis. 'One thing still gets me. This all seems to have been predestined, but I thought we came here mainly because I wanted to?'

'There is free will,' Shalvis assured her. 'It shapes the future, which we can only glimpse imperfectly. Nothing is certain until it has occurred, and it was always possible Alpha would triumph. Right to the last your actions were crucial, as indeed they were in the past, when your sympathy won Kamelion's gratitude. As the Doctor said, do not undervalue the qualities he demonstrated. I think Rovan would have approved of them.'

Peri shook her head in wonder at it all. Her eye caught the red door, the one nobody had opened, which supposedly led to the ultimate treasure. She smiled ruefully. 'Under the circumstances I won't try that one. I guess I can live without knowing.'

'My dear Peri, surely you've worked it out by now,' said the Doctor. And before she could stop him he walked across the chamber and calmly stepped through the red door.

'Doctor!' she cried, but he was gone. For a second she hesitated, then dashed through the door after him.

CHAPTER 24
THE ULTIMATE TREASURE

Beyond the door was darkness.

Peri felt a moment of giddiness and a sensation of rapid acceleration. Rings of light flashed past her. She saw the Doctor's distant silhouette and reached out desperately towards him.

Then came a sudden pressure and the rings of light vanished.

She was standing beside the Doctor on the threshold of a wide archway. Before them a flight of steps led down to a stretch of green lawn fringed by tall, graceful trees. The Doctor gave her an infuriatingly bright and knowing smile, and suddenly she recognised the setting.

It was a doorway of the white pyramid where they had first met Shalvis.

She gaped at the Doctor but he simply put a finger to his lips, ambled lightly down the steps and set off towards the corner of the pyramid, forcing Peri to dash after him. Around the other side the rest were waiting for them.

'What kept you?' Jaharnus asked. 'That tube of theirs got us here quickly enough.'

'Oh, we came by the scenic route,' the Doctor said lightly.

There was an argument in progress.

'For the last time, I don't want to give you an interview,' Arnella was saying to Dynes.

'Not even a passing thought on the Marquis?' Dynes persisted. 'The public might find that rather strange.'

'I don't care what they think.'

Then Brockwell stepped between them.

'Excuse me, Dynes,' he said in his usual diffident manner. 'Over the last few days you have been willing to watch us

275

suffer and almost die on several occasions, for the cheap gratification of your viewers. And now, even when it's over, you continue to annoy the woman I love. Under the circumstances, I think this is a very reasonable response…'

And he punched Dynes carefully on the nose, sending him sprawling backward on to the neat grass and causing the remaining DAVE to weave about in search of a new angle. Dynes clapped a hand to his face, trying to staunch the blood, and stared up at Brockwell in disbelief.

'You know what you've done!' he exclaimed somewhat nasally. 'Assaulted an accredited member of the information media during the execution of his legitimate duty in a situation of high news value. Before eyewitnesses!'

'Sorry, I wasn't looking,' said Loxley quickly.

'Did you see anything, Peri?' the Doctor inquired.

'See what, Doctor?'

'Inspector Jaharnus?' Dynes appealed, now clasping a handkerchief to his face.

'As you reminded me a few days ago, this planet isn't in my jurisdiction.'

Dynes glared at them all. 'Well I have it recorded! That's evidence enough.' And he pointed at the hovering DAVE.

There came a single shot from Jaharnus's commandeered rifle, and the DAVE tumbled to earth in a shower of smoking fragments.

'That felt very satisfying,' Jaharnus admitted. 'What a pity it was watching you when I did it.'

Dynes gaped at her and the smouldering wreckage of the DAVE, then turned to Brockwell. 'There are backup recordings in my ship. I'll still take action against you.'

'So sue me,' Brockwell challenged. 'You won't get much because I'm not rich…' He looked at Arnella and smiled. 'At least, not in any way you'd understand.'

'If it's not too much trouble, could you give our friends a lift back to Astroville?' the Doctor asked, after a decent pause.

'Peri and I are going in another direction.'

'Of course,' said Brockwell, 'We were heading there anyway.' He looked at Arnella. 'We have a lot to talk about, and perhaps certain official arrangements will need to be made – if you think so too, Arnella?'

Arnella looked at him and took his hand, and Peri saw the sadness slowly begin to lift from her face to be replaced by a quiet hopefulness.

'Yes, I think so,' Arnella said simply. Then she turned to the Doctor and Peri. 'Goodbye, and thank you.'

'Good luck,' said Peri.

'Under the circumstances,' Jaharnus said, shaking hands with the Doctor and Peri, 'I won't be needing you as witnesses against Qwaid, Gribbs, and Drorgon.'

'Your investigation is over, then?' asked the Doctor.

'Yes, I suppose it is.' She gave a curious smile. 'Do you think that's what Shalvis meant when she said I was also a seeker?'

'Perhaps. We're all searching for something.'

'But what sort of report am I going to write on all this?'

'I shall assist you, Inspector,' said Loxley heartily. 'There is nothing like a little creative fantasy to smooth the rough edges of life.' He doffed his hat and bowed to Peri and the Doctor. 'Goodbye, my friends. Parting is such sweet sorrow.'

'Farewell! Thou art too dear for my possessing... and like enough thou now know'st thine own estimate,' replied the Doctor in kind.

'That's not quite how it runs, Doctor,' said Loxley, wagging his finger, 'but perhaps I do, at last.'

And he followed the others as they walked away along the path towards the glade where the *Newton* was waiting.

Ignored by all, Dynes had risen to his feet. Now he looked uncertainly at Peri and the Doctor.

'I don't punch,' Peri warned him, 'but unless you want a knee where it'll make your eyes water, you won't even think about it!'

Glowering and still dabbing his tender nose, Dynes disappeared along the path through the trees.

Peri realised Shalvis was standing beside them.

'Now they have departed,' she said solemnly, 'I can show you what Rovan left for those who followed in his footsteps.'

'In his footsteps?' Peri said. 'You mean when we went through the red door? And why did we end up here anyway?'

'Oh, Peri,' said the Doctor in mild despair.

An image was forming before them. It was of a handsome man dressed in plain nondescript clothes. Peri recognised the face instantly from the pictures she had seen in the library on Astroville.

'My friends,' said the five-thousand-year-old recording of Rovan Cartovall. 'Perhaps my actions have been selfish, but at least I am prepared to take the consequences. I do not know what future ages will make of me, and in all honesty I care little. But I do predict that the single question most will ask is: Why? Why did he who had everything give it all up? What strange purpose had he in mind for his treasure? Well here is the truth plain and simple, take it how you will.

'I was bored. I owned everything but myself. I felt trapped within the court and empire, in which I could already see signs of decay. I wanted to live, to experience the true riches of diversity and uncertainty. To find out who I really was, and not simply the figurehead an accident of birth had made me. I hope my sudden departure will give those I left behind cause to pause and reflect on their own motives and intentions, but I have my doubts.

'As to the treasure, it not only bought the cooperation of the Gelsandorans in covering my trail, but it also enabled those who would inevitably follow after me to learn a lesson in relative values. Any who have the means to find their way here are wealthy and capable enough already. If their greed overtakes them then they will reap an appropriate prize. If they want more, then they must come by it through their own labours. This is not hypocrisy, for I must also fend for myself now, as I am leaving all my treasure here. It is a responsibility which I have never had before, but I am rather looking forward to the challenge. I am setting out upon the path that you have also chosen. The trail is uncertain but the rewards, though they may not be material, are compensation enough.

'For of course, if you have not yet realised, the ultimate treasure lies in the infinite possibilities of the universe itself!'

And he lifted his eyes and arms upward to the sky and the stars beyond, and Peri automatically followed his gaze.

As it happened she was just in time to see the *Newton* and the *Stop Press* lifting off from beyond the trees and soar into the air. She watched until they winked out of sight. When she lowered her head again Rovan's image was gone, and so was Shalvis.

They walked thoughtfully back to the TARDIS.

'Are you disappointed?' the Doctor asked.

'I'm not sure. Real life isn't always as satisfying as the storybooks, is it? I thought I might have come away with something more to show for it all. No gold or jewels, not even a bumper sticker: "I've been on the Ultimate Treasure hunt". Only a collection of bruises, about five years knocked off my life through fright, and a story nobody will believe back home.' She shrugged, then frowned as another thought struck her. 'Say, Doctor, what'll happen to this place when Dynes gets through telling the whole world – I mean galaxy – about it? Won't it get overrun with treasure hunters?'

'Do you really think Dynes is the first person who intended something like that? How is it the location of Rovan's treasure has been discovered by so relatively few people, even after all this time? I think the Gelsandorans know how to protect their world and Rovan's trust.'

'I hope so, even though I don't think I like them very much.'

The Doctor looked at her quizzically. 'Nevertheless you

think there's something here worth preserving, despite your feelings about them personally?' he suggested.

Peri frowned. 'Well, I guess being here has been an –'

'Experience?'

'Yeah, you could say that.'

He smiled. 'So you are taking something away with you, Peri. Knowledge, an expanded appreciation of relative values, a raised level of consciousness. Perhaps that's the quest's true purpose.'

'That sounds pretty mystical to me; just like Rovan, the old dropout. Maybe you're a hippy at heart, too, Doctor – yeah, the ultimate hippy! I should have known by the hair.'

'A hippy?'

'You know: the sixties, mind-expanding, flower power.'

'Oh, then. I was otherwise engaged in the sixties. It was a busy decade for me.'

They reached the TARDIS. The Doctor unlocked the door, then paused. 'But talking of flower power, I did once visit a world ruled by sentient flowers.'

'Really?'

'Yes. It happened like this…'

They passed inside. A minute later the incongruous police box dematerialised, and the scented glade was empty once more.

Dynes spent some time after leaving Gelsandor's orbit having the *Stop Press*'s autodoc unit tend his nose. Then he set a course and went to sleep for ten hours, making up for what he had lost over the last few days. The *Stop Press* was in hyperspace by the time he sat down to play back his DAVE recordings and begin editing them.

Except that every single file contained the same message, repeated over and over again, and nothing else whatsoever.

'Dexel Dynes,' said Shalvis, her face staring out at him from every monitor. 'You may recall the promise I made to you at our first meeting. I said you would be allowed to witness everything you wished on Gelsandor during the period of the seekers' quest, and leave Gelsandor freely afterwards. However, I did not promise you could take away any material you gathered for the purposes of further dissemination. The rights you claimed for yourself and used against others under the interstellar convention give you no protection here, since we are not signatories to any such agreement. If you were a better reporter and genuinely interested in things of true value, such as respect and consideration for others, you would have realised long before now –'

Dynes hit the stop button so hard he broke a fingernail.

So, she thought Dexel Dynes would abandon the story of a lifetime as easily as that, did she? Well he'd show her! He'd head back to Gelsandor and get some detailed reconnaissance shots from a safe distance, then make for Astroville and find some innocents he could feed with the location of Rovan's treasure. He'd wire them and their ship up with microcameras so neither they nor the Gelsandorans would ever know it, and get his ultimate treasure hunt story that way.

Still boiling with anger, he ordered his autopilot to reverse course.

The pilot promptly set course for Astroville.

Dynes cancelled the command and ordered it to produce a complete course printout. According to that the last place he had visited was Astroville. There was no set of coordinates for Gelsandor anywhere in the autopilot's memory bank, even though he knew he'd seen the figures flash up on the display board just after he'd made orbit.

But for the life of him he couldn't remember any part of them now.

And he never would.

Also available from BBC Books:

DOCTOR WHO
THE EIGHT DOCTORS
by Terrance Dicks

Booby-trapped by the Master, the Eighth Doctor finds himself suffering
from amnesia. He embarks on a dangerous quest to regain his lost
memory by meeting all his past selves...

ISBN 0 563 40563 5

VAMPIRE SCIENCE
by Jonathan Blum and Kate Orman

The Doctor and Sam come up against a vampire sect in present-day
San Francisco. Some want to coexist with humans, but some want to go
out in a blaze of glory. Can the Doctor defuse the situation without
bloodshed?

ISBN 0 563 40566 X

THE BODYSNATCHERS
by Mark Morris

The deadly Zygons are menacing Victorian London, and only the
Doctor's old friend Professor Litefoot can assist the time travellers in
defeating them. But why are the Zygons stealing the bodies of the dead?

ISBN 0 563 40568 6

Other *Doctor Who* adventures featuring past incarnations of
the Doctor:

THE DEVIL GOBLINS FROM NEPTUNE
by Keith Topping and Martin Day
(Featuring the Third Doctor, Liz Shaw and UNIT)

Hideous creatures from the fringes of the solar system, the deadly Waro,
have established a bridgehead on Earth. But what are the Waro actually
after – and can there really be traitors in UNIT?

ISBN 0 563 40565 1

THE MURDER GAME

by Steve Lyons
(Featuring the Second Doctor, Ben and Polly)

Landing in a decrepit hotel in space, the time travellers are soon
embroiled in a deadly game of murder and intrigue – all the while
monitored by the occupants of a sinister alien craft...

ISBN 0 563 40565 1

Doctor Who adventures out on BBC Video:

THE WAR MACHINES

An exciting adventure featuring the First Doctor pitting his wits against
super-computer WOTAN – with newly restored footage.
BBCV 6183

THE AWAKENING/FRONTIOS

A double bill of Fifth Doctor stories... a rural village hides a terrible
secret from the Civil War in _The Awakening_, while the distant world of
Frontios sees a fledgling colony of humans under attack from the
gravity-controlling Tractators...
BBCV 5803

THE HAPPINESS PATROL

The Seventh Doctor battles for the freedom of an oppressed colony
where misery is a sin...
BBCV 5803